Caught Between

Tayla Crowley

Contents

Prologue

"What the hell?"Jade raised her head, the cacophony of the ringing cell phone bringing her out of her immense concentration.

When Jade Tucker was in her writing mode there were very few people who dared to disturb her. Normally, as a rule she never picked up the cell phone while she was in the middle of a story. Not even if it was the president calling. But the caller id indicated that the call was from Mrs Carter, the mother of her best friend.

Jade pushed herself away from the table where she had been busy clicking at her keyboard and picked up the cell phone which was ringing shrilly on her bed.

"Hello, Jade is that you?" Mrs Carter's voice was still had the sweet edge to it that Jade remembered.

"Hi, Mrs Carter! How are you?"

It had been ages since Jade had last met Mrs Carter. 3 years atleast. Julia's wedding was the last time they had met.

What with Mrs Carter alternating between her house in the suburbs and Julia's house in the city, and with all the writing Jade had been doing it had become quite impossible for them to find time to meet each other.

And the main person holding them together was also missing.

"I'm great, Jade. It's been too long since we last met." Mrs Carter said.

"What with you being such a busy body, always on the go!"

Mrs Carter laughed, "You have been quite busy yourself Miss Jade Tucker. 4 novels in 3 years is a big achievement I believe. Mind you I read all of them."

It didn't matter if any other people in this world read her books or not, but Jade was sure of one thing, her mom, Mrs Carter, Julia and Nicole would always read her books.

"And did you like them?"

"Do you need to ask? I loved them! And don't you think I didn't notice that you used my dialogue in 'Static'."

Jade laughed. She never thought that it could go past the sharp eye of Mrs Carter.

In a way she actually wanted her to read and know that she was thinking about her.

Mrs Carter had always been like a second mother to her, taking care of Jade as much as her own children.

"How is Julia?"

Julia was Mrs Carter's elder daughter, and one of Jade good friends and avid readers.

"Julia is good, very excited for Alec's return though."

"Alec's return?"

Jade who has been balancing on the edge of the bed plopped down onto the floor on getting the unexpected news.

"Yes, sweetie. That's what I called to tell you. Alec is coming back. On this coming Monday. I thought I'll let you know. Isn't it great news?" Mrs Carter sounded as excited as a child going to Disney world for the first time.

"Yes.... Uh... Great news!" Jade tried to sound enthusiastic.

They spoke for some more time, Mrs Carter asking about her mom's health and inviting them for dinner to celebrate Alec's homecoming.

After saying her goodbyes, Jade kept the phone and just sat on the floor staring at the screen.

Alexander Carter was coming back. Her best friend in the whole world was coming back.And surprisingly that was the last thing she wanted.

Chapter 1

JADE

7 years and 6 months had gone by since the last time she had seen Alec, and it had been a little longer since they had spoken to each other. (Jade had been counting.)

Jade had met Alec for the first time on the first day of kinder-garten. And as most kids going to school on the first day, she had been bawling her eyes out, terrified to go in. On the other hand, the ever calm and laid- back, Alec went into class jumping and sporting various band aids all over his hands and legs, while his mother followed him trying to hand him his bag.

They were opposites. In every way possible. But something brought them together.

He was the first one to approach Jade and start talking to her. And she was so surprised that someone was actually speaking to her that her tears stopped in their tracks.

Since that day they became inseparable.

In the coming years as the two of them grew up, it was almost like they were stuck at the hip.

Alec kept Jade from living in her dreamworld while, Jade stopped him from becoming a complete cynic.

They could never keep secrets from each other and as a result they knew everything about the others life.

Their deep friendship resulted in their mothers also becoming good friends.

In high school Jade started getting jealous of any girl Alec seemed to like and Alec on the other hand would get a bad feeling in the pit of his stomach whenever he saw Jade talking to any guy. These incidents led to fights and arguments. But they were still friends. Best friends. They passed of the incidents as friends getting jealous of someone else getting in the way of their friendship. Maybe it was something else. But they did not give it a chance to develop.

Once high school got over and they had to grow up at last, they realised how different they were from each other.

It struck them that life was not going to be as easy as making friends in kindergarten over a mutual love for pb and j sandwiches.

And they started drifting away.

Jade went ahead to get her Masters in English, while Alec did his course in Journalism.

And soon their friendship turned into a series of missed call, mails not replied and meetings cancelled.

On a last try to keep their friendship, they met up for summer break in the last year of their college.

But it was too late, they had grown too far apart to patch things up again.

Soon after, Alec had gone to Thailand to set up Wanderlust his travel company with one of his new friends.While Jade's first novel had been published going on to become a best seller.

Now 7 years later, Jade was a successful author while Wanderlust was doing great in the travel market, having become very famous.

It was almost like they no longer knew each other. Let alone be best friends.

Even for Julia's wedding, Jade for some reason could not make it to the main ceremony and went only for the party after it and Alec left before the party.

So they did not meet.

And now Mrs Carter tells her that Alec was coming back to the city and that would mean they would have to meet.

After keeping the call Jade just sat on the floor and thought about the old days when spending time with Alec was the only thing on her to- do list.

She tried to divert her mind from thoughts about Alec and sat to write again, but her concentration had all but disappeared.

Instead she got up and decided to take a long hot shower.

Before going into the washroom she looked at herself in the mirror on her dresser.

Her black straight hair was almost completely out of the messy top- knot she had tied before she sat to write. And her moss green eyes which normally always twinkled with good humour were blood shot and looked tired.

She was wearing an old T- shirt which she knew didn't belong to her, but had no clue where she got it from, over a pair of faded grey shorts.

In short she looked like a homeless person with a good figure. Not a look she normally sported.

She desperately needed a shower.

After the shower she came out wrapped in a fluffy white towel and with another towel wrapped around her head.

The main objective of the shower for her had been to get rid of the disturbing thoughts of Alec which were moving around in her head.

But after half an hour in the steaming hot water she had still not gotten rid of the feeling of dread in the pit of her stomach.

There was only one person who could help her. Nicole.

She picked up her phone which was still lying on the floor where she had dropped it after the call with Mrs Carter and dialled the number of her best friend.

"Hello!" Nicole said after the first ring.

Jade was always surprised at how quickly Nicole always seemed to pick up the phone.

"Hey, Nic! It's me Jade." She said trying to speak loudly so Nicole could hear her over the racket her children were making.

Nicole had become friends with Jade when they were room mates in college and since then they had always stuck together.

Now Nicole was married to her high school sweet heart, Jason and was the mother to the reckless twins, Noah and Nadia.

"Hey, Jade. Just wait a second I'll go out of this room." Nicole said before covering the speaker and yelling, "Noah , Nadia if you both don't shut up and play like good children I'm taking away your TV privileges for a month."

Jade couldn't help but chuckle. She was unusually proud of her god children for driving her normally cool and calm best friend mad, at the young age of just 3.

"Yeah… So what were you saying?" Nicole said once the noise in the background was a little less.

"Taking away TV privileges is hitting under the belt." Jade said.

"They are going to drive me mad!"

"I love my godchildren!"

"Your training is working. They don't let me sit in peace for more than 10 minutes. Thank God! Mum is coming in half an hour. I'll get some rest." She sounded so relieved at the thought of rest that Jade started laughing again.

"Lilah is coming? That's great! I need to meet you. Can we go out for coffee?"

"Sure.... But what's up?"

"I'll tell you once we meet. See you in half an hour at 'Beans'?"

'Beans' was the local cafe, which was their normal meeting place.

"Okay. See you."

Jade kept the cell phone down for the second time in the day and looked at the clock on her table. It was 10:30 in the morning.

She quickly went to get changed.

Chapter 2

NICOLE

Jade had already been sitting in the cafe for 15 minutes, when Nicole came in, tripping on the edge of the door and stumbling into someone else.

Though Nicole was cool and laid back about almost every issue in the world, she was the biggest klutz Jade knew.

As Jade looked at her, a smile playing on her lips, Nicole walked to the table at which she was sitting. All the while mumbling sorry under her breath.

"Nic, do you always have to be as clumsy as an elephant in a china store?" Jade asked still laughing, as her best friend took the seat opposite hers.

"Go ahead, make fun of your poor, clumsy friend!" Nicole grumbled, "Though, you're looking good."

Jade looked down at the pair of cut off denims that she was wearing with a loose off- shouldered white t-shirt.

"And you're late." She replied.

Before Nicole could say anything to that comment, the waiter came with their orders.

"One cappuccino, one latte and a chocolate pastry." The waiter said as he placed their order on the table.

"Thanks."

"Are you stress- eating?" Nicole asked once the waiter was gone, "chocolate pastry?"

Jade picked up one of the spoons and dug into the pastry, "Nope. Why would you think that?" She said with her mouth stuffed with chocolate.

"Jade I've known you since college. You have one rule, 'stressed spelt backwards is desserts'. You eat chocolate when you're stressed out. So stop the crap and get to the point. Spill!" Nicole said before taking a sip of her coffee and sitting back waiting for Jade to start speaking.

"Aleciscommingback." Jade mumbled with her mouth stuffed, purposely trying to muffle her words together.

"What? Jade stop behaving like Nadia. Swallow and tell me what's up."

Jade swallowed her mouthful of pastry, took a sip of her cappuccino and took a gulp of air before saying, "Alec is coming back."

Nicole gulped her sip of coffee so fast that she almost burnt her tongue in the process, "What? Really? How do you know?"

"Mrs Carter called in the morning to tell me about his return. She was very excited. And she's called mom and me for dinner to their place on Monday. Julia's also going to be there."

Nicole was one of the only people who knew about the whole equation between Jade and Alec.

"No wonder you are stuffing yourself with chocolate."

Jade looked up from the pastry at Nicole's face. She could see that Nicole was trying her best to control her laughter.

"Go ahead laugh!" She said.

Nicole just needed that much encouragement to throw her head back and laugh with all her might.

As she laughed, not one of those cute lady- like laughs, but a real tear jerker her long blonde hair shook in its pony tail.

She was wearing a pair of dark wash jeans and a pretty blue blouse.

"Sorry." She said once her laughter subsided a little.

Her blue- green eyes were twinkling with amusement.

"It's okay."

Jade had a scowl on her face which Nicole immediately noticed.

"Now why are you so stressed it's just Alec."

"Just Alec? You realise it is Alexander Carter we're talking about. My ex- best friend? How can I not be stressed out? I'm going to meet him for dinner on Monday, and I'll have to act all normal when the fact is that we have not spoken to each other for almost 8 years."

Jade shuddered even at the thought of the dinner and shoved another spoon full of chocolate into her mouth.

"You don't have to speak to him much. Weren't you saying just the other day that it has been ages since you last met Julia and Mrs Carter? So you spend time with them." Nicole replied with her characteristic calmness.

"It's not that simple. He's going to be there the whole time. And anyways everyone thinks that we are still good friends and have kept in touch."

"Just chill! It's just a matter of few days. And then he'll go back to his usual life and you can get back to yours."

Jade knew that what Nicole was saying was right. Alec's trips back home never lasted longer than a week or so. His life was too exciting to spend more than that in such a boring place.

But then why didn't the thought of him going back to his normal life, make Jade feel any better?

"I know." She said, softly, "His life is all exciting and glamorous. Why does he want to come here? I mean compared to his my life is going to look boring."

"Now don't you dare underestimate yourself. You have a fantastic life." Nicole said, suddenly she sat up a little straighter, "You know what you should do?"

"What?"

"Dress up really well and look gorgeous. Show him that not only exotic women are pretty."

"You and you're stupid idea that dressing good makes you feel better. That works only with you."

Nicole had been living her life based on this rule of hers.

"It works. And I'm going to prove it! I'll choose your dress for Monday night. I'll come over in the afternoon. Now that's a good idea!"

Nicole seemed really excited about the prospect of dressing her up.

"Monday is my day out with Nadia and Noah. I'm not going to miss out on spending time with my godchildren for Alec."

Every Monday Jade would take the twins out for the day. This outing had two advantages, Nicole got some 'me time' for herself while she would spend time with her beloved godchildren.

"Okay. You take them out in the day and I'll come before you leave for dinner and get you ready."

"You love to dress me up like a Barbie doll don't you? I thought that now that you have Nadia who you can dress up all you want, you would get bored of me. But I guess I was wrong."

Nicole frowned, "Nadia hates getting ready. Can you imagine? My daughter hates getting ready or dressing up."

Nicole was so fond of dressing up, designer shoes and clothes and make- up that when she was young she wanted to be a model.

It was a surprise to all her family members when she grew up and decided to be a English teacher.

She was a teacher at the university and taught the 'English as a foreign language class'.

For the rest of their time in the cafe they spoke about various useless gossips and joked around.

And like always Jade was having so much fun with Nicole that she actually forgot about the impending return of Alexander Carter.

Chapter 3

Unfortunately Jade's luck with forgetting about Alec's visit was not that good.

On Monday morning she woke with a churning feeling in her stomach. Not even the thought of spending the whole morning with the twins helped Jade to get rid of the churning.

And her talk with her mother the previous day had made matters worse.

Sunday afternoon Jade had been interrupted again while she wrote by her mother's call.

"Jade, did you get a call from Mrs Carter yesterday?" Amanda Tucker exclaimed in a way of greeting as soon as Jade picked up the phone.

"Hi mom! I'm doing good. How are you?" Jade had replied sarcastically while she moved away from the laptop, preparing herself for a long conversation.

"Being sarcastic is not lady- like, Jade." She said, but Jade could here the smile in her voice, "But answer my question. Did you hear from Susan?"

"Yes I did mom. I know Alec's coming for a visit." The thought was still making her shudder.

"But do you know the reason why he's coming?"

Jade had mentally gone over her full conversation with Mrs Carter trying to remember if she had mentioned the reason for his visit. But nothing came to her mind.

"Not really."

"Well, I was speaking to Susan and she told me that Alec is coming back home to introduce his girlfriend to the family. Isn't that sweet? And if he is coming back all the way from Thailand, their relationship must be pretty serious, right? Alec in a serious relationship. Nicole married with adorable twins. When are you going to get settled and give me the grandchildren that I deserve?"

Amanda had been rattling on but Jade had stopped listening at the mention of Alec's 'serious' girlfriend.

"Wait.... Alec's girlfriend?" She managed to croak out.

"Yes. Her name is Emmaline Burns. She works in the PR firm which does all the publicity for Wanderlust. Isn't that cute?"

Amanda being a librarian, living in the world of romance novels, found a lot of things cute and adorable.

"Uh… Yes…"

The rest of the conversation had been carried out solely by her while Jade had been thinking about the development in the case of Alec's return.

She had just made agreeing noises in the right places till Amanda was satisfied.

Now as she remembered the conversation she groaned and buried herself under the covers once again.

Today's dinner was going to be bad. A nightmare.

At last, after groaning, mumbling and just simply complaining for half an hour, Jade got up from her bed and went for a bath.

She was supposed to pick up the twins from the Bradshaw house in a hour and a half.

She quickly took a shower and changed into jeans and a comfortable tank top.

Comfort was on top of the list while deciding on what clothes to wear when going out with the twins, because she knew she was going to spend most of her time running after them.

She locked her apartment and left for Nicole's house in her car.

Nicole lived practically on the other side of town.

She reached the pretty cottage which belonged to her favourite family and Jade rang the doorbell.

From outside the house looked serene and peaceful.

But Jade could clearly hear the sounds of yells and screams coming through the wooden door.

"Hi!" Nicole said on opening the door.

She had Nadia propped on her hip, who was busy stuffing her mouth full with her mothers blonde hair.

Behind Nicole, Jade could see Jason trying to pry Noah away from a potted plant.

"Hey!" Jade said with a bright smile.

The twins could brighten her mood no matter how grumpy she felt.

Once Nadia noticed Jade standing on the doorstep, an angelic smile immediately lit her pretty, cherubic face.

She extended her hands and yelled as loud as she could- which was pretty loud-, "Jady!!!"

Taking the clue Jade took Nadia out of her mother's arms and tickled her under her chin, which made the kid giggle and laugh.

The sound of his sister laughing was successful in taking Noah's attention away from the plant and made him focus on the presence of Jade.

Immediately he started wriggling and throwing his hands about. Jason put him down and he ran to Jade and stood hugging her knees.

"Hey Jade welcome to the mess, which is our house."

Though Jason sounded fed-up as he picked up the cushions and toys from the carpet and placed them in their right place, there was a bright smile on his face.

Jade could see why Nicole had fallen for Jason in high school. He was tall and broad- shouldered with dark brown hair.

His eyes, which were a sharp blue colour always had a look of absolute amazement in them.

"Hey Jason!" Jade walked into the house with Nadia still in her arms and Noah dragging behind her, his arms wrapped tightly around her knees, "How's the Lawrence case going?"

Jason was a partner at one of the biggest law firms in the city. He was successful and extremely good at the job he did.

"It's going good. I'll be wrapping it up soon." He said, giving Jade a special smile for remembering.

"He's acting all laid- back in front of you but Jade you don't have any clue how tensed and worried he was a few days back."

Nicole commented as she tried her best to pull Noah away from his tight grip on Jade's legs.

"Did you have to break my bubble in front of Jade?" Jason gave a mock- frown.

Nicole and Jade laughed.

"And how is my favourite goddaughter?" Jade said looking at Nadia in her arms who was frowning at the lack of attention.

"I'm dood!" She exclaimed loudly.

"It's good Nania. I am good Jady!" Noah corrected his sister from below.

Having come into the world five minutes before Nadia, Noah took his job as elder brother very seriously.

"Now are you? And show me that big bruise your mom was telling me about."

Noah proudly held out his arm and Jade could see a big ugly bruise on his elbow.

"I gave him that vruise!" Nadia said proudly.

Having picked up all the stuff from the floor Nicole came and sat next to Jade on the sofa where she was sitting with both Noah and Nadia on her lap.

"Nadia that's nothing to be proud about. Hitting your brother is not good." She said sternly.

In reply to the accusation, the 3 year old angel just gave a dazzling smile to her mother.

" My pretty daughter thinks that a smile can get her everything." Nicole laughed.

"Well she does get everything when she smiles. She's going to be a real heartbreaker when she grows up." Jade replied.

"Let's not talk about heartbreakers. She's not having a boyfriend till she is 30." Jason entered the room with the twins' bag in his hands.

"Says the guy who married my best friend when she was just 22." Jade smiled, taking the bags from him.

One with a Barbie on the front and the other with Winnie the Pooh.

They headed towards the door, with Jade clutching the hands of Nadia and Noah and carrying the bags on her back.

"Be safe. Nadia, Noah don't trouble Jady. Come soon, you don't want to be late for dinner do you?"

In the confusion of all the havoc created by the twins, the dinner had slipped from Jade's mind, but Nicole's reminder brought the churning feeling back to her stomach.

"Yeah.... See you in the evening." Jade said quickly before settling the kids in the car and getting into the driver's seat herself.

It had been decided earlier that Nicole would come in the evening to help Jade choose the dress she would wear for the dinner and also to pick up the kids.

Dinner. Even the word made Jade sick. She shook her head, smiled at Jason and Nicole and drove ahead.

Today was her day with the twins and No one was going to spoil it.

Not even Alexander Carter. Definitely not Alexander Carter.

Chapter 4

M ATT

"Jady ice- cream!" Yelled Nadia from the back seat of the car where she was strapped in, just as Jade was parking in from Jo's the local ice- cream parlour.

Immediately, not to be left behind Noah also yelled, "Ice- cream" as loud as he could.

Jade had spent the whole morning at the zoo with the twins. She had mostly been dragged around from one animal to the next.

Till it was time to leave, Jade was drained out but at least there were no more thoughts of meeting Alec in the evening.

It was 2 and the twins wanted ice- cream. And that's what they would get.

As Jade made it a habit to give them whatever they wanted on their days with her. In short, she spoilt them rotten. Even their teeth.

"Yes guys! See we've reached Jo's! Now who wants a sundae?" Jade said once she had parked the car.

As the twins yelled and laughed, she got down and started helping them out.

"I want to take Horsy too!"

Nadia said dragging out the huge stuffed horse, Jade had bought for her from the gift shop at the zoo.

"And I want to take Ally!" Said Noah bringing out his stuffed alligator.

"Now, I think that Ally and Horsy will be safer and happier in the car. Let's leave them here. What if some other kids like them and want them for themselves?" Jade bent down till she was at eye-level with the twins and said.

"But Jady! Ally wants ice- cream too!" Noah insisted with a pout.

"So does Horsy!" His sister followed.

"Of course they do!" Sighed Jade and stood up with a smile on her face. "Come let's go."

The twins knew that Jade couldn't say no to them if they brought out the heavy duty guns, the pouty, puppy dog faces. And they took complete advantage of Jade's weakness.

Jo's had been opened by Johnathan Bailey the year after he left high school. And since then nothing had changed in it. The ice cream still had the same flavours and 50 different toppings.

The place still had the same bright coloured chairs and tables.

One addition was that old Jo now sat in one of the chairs everyday, having been pushed out from behind the counter 5 years back as his son Jo Junior and daughter- in- law took over the management of the place.

He sat there everyday and directed everyone about.

Jade had been going over there since she was small.

First she used to go there with Alec to enjoy the sundaes and joke around, then afterwards she used to go there with Nicole to enjoy the thick shakes.

And now Jo's was the place for her and the twins whenever she took them out.

The bell on the door tingled as Jade walked in with the twins and the huge soft toys.

"Hey Mr Bailey!" She said seeing the old wrinkled man sitting at his usual place.

"Jade! Here with the twins again are you?" Old Jo exclaimed.

He had seen Jade grow up into the successful, kind woman that she was now.

He still remembered her coming in with scraped knees and tear stained cheeks at the age of 5. The only cure to the scraped knees was a chocolate chip cone.

"Yes. They wanted sundaes." Jade smiled at Jo Junior standing behind the counter.

Jo had been two years ahead of them in school.

"Like they always want on their day out with you." He said as he started making their usual triple chocolate sundae.

"Come here little ones! Show this old man your toys. Come!" Old Jo said from his place.

The kids gleefully ran to him and showed of their possessions with pride.

The ice- cream parlour was filled with the locals.

Jo's was the most famous place in town for all youngsters.

Jade smiled at all the town people she recognised and then turned back to Jo who had finished preparing the huge sundae.

"Here you go Jade. 1 triple chocolate sundae for my favourite author and her godchildren."

He smiled as he handed her the big bowl.

"Favourite author? Don't tell me you've read even one of my novels." Jade laughed.

"I haven't but Ronnie reads out some parts to me."

"Now that's romantic!"

Jo blushed, "Now now! Don't go getting ideas!"

Jade flashed one last smile to Jo and walked to where the twins were sitting with his father.

"Sundae!" Both of them yelled as soon as they saw Jade come towards them with the sundae.

"Yup. Come here."

She placed the sundae on the table next to old Jo's.

The twins pounced onto the ice cream with gusto.

It was almost like they had not eaten anything for years.

"Guys chill! The ice cream isn't running away!" Jade said, "No Nadia don't lick your fingers! We have tissues."

But Nadia, who was enjoying the occasional treat, didn't pay any heed to Jade's words as she put her fingers into her mouth and licked of the chocolate sauce on them.

"Let them be Jade. I remember when you and the Alec Carter used to come in with your mothers. They used to be worried that you both would choke on the cold ice cream." He guffawed from the next table.

Jade clearly remembered those days when they used to hold competitions to see who could eat the most.

"Don't encourage them old Jo!"

She turned around with a smile and spooned some ice cream into her mouth.

The chocolate burst in her mouth and almost moaned out loud.

This was what she needed to make her life better.

The bell on the door rang again to signify someone else had entered the parlour.

But Jade was busy laughing with the twins and having the ice cream that she didn't care till she heard someone clear their throat from behind.

She turned around with the spoon still in her mouth and she had a strong suspicion that there was ice cream on her nose.

"Hi Jade!"

There in the parlour stood Matt Damon with all his good looks.

He was dressed in a casual white shirt with blue jeans.

Jade stumbled and quickly took out the spoon from her mouth, "Hi!"

"Hello, Nadia and Noah! Your day out with Jady is it?"

Jade swallowed as Matt bent over the twins and tickled them.

Jade had gone out with Matt for almost a year before they broke up.

And she could still see why she had agreed to go out with him.

His dark brown, almost black hair, was falling on his forehead, as he flashed his breath stopping smile at the twins.

"What brings you here?" She said after clearing her throat.

"I was just craving Jo's ice cream." He said, "Is anyone sitting here?"

Jade looked at the seat at which Matt was pointing at.

"No. Please sit."

Matt took the chair and turned it around before sitting down with the back of the chair to his chest.

"So what else is going on?"

Jade looked up into Matt blue eyes, "Nothing much. Just normal."

"Just normal?"

"Yeah."

Matt just looked at Jade with his head tilted and his eyes narrowed.

"What?" She asked at last.

"Nothing. You just look good." He replied matter of factly.

"Matt-"

Jade was interrupted by the ringing of her phone.

She picked up the phone and saw that it was from Nicole.

"I'll just take this call."

"Sure. Go ahead!" Matt said and turned towards the twins and started talking to them.

"Hey Nicky?" Jade said picking up the call with one eye still on Matt.

"Where are you?" Nicole said without any greeting whatsoever.

"At Jo's. Why?"

"Ice cream, Jade? Seriously? If they get a cold I'm sending them to your place."

Jade laughed, "They won't. And anyways did you call to tell me this?"

"Oh yeah! No. Did you forget about dinner today?"

"I wish I could." Jade sighed.

"Well you are going to be late if you don't come back now. I've to get you ready." Nicole exclaimed.

"Nicky!"

"I'm leaving the class. You better be at your apartment before I reach there." Nicole warned before hanging up.

The last thing Jade felt like doing at the moment was get ready.

"Any problem?" Matt asked looking at the expression on Jade's face.

"No. It's just Nicole."

"Oh!"After their break up it had always been awkward between them.

Their relationship had not ended in a bad way but they had had a disagreement about the future of the relationship.

While Jade never looked for anything serious in her relationships, Matt wanted them to move in and move ahead in the relationship.

This must have been like the second or third time they had met since the break up.

"We should get going."Jade said to the twins and also to Matt.

"No Jady!" Nadia whined.

"We no want to go home." Noah said.

"Come on sweets! Mom's waiting. And we're not going home, we're going to my apartment."

That got them going.

The twins loved Jade's apartment especially because of the big LED tv she had.

"I'll drop you to the car." Matt said helping Nadia get of the chair.

He did not listen to any of Jade's protests and insisted to drop them to the car.

After securing the twins in their seats, Jade stood up and faced Matt.

"Thanks!"

"No problem." Matt looked at her with his intense look, "I wanted to talk to you anyways."

"About?" She asked.

She avoided to look into his eyes.

"I miss you Jade." He said, "I really want to get back together."

She was so stunned at his words that Jade just stared at him.

"Matt-"

Before she could continue Matt bent and placed his lips on hers in a soft kiss.

For a second she forgot all the bad things in her life and concentrated on the kiss.

She remembered the carefree and frivolous relationship she had had with Matt.

The days she had spent with him had been really good. He was one of the sweetest guys she had ever met and had really fallen for him.

But then she remember how he wanted more from what they had. Much more than she could even think of giving.

"Matt."

Jade sighed and nudged him away softly.

"Jade?"

His lips were swollen as he looked at her.

"We can't do this. I really like you and you are a great guy. But Matt I cant give you what you need from this relationship. I'm sorry."

Matt cupped her face in his big hands, "Jade I understand. But-"

"Your a great guy Matt and I'm sure you'll find a girl who wants the same things from life as you do. It's just not me." She said softly placing her hands on his.

"Sadly!" Matt sighed stepping back.

"Sadly." She agreed, "Bye Matt. See you."

Jade stood on her toes and placed her lips on his cheek in a soft kiss.

"Bye Jade."

She got into the car and took a deep breathe.

"Jady! Were you kissing Matty? Like mom kisses Daddy?" Nadia asked.

Jade laughed, "I guess I was."

She left for her apartment with thoughts of the coming dinner pushing out the thoughts of kiss from her head.

Chapter 5

ALEC

In the 8 years that Alec had been away from his home town, Millbrooke had changed very little.

It still had the cosy small town feel to it.

As he looked out of the window of the rented car he had taken from the airport in Chicago to drive the 8 miles to Millbrooke, he saw the Main Street.

It looked the same just with a few more additions in the long line of shops and food joints.

There were a few boutiques and some of the food chains had opened their branches there.

The feeling of coming back home was surprisingly nostalgic.

They passed the kindergarten school where he had met Jade for the first time.

Jade Tucker, his best friend!

Coming back home meant that he would meet her once again after almost 8 years.

Mom had said that she had stayed in Millbrooke itself.

Alec wondered how her life was now.

The crazy, funny girl he remembered had gone on to be one of the most popular authors in the country, and Alec could not be more proud.

He couldn't wait to meet her.

Just then they passed Jo's ice cream parlour.

Though there were some small changes in the town that Alec noticed Jo's was still exactly the same.

With it's colourful boards and chairs it still looked like the cheerful place he remembered.

He slowed down and entered the parking lot of Jo's.

"Where are we going? Have we reached?"

Emma's British accent from the passenger seat reminded him that he was not alone in the car.

"You have to try Jo's ice cream! It's the best in the world. I thought we'll just make a quick stop and then go home." He said before quickly getting into one of the empty spaces.

Emma snorted, "Best ice cream in the world? No ways! The best ice cream I had was in London. This is just a small town how good can it be?"

Alec did not even attempt to argue with her.

Emmaline Burns had very strong ideas and opinions and it was extremely hard to change them.

"Come."

He opened the door and stepped out.He took a huge breath, breathing in the clear air without any pollution after years.

He stretched waiting for Emma to adjust her make up and step out of the car.

He looked around the parking lot.Suddenly he spotted something that made him stand up straight and look carefully.

There on the other side of the parking lot four people were coming out of the ice cream parlour.

There were two kids who looked so similar that they had to be twins.

Holding the girl in one hand and a huge stuffed horse in the other was a man.

He was dressed casually and even from this far Alec could see that he looked good.

On the other side of him was the other kid, a boy with a stuffed alligator in his hand.

The man and the kids were laughing and enjoying the short walk to the car.Just a few steps behind them was a girl.

She was tall with long legs and a thin waist.

Her black hair was straight and almost till her waist. She was wearing a tank top that showed of her bare arms.

She was tanned and Alec could see that she was stunning.

It was Jade.

He was sure. Though he could not see her face properly he was confident that it could not be anyone else.

The way she carried herself confidently and gracefully.

Was this her family? Mom had not mentioned anything about her marriage. And surely she had not said anything about twins.

And why was he feeling sick at the thought of her marrying some jerk?

There was no reason for him to be jealous. He should be happy for her and instead here he was getting a sudden urge to punch the man who was helping her strap the kids in the back seat of the car.

When the kids were strapped and secured Jade stood up and faced the unknown guy, with the white shirt which was spotless.

Who's white shirt is spotless? Thought Alec.

They spoke for a few minutes and then to Alec's surprise the guy bent and started kissing her.

Alec felt the acid burn in his throat as he clenched his fist.

He knew he was being silly. What difference did it make to him if Jade was kissing people in random parking lots?

God knows he had done more than enough kissing himself since the last time he had met her.

To his relief, Jade pushed the guy away. Well if he had to be honest she nudged him away.

The guy cupped her face and they exchanged a few words.

Alec was almost stalking Jade now, but he didn't care.

She stood on her toes and placed a soft kiss on his cheek, before turning around, getting into the car and driving away.

The guy stood for sometime before he too got into a car and drove away.

"What are you looking at? I thought we were going to have ice cream." Emma asked as she came to stand next to him.

Alec gulped the knot that was lodged in his throat and said, "Nothing. Come on."

She took his hand and they walked towards the ice cream parlour.

The bell on the door rang as they pushed it open and stepped into the parlour.

It still had the sweet smell of sugar, milk and waffle. A smell Alec could never forget.

"Is that you Alexander Carter?"

The gruff voice made Alec turn and he was face to face with old Jo.

He was more wrinkled than he remembered, with a shock of white hair on his head.

"Old Jo! Who did you think it was?"Alec went and gave the old man a tight hug.

He was the superhero of his childhood.A superhero who had an ice cream cone in one hand and a ice cream scooper in the other.

"It's been years." Old Jo said once they stopped hugging.

"8 years is a long time. And how have you been?"

"Good good! Except for the fact that my son and daughter in law pushed me from behind the counter. I'm not allowed to work anymore. My own shop that too. But no!"

Alec laughed. It must have been quite a feat on Jo Juniors part to stop the adamant old man from doing the work he so loved.

"You've been betrayed by your own family have you?"

Old Jo guffawed.

"Now enough about me. Introduce me to the beautiful young lady with you."

Alec put his hand on Emma's waist and said, "This is Emmaline Burns. Emma this is Jo Bailey. The owner of the best ice cream place."

"Nice to meet you, Mr Bailey." Emma said in her clipped British voice with a smile.

"British are you? Always liked the English women. What with their strong accents and manners." Old Jo said much to Emma's amusement.

"Uh..." She started saying something.

"Now our Mr Bailey has always been a ladies man." Alec said.

Again Old Jo laughed loudly.

Alec said a quick bye to the old man and went towards the counter.

"Alec Carter?" Jo junior asked with disbelief.

"The same." Alec smiled.

"I didn't know you were in town. How have you been?" He said coming out from behind the counter and hugging Alec.

This is the thing of small towns.

Everyone knew everyone's business and everyone was glad to meet you.

"I've been great! Heard you took over the parlour?"

"Oh the old man needs to rest and as long as he works in the parlour he can't rest. So now I work and he sits there and orders me around."

They laughed.

Alec had been in the basketball team with Jo and they had always been good friends.

"This is Emma by the way." Alec said introducing Emma to him.

"Hello, ma'am! And what can I get you both?" Jo asked.

"I'll take my usual, cookie and cream cone. Emma?" Alec said.

"Umm... Strawberry?" She said.

In her beige ironed skirt suit she looked out of place in a colourful and fun place as the parlour. And she felt equally out of place.

"I'll serve it up in a minute." Jo said getting busy with the cones.

Alec turned towards Emma and said, "Why don't you go and catch a seat I'll get the ice cream."

Emma gave a parting look and walked in the direction of the empty booths.

The only booth that was empty was the one right next to old Jo's. As she took the seat, the old man started talking to her.

Emma winced and replied to him.Alec laughed and turned back to the counter.

Now he could ask what he wanted to.

"Jo was Jade here a few minutes ago? I saw her leave but I didn't recognise the people she was with."

Jo turned around from the ice cream storage, "She was here with the twins."

"The twins?" Alec asked.

"Of I forgot you don't know. Nadia and Noah Bradshaw are Nicole and Jason Bradshaw's twins. They are three and notorious." Jo said.

"Jason and Nicole got married?"

"It's been 5 years now."

Alec was surprised at all the developments in the lives of his friends that he had missed out on in the last 8 years.

"That's a surprise." He made a mental note of calling up Jason the first chance he got and then continued, "And that guy?"

"Oh that was Matt Damon. He is the new doctor in town. Not so new anymore. It's been 4 years since he moved here." Jo said, "Here you go!"

Alec took the ice creams from Jo's hand and passed the money to him.

"Thanks Jo. By the way are they dating?"

Jo smiled.

Working at such a place which was frequented by almost everyone in town he knew gossip about everyone.

And he had been interrogated about people so often that he was quite used to it.

Guys asking about single girls. Girls asking about their ex's new girl. It was routine for him.

Jo placed his elbows on the counter.

"They were dating and I didn't hear anything about a break up. So I guess they still are." He shrugged. "Why don't you ask her yourself?"

"I'm going to do that. Didn't get a chance today." Alec said quickly.

"Okay. Enjoy!"

Alec smiled and took the ice cream to where Emma was sitting. She looked tortured.

Alec sat next to her and handed her the ice cream.

Old Jo stopped talking to Emma about the English women he had met in his youth.

Someone had ordered for Jo's special sundae and the old man started issuing orders to Jo who was making it.

Emma sighed and turned to Alec, "He can talk a lot!" She said.

"Oh yes he can!" Alec took his first bite of the ice cream and he remembered all those times he used to come here with Jade to have ice cream when they were small.

He had many memories in Millbrooke, that he had left behind.

And now that he was back those memories were not going to let him go easily again.

Chapter 6

Emma looked around at the streets and shops going past the window as they drove through the town of Millbrooke.

Having lived all her life in a crowded and energetic city like London, this laid back and small town made her feel uncomfortable and out of place.

The people walking on the streets were all casually dressed even though it was a Monday morning.

Everyone was smiling at each other and giving cheerful nods.

How would it feel to live in a place where everyone knew you, and you knew everyone?

Even in the ice cream shop where they had stopped earlier, which Alec had been praising so much, that old man had started a conversation with her as if he knew her since the beginning of time. It was unsettling and a bizarre concept for her.

Her beige skirt and jacket looked as out of place, as her pale skin.

Everyone over here sported a healthy tan that one could get, only by spending whole days out in the sun.

To make things worse, Alec had been acting really different ever since they entered the town.

He was lost in his own thoughts and was barely talking to her at all.

She turned in her seat to look at him with a critical eye.

She had met Alexander Carter for the first time at a meeting in her office in London.

Emma worked for Bridge and Co. a PR agency in London and Wanderlust, Alec's travel company was one of the biggest clients their company had.

She had been promoted a few days back when her boss had taken her along for a meeting with Wanderlust.

That's when she met Alec in the conference room.

He had stood completely out of place with his sandy brown hair and blue eyes, dressed in a casual shirt and jeans.

But the smile which he flashed at her when they were introduced had stopped her heart.

He was handsome, in a rugged outdoorsy way.

And the fact that Wanderlust was doing great and making Alec and Derek the owners rich in a very short time also helped his case.

It was not long before they started dating and if everything went according to her plan they would be married by the end of this year.

It had been her plan to come to Millbrooke and meet his family. She wanted him to introduce her to his mom.

She knew very well that, meeting the parents was the first step to the nuptials which she was already planning.

She herself had taken him to meet her parents a week before they left for America.

And to say that the meeting had been a success would be an underestimation.

Mother had loved the fact that he was handsome and well mannered. While Father had been clearly impressed by the success of Wanderlust and all the plans they had for its future.

Her parents had made it very clear to her, very early in her life that she had to marry well to live a good life. And not only for love. Marriage was a thing which had to be well thought through and planned ahead of time.

And Alec met all their expectations.

So she had convinced him to take her to Millbrooke. But that was before she knew what a small town this was.

The air was so clear here and the streets silent, without any honking or shouting. So silent that she almost had a head ache.

They had been driving for hours and it felt like they were heading in the direction of the end of the world.

"When are we going to reach, Alec?"

Alec turned to see Emma who was pouting.

"In a few minutes. We're almost there."

Emma smiled, "I can't wait to meet your mother and sister! I'm so excited."

Alec smiled back before turning his attention back to the road.

They passed a garden with huge, shady trees and took a turn into a street lined with big houses.

The houses had nice front yards with flowers and well mowed lawns.

Alec parked his car in front of one of the houses.

Now this was the kind of thing Emma was thinking about.

Emma knew that Alec had lost his dad to a car accident when he had been 9.

And Jackson Carter had left them all the money he had earned from his hotel business.

She had known that even without Wanderlust, Alec was rich.

Julia, his sister now took care of the Carter hotel business.

"We're here."

Alec said getting out of the car and stretching.

The house looked the same.

This was the place where he had grown up. He had spent all his childhood and teenage years in this house and had made thousands of memories here.

That was the garden in which he had played in with Jade.

He knew that when he stepped in the house, it would have the same smell of lemongrass and home cooked food.

Emma got down from the car after Alec, slowed down because of her towering heels.

"It's beautiful!"

"Yes it is."

Alec sighed and turned towards the car to remove their luggage.

"Won't there be someone to take the luggage?" Emma asked when she saw Alec taking out her three Louis Vuitton suitcases from the trunk.

"Only mom and Julia are in there right now, Emma. I told you Steve will be coming day after to meet us."

Steve was Julia's husband who was in Chicago taking care of the hotel in the absence of Julia.

"I didn't mean Steve. I meant servants or something."

Alec heaved the last suitcase out and gave her a incredulous look.

"Em we don't have servants here."

"But there must be someone who takes care of the whole house. Cleaning, cooking and stuff."

"Mom does all the cooking and most of the cleaning on her own. The cleaning lady comes once in two weeks to give her a hand."

"What?"

This was absurd. Such a big house and no servants. No one to do the cooking.

She and her parents lived in a house which was the same size as this one and they had help coming in every day.

And she couldn't remember the last time Paula Burns, her mother had entered the kitchen.

"I know. I keep telling mom that we should sell this house and she should move into a smaller one. She's too old now to take care of such a huge house. But no, she says she entered the house as a bride and won't leave it till she dies."

Alec heaved the bags up the stairs as Emma stood without lifting a finger, appalled at the thought of selling this beautiful house.

"Are you going to stand there?"

Alec had reached the door and was about to ring the bell.

Emma ran up the front yard and the stair as fast as she could in her heels.

"Don't be nervous about meeting mom. She's the sweetest person on earth." Alec gave her hand a reassuring squeeze, mistaking her delay for hesitation due to nervousness rather than surprise.

He rang the bell.

A scrambling noise came from inside, and someone said loudly, "They're here!"

The door was pulled open and there in the middle of the doorway stood Susan Carter.

She saw Alec standing on the threshold and immediately hugged him tightly.

"Oh Alec! Too long it's been too long. I thought you forgot your old mother."

When they separated, Alec had a huge grin on his face and his mom had a bigger smile and tears on her face.

"Now now mom. You are not even close to old and how can I forget the most beautiful woman on earth." Alec said.

Susan Carter looked the same.

She was shorter than him by almost a foot with sandy blonde hair like his and dark green eyes.

Her smile still was beautiful though now there were a few more wrinkles around her eyes and lips.

She had a well maintained body and was dressed in fitting slacks and a loose shirt.

"And you must be Emmaline!"

To Emma's surprise she found herself being hugged by Susan.

Emma belonged to one of the proper British families, where manners and politeness were prided. From a young age certain things had been drilled into her. One of the main things being that it was absolutely necessary to hold yourself aloof from everyone.

So hugging was definitely not something her parents approved of. She couldn't remember the last time she had hugged her parents let alone anyone else.

She stood awkwardly and patted her back with her hands till Susan let her go.

"You can't believe how happy I am to meet you." Susan gleamed up at her.

Emma gave a bright smile and said, "Im pleased to meet you too, Mrs Carter!"

"Oh call me Susan."

"Okay Susan. And let me tell you, this town is absolutely charming."

"There's the British accent. I was waiting for it. Mom are you planing to leave them standing at the door or are you going to let them come in."

A pretty looking woman, who looked to be in her early 30's stepped out from behind the half open door.

This must be Julia, thought Emma.

She had the same eyes as Alec, but her hair was darker almost brown.

She had a smiling face and she was as tall as Alec.

Her brown hair was long and left open to curl till her waist.

She was dressed casually in jeans and a white t- shirt.

"Hey bro!" She hugged Alec tightly once they had been pulled in the house by Susan.

"Hey Sis!" Alec pulled Julia up from the floor and twirled her around once before letting her down.

"Hello Emmaline."

Emma shook the hand extended by Julia.

"Please call me Emma."

"Come in! Come in! Julia help Alec get in the bags. Emma, you come with me."

Susan pulled Emma into the living room behind her.

The house was decorated in a cozy fashion with soft sofas and plenty of knickknacks.

There were fluffy cushions and the wall was painted in warm colours.

The decoration was nothing like anything Emma had ever seen in anyone of the houses she had frequented in London.

Back there, all her family friends had houses which were carefully decorated by interior decorators. The owners didn't have a say in what went where.

If there were books on the shelves, they were there not because someone in the house liked reading them, it was because they looked good with the colours of the room and it gave an intellectual feel to the room.

Her house in London and all the houses she had visited over years for dinner parties and tea parties, didn't have the homey feel to it.

The Carter house had an individual touch to it. There were photos all around, and paintings by Julia and Alec.

The house was smelling of something delicious and the smell seemed to be coming from the kitchen.

"Steve's great." Julia said coming into the living room with Alec.

"Mom do I smell chocolate chip cookies?"

Alec said sniffing the air like a dog.

"Yes. But no cookies before lunch."

Alec felt great coming back home. He loved that the house always had a cozy feel to it. He loved that he could be himself in the house. And most of all he loved that he was meeting Julia and mom after so long.

He went and plopped down next to his mom on one of the sofas opposite where Emma was sitting.

He hoped that in those three suitcases, she was carrying something a little casual.

Because right now sitting in the casual living room of their house, Emma's suit looked even more out of place.

"Lunch is ready. I thought you both can freshen up a little and then we can have lunch together. I'm sure you must be tired Emma."

Emma gave Susan a smile and said, "That will be perfect."

"Great! Julia go show Emma where the guest room is. Alec you know where your room is."

Susan headed into the kitchen.

"Guest room?"

Emma turned towards Alec.

Did they really expect them to stay in different rooms?

They two of them had been living together for almost a year now. It was part of her plan leading to their marriage and now they were going to stay in different rooms.

"Emma, mom is old fashioned. And though she clearly knows that you both have.... You know.... 2 years is a long time. But I don't think she'll be comfortable with you two living in the same room."

Julia stuttered and made herself busy trying to pick the bags.

"But...."

"Emma... Let's adjust. It's only for a few weeks." Alec interrupted her.

"Okay."

Together they carried all the bags to the second floor where the guest bedroom was.

Not only was she expected to live in a different room, but Alec's room was on a different floor altogether.

The guest bedroom was really pretty with a huge double bed and pale blue walls.

From the window the pretty garden could be seen and on the walls there were paintings of flowers and gardens.

"The room is really pretty."

Julia smiled.

"Mom did the decorations herself." She kept the last bag on the floor, "Now we'll go. You freshen up and we'll meet for lunch in half and hour?"

"Sure."

Alec who was standing next to Emma gave her hand a squeeze and walked out of the room behind Julia, leaving Emma alone in the room.

Was this really a good idea? Thought Emma flopping down on the bed.

Chapter 7

A MANDA

"You look great!"

Jade gave Nicole a self conscious smile as she stood in front of the mirror fidgeting with the dress.

Nicole had selected a navy blue sleeveless dress for her to wear for dinner at the Carter house.

Jade had bought the dress from a small boutique 2 years back during one of her rare trips to New York.

And she had never worn it.

The hemline of the skirt came barely till mid- thigh, and though the colour was very pretty and brought out the green of her eyes, it made her self conscious.

"Jade stop fidgeting. You look beautiful."

Nicole was sitting on the bed going through all the earrings Jade owned, trying to figure which would look good.

"You mean that? Don't you think it's too much?"

Jade stepped away from the full length mirror and looked at Nicole.

She had come from Jo's ice cream parlour, to find Nicole waiting in front of her apartment.

The twins had immediately been ushered in by their mother. After a quick wash up, they had been settled in front of the TV and Nicole had started getting Jade ready.

Even now almost an hour later the cute cartoon noises were coming from the living room.

"Yes I mean it! You wait and watch one look at you and Alec will forget all about his girlfriend with her British accent."

"I'm not trying to steal Alec away, Nicole."

Jade turned back towards the mirror to hide the blush that had crept onto her face.

"I know that Jade. But sweetie, he's the dumbass who didn't realise that you were in love with him."

"Nicole!"

That was the thing Jade had been trying to avoid since she heard that Alec was coming back to town.

The reason why she was so reluctant to meet Alec after so many years was not only that he was her best friend and they had lost contact.

But also because, she, Jade Tucker, had made the biggest mistake in the world and had fallen in love with her best friend.

And when, Alec had moved out of town, attracted to all the unknown things out in the world, he had taken one thing with him. A piece of her heart.

Nicole was the only person she had told about it.

"What?" Nicole came to stand near her, "It's the truth!"

"It was the truth. I'm no longer in love with Alec. It was 8 years back and I have grown out of that stupid infatuation."

"Grown out? Really? You were the one who was stress eating when you heard that he was coming back."

"That's a different matter."

Jade started combing her hair. She knew that Nicole was telling the truth, but admitting it would make it more difficult to face Alec in the evening.

8 years and about 15 relationships later, she had still not managed to find someone to replace Alec in that corner of her heart.

"Jade you can lie to me, but not to yourself."

Just as Nicole was going to say something else the doorbell rang.

Nicole gave a look to Jade that made it clear that they were not done with the conversation and went out to open the door.

Jade finished coming her hair, put on her black high heeled pumps and followed Nicole out.

"Jady you look pretty!"

Nadia dragged her eyes from the cartoons and looked at Jade.

"Thank you, sweetie."

Nicole gave her 'I- told- you- so' look and pulled open the door.

"Hello Nicole! How are you? Haven't you become too thin?"

Amanda Tucker bustled into the room, giving Nicole a tight hug on the way.

She was wearing a pale peach shirt over grey well fitted slacks and her blonde hair, which was liberally streaked with grey and cut till her chin was open and swinging around her face.

"Nadia! Noah! Am I going to get a hug?"

The twins ran into Amanda's arms with huge grins on their faces and when they came up each was clutching a lollipop in their hands.

"Mommy see! Amanda Nana gave us lollies!" Noah said showing of his lollipop proudly.

"I can see that. I think the Tucker women have taken it up on them to spoil your teeth."

Amanda laughed, "Now the least I can do is spoil them."

"Hey Mom!"

Jade got up from the sofa, from where she had been looking at the scene.

"Jady! Now don't you look pretty!"

Jade hugged her mother.

One thing Jade loved about her mom was that, Amanda Tucker was always cheerful. No matter what was happening she had a comforting smile on her face and a twinkle in her eyes.

And she had the magical power to make the people around her also happy.

It was just an Amanda thing.

"See I told you!" Nicole said as she opened the lollipops for the twins.

"You don't look bad either mom."

Amanda raised an eyebrow, "Really? When do I ever look bad?"

Jade laughed.

That much was true.

All the people in town always told Jade, that in her youth, Amanda had been one of the prettiest girls in town.

With wavy blonde hair, green eyes and a sunny personality, she had the power to attract everyone to her.

Everyone told Jade that she looked exactly like her mom.

Now in her 60's Amanda had aged beautifully.

She had a well maintained figure and her blonde hair suited her style.

The secret to her figure almost being better than Jade was the jogging she did every morning before going to the town library where she had been working as the head librarian since before Jade was born.

"And how was your day with the twins? And how was the kiss with Dr Matthew?"

"Kiss? Matthew?"

Nicole had a stunned look on her face.

Jade was not surprised that her mom knew about the kiss in front of the ice cream parlour.

The library was the centre of all the gossip around town and Amanda Tucker knew everything about everyone.

"Who was I caught by?"

Jade walked into the kitchen, followed by a smirking Amanda and a confused Nicole.

"Elizabeth Johnson, saw you while coming out of Jo's with her grand daughter."

Jade laughed, "Next time I meet Mrs Johnson we need to have a talk."

"Okay will someone tell me what's happening?"

Nicole plopped onto one of the breakfast chairs.

"Nothing is happening." Jade filled a glass with water and handed it to her mother, "Matt was coincidentally at Jo's at the same time as me and the twins. He sat with us and then offered to drop us till the car."

"And?"

Nicole urged.

"And then he kissed me."

"Just like that?"

"Yeah just like that. He said he missed me and wanted to give our relationship another try."

Amanda raised an eyebrow with a smile playing on her lips.

Jade was sure she was already thinking about cute babies who looked like Matt with the same green eyes as her.

"And what did you say?"

Nicole looked so eager to know the answer that it was almost funny.

What would be the best way to answer this?

Telling the truth would make Nicole think that she refused Matt because of their conversations tom earlier, about Alec.

And lying about it would make mom dream even more.

"I told him that I need some time to think. And I'll tell him later."

"And what is your answer going to be?"

Nicole was propped her elbows on the table.

"If I already knew what my answer is going to be I would have told him earlier."

Nicole scowled and sat down again.

"But still. What do you think? You two were very good together."

Amanda had always liked Matt.

And when the two of them had been dating, she had really thought that they would have ended up together.

But suddenly Jade had gone and broken their relationship. Shattering all the dreams that she had been seeing.

"I don't know, mom."

"Okay let's forget that. But how was the kiss?"

Jade had to laugh at that. Her mom could change her mood no matter what.

"Like kisses with him always are."

"Since neither me nor your mom has ever kissed him. That answer is completely invalid."

"The kiss was sweet and intense. He is a really sweet guy."

"Oooo!"

Jade laughed again. Her best friend and her mother were really the best remedy to her sucky mood.

"We should leave. We'll get late otherwise."

Her moms words got the churning back in her stomach.

"Yeah. I guess."

Nicole got up from her seat and started adjusting Jade's hair.

"Now just remember you look gorgeous. And you're going to tell me what happened as soon as you come home. I want a detailed description of Emmaline Burns."

Jade laughed, "Yes Nicky!"

They started leaving. Just as they were about to leave Jade remembered that she had left her purse in her room.

She went back in while Nicole for the twins ready to go home.

She picked up her small silver bag and stood in front of the mirror for a second.

She really was looking good in the dress.

She smiled at herself, "Maybe Nicky was right."

Please god let the dinner go good, she thought before following her mom out of her apartment.

Chapter 8

JULIANA

After saying their goodbyes to Nicole and the twins, Jade got into her mom's car.

"Are you excited to see Alec after so long?"

Amanda asked while backing out of the apartment building.

"Yeah... Yes I am." Jade stuttered. "I can't wait to meet Julia and Mrs Carter either."

Julia lived in Chicago with her husband, where they ran the hotel business which had been in the Carter family for generations.

Jade didn't ever miss a chance to meet them whenever she went to Chicago.

But it had been almost a year since she had last visited Chicago. And it had been more than two years since she met Mrs Carter.

"Susan is so excited, you have no idea."

Jade smiled. She had such good memories with the Carter family. She was not going to let her stupid feelings for Alec come in between a good dinner with her favourite family.

The Carter's lived about 15 minutes from Jade's apartment.

On the way, Jade was kept entertained by all the gossip of the town her mom collected in the day.

"We're here."

Jade looked up at her moms words.

They were parked in front of the huge white house which belonged to the Carter family.

Some architects who were in love with buildings, often say that buildings or houses have vivid and bright personalities like human beings.

If that was true, the Carter house had surely a personality like an old, regal woman.

Standing in all it's glory of white walls and huge decorative gardens, it had stood there watching years go by.

The house had witnessed the wedding of Mr and Mrs Carter, the birth of their daughter Julia and son Alec.

The house had been there to witness the whole days Jade herself had spent in its cozy rooms and beautiful gardens.

This house was as much a home to her as her apartment or her mom's house on the other side of town.

She had spent some of the best days of her life in it. Days that she will never be able to forget.

"Let's go!"

Jade saw her mom get down. The prospect of going in and meeting Alec and his girlfriend brought the churning back.

There was no backing out now. She couldn't turn back.

Don't chicken out, Jade!

She took a deep breath and stepped out of the car.

They walked up the front yard and up the stairs together.

They rang the bell.

It's show time!

"You both could have told me earlier that you have invited Amanda and Jade for dinner. We would have been prepared." Alec said as he put the buttons of his light blue shirt.

After lunch when he and Julia were sitting on the front porch enjoying Moms cookies, Julia had told him about the dinner.

Emma had been asleep in the guest room trying to overcome the jet lag.

"Is it a problem, Alec?"

Julia was not concerned about how her brother felt about the dinner guests.

She was worried that Emma wouldn't be comfortable meeting new people the day she came.

She herself came to know about the homecoming dinner that morning when she had come home to see mom making food for company.

She understood that mom had been so excited about Alec's return that she couldn't stop herself from inviting her best friend.

It was a wonder she had not invited the whole town.

But she didn't expect Emma to understand Mom's behaviour.

"Of course not, Jules. I'm dying to meet them. It's been ages."

Alec said once he was done with the shirt.

"And Emma?"

"She's glad she gets to meet Jade. Don't worry so much."

Alec came up and gave his sister's shoulder a light squeeze.

His mom's plan had actually made his plan of meeting Jade as soon as possible, easier.

"Okay."

Julia looked so worried that Alec had to laugh, "Jules chill! Everything will be fine. Emma's not as hoity- toity as she seemed this morning."

"Hoity- toity?"

The two of them laughed aloud together.

It was just like old times.

Julia and Alec had always been very close to each other. Maybe because they had lost their father at a very young age and that had left them with only their mother and each other.

Julia was 3 years older than Alec, but that didn't make a difference to their teasing and fun relationship.

"You do look pretty."

Alec said once they had caught their breathe from all the laughter.

"Is my younger brother giving me a compliment?"

"I'll deny it if you say it in front of anyone. But yes."

Julia smiled, "Thanks."

She was really looking quite good, in a black dress with full sleeves and the hemline till a little above her knee.

A dress which had been given to her by her husband Steve, on her previous birthday.

"So when are they coming?"

"Anytime now."

Julia got up from her place on the bed in Alec's room.

His room was the same as he had left it, with pictures from all over the world stuck on the walls and photos of her, Jade and their mom next to them.

It was a mess of pictures and vivid colours. A mess, which he had made lovingly and painstakingly.

She looked at her brother.

Alec looked the same, with his sandy- brown hair and handsome face.

His blue eyes still sparkled with good humour.

He was tanned and leaner than when he had gone.

But there were lines near his eyes now, making it clear that running Wanderlust, was not only fun and games.

"I really did miss you, Al."

"I missed you too."

Just then the bell rang.

"That must be them."

Julia started leaving the room.

"You go open the door, I'll call Emma."

Alec said taking the stairs two at a time towards Emma's room.

He was just hoping that she had opted for something a little casual this time.

Something other than the suit she was wearing that morning.

He was used to seeing her dressed that formally.

Emma was that kind of girl who was always perfectly prim and proper. The kind of girl who had pearls in her ears and wore sweater sets all the time.

"Emma?"

The door to the room was open and she was standing in front of the mirror looking critically at herself.

"Hi. Do I look okay?"

Emma was wearing a pair of slate grey slacks and a dark blue shirt. Her hair was open and fell till her shoulder.

This was the most casual Emma could be.

"Good." He said shoving his hands into the pockets of his black jeans, "they're here."

"Oh! Let's go then."

Emma followed Alec out of the guest bedroom.

"Tell me again who all are coming?"

"Only Amanda Tucker, mom's best friend and her daughter, Jade."

"Your best friend?"

Alec had told Emma everything about his friendship with Jade.

Even if he would not have told her, she would have guessed from the amount of pictures they had of the two of them in the house and he had in his apartment.

"Yes my best friend."

"Okay. Let's see how it goes."

Loud voices were already coming from the living room.

Yes, let's see how it goes, thought Alec before entering the living room.

Chapter 9

Susan opened the front door to see her best friend Amanda and Jade, Amanda's daughter standing over there.

She squealed and hugged Amanda though they had met just the previous day for lunch.

Then she pulled Jade into a tight hug.

"Hello Mrs Carter!"

Jade laughed when she held her at arms length.

It's had been too long since she had met Jade.

Her dark brown, almost black hair had grown out in curls and her green eyes were still sparkly.

Susan still remembered when Alec had got Jade over for the first time, both of them laughing and joking, wearing their kindergarten uniforms.

Jade had changed a lot since then, but she was still her Jady, she was still like a daughter to her.

"Hello Jade!"

"Now Mrs Carter, soon I'll start looking older than you. Have some pity on the minors!"

Susan laughed, "Flattering me won't help. I've not met you for days. And you calling me Mrs Carter even after so many years makes me feel like I'm 90."

Jade had this thing with Susan, as a rule she never called her anything but Mrs Carter.

It always irritated her.

"Nope. I like calling you Mrs Carter."

They laughed.

"See who's here."

Julia stepped into the living room with a huge smile on her face.

"Juliana Ashby!"

The girls hugged.

"You look pretty!"

Julia said once they separated.

"You don't look too bad yourself. I love that dress. Is it the one Steve got for you?"

Though they had not met for almost 2 years now, the girls had made it a point to keep in touch through phone calls and mails.

"Yes."

"Steve surely gets extra points in my book for that dress. He's got quite a good taste."

"He chose me, didn't he?"

Jade laughed.

"Now who's keeping the guests at the door?"

Susan asked coming to stand behind Julia with her hands on her hips.

"Since when are Amanda and Jade guests in our house?"

Julia asked, letting them enter and go towards the living room.

"So you noticed me? I thought that in your excitement to see Jade you forgot all about me."

Amanda mock frowned. She had always had a soft corner for Susan's elder daughter.

Out of all the kids she had liked reading the most. Julia had spent days in the library reading till her eyes watered during her high school and college years.

"How can I forget you, Amanda? Is it even possible?"

Julia smiled and hugged her.

"I'm meeting you'll after so long." Jade sighed and plopped onto the sofa in the familiar living room.

She knew this house almost as well as her own.

"Is Jade Marie Tucker becoming sentimental?"

Jade turned in the direction of the stairs leading to the floors above at the sound of the familiar voice she had missed so much.

And there just below the staircase stood Alexander Carter.

The guy who she had been in love with for years, and who was most importantly her best friend.

He looked the same. His sandy brown hair was still ruffled because of his fingers which he always ran through them.

His eyes had a few more lines near them but were still the crystal blue colour she remembered them to be.

He had grown a little broader in the shoulder and taller since the last time they had met and he was tanned a golden brown..

"Have you ever seen me become sentimental?"

Jade replied with the wicked expression she reserved just to use on him.

"Do you seriously want me to remind you of our graduation?"

Alec flashed her his famous crooked smile in triumph.

"At least I was not the one who cried while watching Titanic every single time."

"I was not crying. The salt from your stupid popcorn went into my eyes."

Alec said indignantly. This was one of his sore points.

"Yeah right!" Jade laughed.

They came towards each other and hugged, forgetting all the years that had gone by.

"How are you?"

Alec asked holding Jade back but still not letting her go.

"How do I look?"

"Just like you do on the cover of your novels." Alec said.

"You have seen my novels?" Jade raised one eyebrow.

"Some of them. And how do I look?"

"Like you did on the cover of Forbes last month."

Alec laughed, he remembered that a picture of Derek and him had been on the cover of Forbes magazine the previous month, along with an article about the success of Wanderlust.

He just smiled at Jade for a few minutes before stepping back and letting her go.

"Amanda!" He exclaimed when he saw her standing behind the sofa with her characteristic smile.

"Alec!" She copied him before he pulled her into a hug.

"This is what I was missing out there. I didn't get to see the pretty Amanda Tucker everyday."

"Is that so?"

Jade looked around. This was the family which she remembered from her childhood.

Before Nicole, Jason and the twins were in her life, her life rotated around her mother, Mrs Carter, Julia and Alec.

This was all she knew in her life back then. And she had been satisfied with that.

"Won't you introduce us to Emmaline?"

Jade heard her mom ask Alec who had been joking with her.

"Oh yeah! Em! Why are you standing over there come here."

From the shadow of the staircase a girl stepped out.

She looked about their age, with a beautiful face and long blonde hair.

She looked around the room warily with her green eyes and gave a small, formal smile.

"Hello."

Her voice was polished and smooth.

The way she was dressed and carried herself reminded Jade of the heroines in the regency novels she used to read.

She had a way of walking and holding herself that was calculated and belonged to a different era completely.

"Emma, this is Amanda Tucker, my childhood crush who also happens to be my mom's best friend."

Alec said throwing his arm over Amanda's shoulder.

"Hello! Don't listen to him. He's always liked to fool around. I could tell you stories from his childhood that will give you blackmail material for the rest of your life."

Alec stepped back with a pout, "Hey!"

Everyone laughed. While Emma smiled politely.

Jade went and stood behind Mrs Carter hugging her from behind.

"Hi, I'm Jade Amanda's daughter."

She said bringing a smile to her face with great difficulty.

"And my best friend!"

Emma turned toward Alec and smiled, "I've heard a lot about you from Alec."

"Now have you?"

Jade was surprised, she had not expected Alec to have mentioned her in front of his girlfriend ever.

"Yes, Alec loves telling me stories about Millbrooke."

Emma said giving her a challenging look.

This had to be interesting. Was Emma really a little jealous of her. Or was it just a misunderstanding on her part. The evening would tell.

Chapter 10

"So Jade, I hear you are an author."

Jade looked up on hearing Emma's voice.

They all had just settled down in the living room with glasses of red wine.

"Yes."

Jade decided to keep her reply small because she didn't really like the tune in which Emma had asked the question.

Actually she didn't really like Emma. Period. She tried to convince herself hard, that her dislike towards her was not because of her relationship with Alec, but because of her nature.

In the few minutes she had spent with Emma, it had become clear that she had a way of making the other person feel a little inferior.

She looked down her nose at everything. From Jade's dress to the dessert Amanda had brought with her.

"Have you read any of her books Emma?"

Emma turned to look at Julia, who was sitting next to Alec on the love seat.

"Not really. I don't read much fiction. I always feel that the media influences the writers of fiction novels."

Jade who normally loved the British accent, having had a crush on any guy who sported one, found Emma's way of speaking really annoying.

"In what way?" Jade asked.

"Take for example the current rage of Feminism that is there in the media. They hype it up so much that it's almost like no girl is safe anywhere. It's ridiculous."

"Girls are really not safe anywhere. And anyways it's not only about that. It's about equality. For men and women. Same rules and same rights."

Jade realised her reaction was a little aggressive and loud than what was strictly required but she couldn't help it.

"There is equality. I mean, if... When Alec and I, we get married, he will allow me to work. It's not like he's going to tell me to sit at home."

Jade almost winced at the idea of Alec ever marrying this devil with an angel's face sitting opposite her.

Emma had her all riled up while she herself sat casually sipping wine from her glass.

"Allow? Why does he have to 'allow' you to work? Why does he have a say in whether you work or no? It's your life."

"He'll be my husband. Of course he will have a say, in my life." Smirked Emma.

"This is where we go wrong. If men have a say in their wives or daughters life. Whether they should work or no. Study or no. Go out or no. Then women too should have a say in their lives. You should also give him permission to work."

Emma giggled before saying, "Don't be ridiculous."

She actually giggled.

Like they were in third grade discussing some new cartoon, instead of discussing feminism.

"That just proves your not a feminist. Totally not."

Jade felt like going and shaking Alec by his shoulders and asking him why he was wasting his time with this... This... She couldn't even come up with a name for her.

"No I'm not a feminist. Though I do support gender equality."

"That's like saying I don't want water, I want H2O." Said Jade sarcastically.

"Okay.... Let's change the topic."

Julia said sensing the tension in the room and trying to cool it down before Jade and Emma started fighting and abusing each other.

The others had just been staring at the two of them while they had thrown words at each other.

The only thought in Alec's head was, where the hell was all this about marriage coming in?

"I'm sorry. I guess I got a little excited."

Jade said guiltily.

She expected Emma to also apologise or at least say something. After all they had been arguing for the last five minutes without giving anyone else in the room a chance to hold a normal conversation.

But the skank just sat there calmly sipping her wine and eyeing Jade.

"That's okay.... Umm.. Why don't we go and start eating?" Susan said awkwardly getting up.

"That's a good idea. I'll help you set the table."

Alec jumped up happy to have an opportunity to leave the room and get away from the tension.

"I'll come too."

Jade said, she just wanted to go as far away as possible from the eye of Emma.

She got up and followed Alec out of the room towards the kitchen.

As she was passing next to Emma something happened and the glass of red wine in her hand slipped and fell right on Jade's dress.

"Oh God!"

The front part of her pretty dress was dripping and had a huge stain on it.

"I'm so sorry!" Emma got up from the chair and with a panicked look on her face.

"It's okay. It was a mistake." Jade said automatically trying hard to wipe the stain away with the tissue Julia handed her.

Or was it?

"Come with me I'll help you out."

Julia said guiding her towards her room.

"No no.... My mistake I'll help. Anyways she's closer to my size than yours."

That was true. While Julia was rod thin and a lot taller than Jade, Emma had a curvy figure like her and was just a little shorter than her.

Jade followed her to the guest room of the house.

The room now sported 4 huge, designer suitcases. The dressing table was covered with various creams and more make up than any mall.

On the bed there was a book with a very important looking man wearing a suit on the cover.

Emma went to the cupboard and took out a light green dress, which would have looked better for a tea party on the front porch than a small dinner with friends.

She handed the dress to Jade and said, "Here you go. Put it on."

"Thanks."

"Listen to one thing. You can act as superior as possible, hug Julia and Susan, show off that you know Alec since the beginning of time. But he's mine. This family is going to be mine. And if you know what's good for you, you'll start behaving accordingly. Understand?"

Jade was surprised by the challenging tone of her voice. She was so taken aback that for some time she couldn't answer.

Once she got her voice back she said, "You are not married to Alec. And they will always be my family, always. It's doesn't matter how many blonde women with sophisticated British accents come into Alec's life he will always be my best friend. Get that in your mind!"

Emma scowled, before she could say something to that there was a knock on the door and Julia poked her head in.

"Hey! I came to check if everything is okay."

"Yup... Everything is fine." Emma lied smoothly, "I was just saying that I'll leave Jade to change and go down."

"You go ahead Emma, Julia why don't you stay here and help me please."

Jade said as sweetly as she could.

"Okay."

Emma flashed one last diabetic smile at Jade and walked out of the room.

"Phew! The sparks that the two of you are giving off!" Julia said dramatically, before plopping down on the pillow.

"I can't believe Alec is dating this brain dead girl."

"If you'll keep arguing like this, Alec is going to have a tough time."

Jade glared at Julia who shrugged and picked up the book lying on the bed.

She removed her pretty dress and started putting on the dress which Emma had given her. The only thing she could say about it was that it was green and it fit her.

"We were not arguing. We just have different opinions."

"That's the understatement of the year, Jade." Julia looked up from the book and almost burst out laughing, "1975 called, they want their dress back."

Jade stood in front of the mirror looking at herself.

The dress was hideous with a stiff collar and pearl buttons running it's length.

It made her look pale and sickly and clashed horrifically with the light make up she had put on before coming.

"Who wears such dresses?"

Jade sighed and picked up her own dress. She didn't have any other option but to wear this dress. It did fit very well.

"Emma obviously does."

Julia face was a picture as she tried hard to control her laughter.

"Go ahead. Laugh. You know you want to."

Julia just needed just that much encouragement to burst out in hysterics.

Jade looked like a governess from years back. The dress was till a little below her knee and it made her legs look horrible.

"Okay sorry. Let's go, anyways it's just us." Julia said once she got her breath back.

Jade sighed, "Easy for you to say."

"Come on!" Julia pulled her out of the room and towards the stairs. As they were headed down she said, "Was I the only one who thought that she dropped the wine on purpose?"

"I don't know Jules. I really don't know."

The walked into the living room together, Jade thoughts stuck on the conversation she and Emma had had in the guest bed room before Julia had come in.

As soon as they entered the living room the flow of conversation stopped as everyone had turned to stare at Jade.

"Uh…You…Jade…" Alec stuttered finding for something to say as a compliment.

"I'm so sorry I didn't think the dress would make you look pale. I guess you are a little darker than me." Emma said standing up.

That bitch, thought Jade.

But she smiled instead, "I guess."

"I'll give you something else to wear."

"No it's okay. It's just family anyways." Jade said declining Emma's offer.

"Let's have dinner?"

Susan offered when no one could come up with anything good to say about the dress Jade was wearing now.

"Yes let's go. I'm starving and I thing I saw Susan's special chicken."

Amanda said too cheerfully ushering everyone to the dining area.

Jade went to take her seat on the Carter dining table. All through the years she had had so many meals in the house that she even had a fixed place on their dining table, right in between Alec and Julia.

But before she could reach her chair, Emma plopped into it and started talking to Amanda who was sitting right opposite to her.

Julia looked at Jade, unsure of how to react. It would have been rude to ask Emma to get up and God knows she had been rude enough earlier.

Jade shrugged and sat next to her mom opposite Alec.

As usual the food was beyond delicious.

Susan Carter was first and foremost a great cook.

The conversation came to a still while everyone concentrated on eating after complimenting Susan.

"Jade I heard Jason and Nicole had twins." Alec said breaking the silence.

"Yes Nadia and Noah. They are my godchildren."

Jade smiled at the thought of the over energetic twins.

"They are even more troublesome than what you and Jade were when you'll were young, and mind you that's quite a feat."

Amanda piped in after taking a sip of her wine.

"I've not met Jason for years."

"You have not come home for years." Jade replied to Alec's statement.

They shared a look which made Julia start talking before a fight broke out, "We should all catch up one day. Go out for drinks or to dance. Alec, Jade, Emma, Jason, Nicole, me and even Steve when he comes."

"That's a good idea!" Alec exclaimed.

Jade just nodded. All of them going out would mean that she would be the only one alone. While the other couples enjoyed themselves. Not a way she wanted to spend her evening.

"I forgot to tell you Alec. I have to go to Chicago tomorrow for two days." Emma spoke after a long time.

Till then she had just been eyeing everyone. She had this way of looking at people, her light green eyes noticing everything. It was a little creepy.

"Chicago? Why?"

She smiled at Alec, "Mr Bridge asked me to go and check up on some things in the Chicago office. I have to go as soon as possible. Preferably tomorrow morning."

"Okay. I'll get you a cab in the morning." Alec said going back to his chicken.

"You could come back with Steve then. He's coming two days later himself."

Julia had asked Steve to leave the hotel in the care of the more than capable manager.

They needed to take some time off and spend it with each other desperately. And they also had some news to give to everyone.

"Okay."

Emma replied.

Dinner was a quiet affair, with very few words being spoken.

They enjoyed the chocolate soufflé Amanda had got for dessert and then it was time to leave.

"We'll plan something soon." Julia said referring to the idea of all of them meeting up.

"Yeah. Sure." She turned to Emma and said, "I'll send the dress to you later."

"No that's okay. You can keep it with you. As a reminder of me." Emma smiled sweetly.

Like she would ever be able to forget her, thought Jade.

"Bye Jade and Amanda!" Susan smiled at them while they got into the car.

Alec just waved with a hesitant smile.

Hesitant was the word for the interaction Jade and Alec had had the whole evening.

They had not spoken much after the first conversation.

"It was a good night over all." Amanda said once they started driving off.

"Yes."

Her cell phone, in her clutch beeped signalling the arrival of a message.

Hey!

It was a message from Alec. It came as a surprise to Jade that he still had her number.

Hi!

She relied quickly curious to know, what he wanted to say.

We need to talk. Can we meet up tom at Beans for coffee?

Jade didn't know how to reply. The last thing she wanted to do was to meet with Alec alone.

But she couldn't just say no, could she?

Okay. At 4?

Okay. The reply came immediately.

Coffee with Alec would be interesting if not anything else.

Amanda dropped Jade at her apartment.

After saying bye and goodnight, Jade went up to her apartment, happy to be back.

She got out of the hideous dress and pushed back the strong feeling of burning it before pushing it to the back of her cupboard.

Just when she had changed into a tank top and shorts and was about to go to bed her cell started ringing.

The caller id said that the call was from Nicole.

She sighed and picked it up because as far as she knew her best friend, Nicole would keep calling till she didn't pick up.

"Hi!" Nicole said when Jade picked up the phone.

"Hello! Shouldn't you be in bed?"

Jade tried to remove the exhaustion from her voice.

She was drop dead tired, after spending the morning with the twins, the encounter with Matt, getting ready and of course all the drama with Emma.

"Forget about bed, tell me what happened."

Jade laughed, "You want to know everything?"

"Yes everything."

So Jade recounted all the events of the evening not leaving a single thing out.

By the end Nicole was laughing out loud, "You had quite a event full evening."

"You bet!"

"This Emma sounds interesting."

"I can't wait till you meet her." Jade said.

If she had clashed with Emma, Nicole's encounter with her was bound to be hilarious.

"You must be tired. Go to sleep. And all the best for tomorrow's meeting with Alec."

"Don't remind me about that."

Nicole giggled, "Go to sleep."

She kept the phone and fell face down on her bed. She was asleep before her face hit the pillow.

The next morning when she woke up it felt like she had slept for less than five minutes.

She really wanted to throw the alarm clock and bury her head in the pillow again.

But she knew she had to complete some writing in the day. So she pulled herself from the bed and went straight into the washroom.

Her blue dress which now had a very big stain on it was still lying on the sink where she had left it last night.

Looking at it brought back all the things that had happened last night.

While having a bath and getting ready the only thing she could think about was what she was going to say to Alec when they met in the evening.

Last night, there were other people around her. People she could talk to while avoiding Alec the whole time. But that was not going to be an option today.

She had her two cups of black coffee while replaying the events of yesterday in her head.

By the time she was done it was pretty clear that she won't be able to right anything with all the jumble of thoughts in her head.

So she put on shorts and a sports vest, tied her hair into a pony and went for a run.

Maybe a run would clear her mind.

Who was she kidding? Nothing would help her get rid of the dread of meeting Alec. Except for maybe a bottle of whiskey and a strong hangover.

Chapter 11

Jade came back from her run to find her mother waiting outside the apartment.

"Mom, how long have you been waiting?" She asked.

"Oh I just reached. I was just going to give you a ring."

Jade went ahead and opened the apartment, "Come in. And what brings the busy Amanda Tucker to my humble abode?" Joked Jade.

Her mother was looking a little stressed and serious, which was highly unusual for Amanda Tucker.

"Ummm.... Stuart called in the morning." Amanda said once they sat on the sofa. She fidgeted with her fingers waiting for Jade to say something.

"Who?" Jade asked, even though she clearly knew who her mom was talking about.

"Jade! Your dad called in the morning." Sighed Amanda.

"And?"

"He said he's coming back."

Was this a joke? Seriously! All the people in Jade's life who had left her were coming back in the same week. And she didn't know how to deal with everyone.

"Why?" She asked.

There was no expression on her face. Amanda was almost scared to say anything further.

"He said his work in London is over." She said almost in a whisper.

"Is he bringing his Spanish girlfriend with him?"

Jade sounded so much like a whiny teenager in that one sentence that Amanda almost laughed.

Jade noticed the look of amusement on her mothers face and glared.

"First off, she is his secretary. And second thing she is Mexican not Spanish."

"Mom you want to neglect all his affairs, go ahead! Turn a blind eye and a deaf ear. I'm not doing anything of that sort."

"Jade! It's your father you're talking about. Mind your tongue."

Jade gave a bitter laugh, "Father? Stuart Tucker is not my father. Being a sperm donor does not make him my father."

"Jade!"

"Mom this is ridiculous! He went away when I was 8! 8! He never did anything a father does. So I'm sorry if I don't have any 'fatherly feelings' for him." Jade said viciously.

Amanda sighed, "Jade he sounded serious this time. He apologised. He said he wants to-"

"Apologised?" Scoffed Jade, "He apologised and you believe him?"

"He's my husband." Stated Amanda.

"Was your husband. Don't forget you'll have been separated for more than 14 years now."

"He deserves a chance!"

"He does not deserve anything! And we have already given him too many. You still love him, mom. You know it. I know it. Even he knows it. And that's what he takes advantage of every time." Jade moved closer to her mom, who had dropped her head into her palms and put a hand over her shoulders. "He takes advantage of you. And you let him. He comes back every 2 or 3 years says sorry you take him back and then he's gone again. And every time it takes you months to get over it. Why do you let him behave like this to you? Why?"

"Because I hope. I hope Jade that maybe this time I'll get my old Stuart back. I'll get back the Stuart I had fallen in love with. I can't stop hoping Jade. I know he has affairs. I ignore them but I'm not blind. But every time he comes back, Jade, I can see the old Stuart deep down. And I know he will come back one day."

Jade saw that her mom was crying and this was what disgusted her, this pain that her mom felt.

Jade sighed, she could never see her mom cry, that was her biggest weakness.

"Mom he's a jerk. But he's a jerk you're in love with. This is the last chance I'm giving him. I mean it, last. I'll come with you to meet him."

Amanda smiled through her tears and said, "You know why I get through all the hurt every time? Because my daughter is an angel. Your dad, who you call a jerk, gave me one great gift and that was you Jade."

Jade smiled and hugged her mother,

"I'll go get tea for you sit. And no more crying."

At least for now. Since dad was coming back it meant more crying was on its way.

Jade had got used to not having her father around. After all 14 years was a long time.

She was 8 when one night she woke up to the sounds of her mom crying while her dad packed his suitcase and went out of the house.

He didn't come back.

Jade learned to live her life with only Amanda playing both the roles of father and mother. And she did a great job.

A year after that Alec and Julia lost their father. Jade was there the whole time to comfort them having gone through the same hurt and felling of absolute abandonment they were feeling.

It was difficult but it got less painful after two years.

That was the first time he came back. He apologised to her mom and came back to the house.

Jade had been naive back then she had been overjoyed to have her dad back.

For a few days life was just like before.

But Stuart Tucker didn't like the life he had in Millbrooke. It was too boring for him.

So he packed his bags and left again. Breaking Amanda's and Jade's heart again.

There had been affairs. Plenty of them. But after a point they had started ignoring them.

This routine had continued for years now. He came back after a long spell of disappearance. Apologised and acted all normal.

And then he packed up and left.

During his time away from home they had no contact with him. No presents for birthdays and Christmases. No phone calls. No mails.

But she was used to it.

He was coming back again. He would leave again. And in the process he would break her moms heart again. It had become a vicious cycle. That Jade could do nothing to prevent.

Amanda still loved him. And she would accept him no matter what. But Jade was not naive any longer.

Jade went into the kitchen and started making tea. As she was waiting for the water to boil she saw her cell phone lying on the table.

She checked to see if there were any messages and was surprised to find a message from Alec.

Hi! It said.

According to the time shown on the screen the message had been sent 10 minutes back.

Jade thought for a moment before replying.

Hey! She sent.

One exclamation mark just like him. Not to excited, not to bored. She thought before pressing the send option.

She knew that if she had didn't get busy fast she would spend her whole time waiting for Alec's reply so she closed the cell phone, kept it aside and got busy making the tea.

Though a part of her mind was still on the message.

As she poured the tea into two cups, her cell phone buzzed. She got so startled that she almost spilled the tea on the kitchen table.

She purposely kept the kettle extra slowly, wiped of the few drops of tea that had fallen, with a cloth and walked slowly to the cell phone to check.

She didn't want to be disappointed of the message was not from Alec.

But it was.

She knew it was silly but she felt a surge if happiness.

The message said, Remember about our meeting?

Of course she remembered. How could she possibly forget about it when it was giving her a constant stomach ache?

She didn't type that though.

She slowly typed out, Yes.

Almost immediately after she pressed the send button Alec's reply came.

The thought that he was actually waiting for her to reply felt really good.

At 4?

Yes.

Jade sent it purposely being short. She didn't want to seem excited at the prospect of meeting him.

I'll be waiting, came the reply.

Okay.

She sent the last message and kept the mobile.

If the week continued to be like this there was a strong possibility that she would have ulcers by the end.

She sighed and took the tea out to her mom. Trying very hard but unsuccessfully to stop thinking and worrying about her meeting with Alec that evening.

Chapter 12

"You sure you don't want me to get anything for you?"

Jade looked up to find Kevin standing next to her. Kevin worked part time as a waiter in Beans. And the other half of his time he was studying to become a doctor.

Nicole and she visited Bean so often that, they almost knew everything about him.

At least all the things his mother didn't know about him, since that Jade knew from before. Beth Green worked with Amanda at the town library and she had a habit of telling pretty interesting stories about her son.

"I'm sure. I'm waiting for someone."

Jade replied and took a sip of water.

Alec was late. It was 4:30 and he still wasn't here.

Jade had been sitting there for half an hour now without anything to do passing her time by having glasses of water and speaking to the people she knew who entered the cafe.

Thankfully that happened in plenty.

"I know you told me earlier. But that person is sure making you wait a lot." Kevin said raising an eyebrow.

He was very handsome with black wavy hair which flopped on his forehead and green laughing eyes. He had a confident way of speaking and a charming personality.

All this attributed to the fact that Beans was always crowded with teenage and college girls, waiting for their chance to talk and flirt with him.

"Don't you have some book about blood and innards you should bury your head in?"

Jade knew that whatever free time Kevin he had from the work he spent studying.

Kevin smirked, "I was just asking." He threw up both his hands.

"Thanks for asking. I just want another glass of water. Thank you."

Kevin filled up her glass with the jug he was already carrying, he had known she wouldn't order till whoever she was waiting for came.

"This is your 4th glass. You'll have to get up to go to the washroom in the middle of your meeting."

Jade looked up at the dimples on Kevin's face and laughed, "Now go!"

Kevin was the closest thing she had to a little brother, and he sure played his role to perfection.

She had actually had plenty of water since she was dropped at Beans at 4 by her mother.

She felt like a teenager asking her mom to drop her but she didn't have any other option.

Her car had refused to start when she was leaving and her only option was asking her mom to give her a lift, who was on her way home after spending the whole morning with Jade.

But that meant that she would have to get a lift back home from someone.

Alec seemed to be the most sensible option, but that was the last thing she would do. She didn't want to owe him one on the first day they met. Technically the second, but who was keeping track.

Just then the bell on top of the door of the cafe rang signalling that someone had entered.

Jade looked up and was relieved to see that it was a haggard looking Alec finally.

Then the feeling of relief was replaced by a churning nervous feeling at the pit of her stomach.

He came in carelessly running his finger through his already messy hair.

"Hi! I'm so sorry I'm late. I really really am! I got a call from Derek just as I was leaving." He said taking he seat opposite to her.

He was dressed in dark wash denim jeans and a black t- shirt, which was tight enough to show the outline of his washboard abs.

Jade pulled her eyes away from Alec's abs with some difficulty and said,"Its been 8 years that doesn't mean I don't remember you. Don't forget I knew you better than you knew yourself. Alec Carter can never be punctual. Even if someone offered him a million dollars."

"That's true enough, little- Miss- Know- It- All!" Alec laughed.

Jade had missed his laugh. Alec always laughed with his whole body. And it was one of the things she had loved about him.

Little- Miss- Know- It- All had been Alec's nickname for her when they had been young.

Growing up with a librarian as a mother, had many advantages. One of them was that Jade always knew some baseless stupid trivia about every single thing.

And as a teenager she had taken it upon herself to annoy Alec with all the facts and trivia she had picked up from her mom.

That's when he had come up with the name for her. Back then she used to get super angry on him whenever he called her that.

But now she just smiled with the memory of all the stupid things they used to do.

Before she could say anything Kevin came and stood next to them with a notepad in his hand and a Beans apron tied around his waist.

"Welcome to Beans! What can I get you'll today?" He asked in his usual way but with a smirk in the end for Jade's benefit.

"Why didn't you order before I came? You should have." Alec asked finding out that there were no cups on the table already.

"It's okay. I thought I'll wait for you."

"She kept herself entertained with many glasses of water." Kevin piped in once Jade finished talking.

Alec laughed again and then ordered, "One black coffee with three spoons of sugar for me. And one cappuccino with little milk and two spoons of sugar for the lady."

Kevin nodded after writing down the order and left.

"You remember?"

It came as a surprise to Jade that even after so many years he remembered such a trivial thing as the way she took her coffee.

"Of course. Don't forget your not the only one who knew everything about me." He said, "Anyways you look pretty."

Jade looked down at the denim cutoffs she was wearing below a faded old blue shirt.

It was nothing special and she had just thrown it on, before leaving.

"Since when did Alec Carter start giving me compliments?"

Alec shrugged and they smiled at each other for a few minutes.

They could never be awkward with each other for long. They were just too good friends for that.

"I really missed you." Alec said suddenly.

"Now did you?"

"Yeah.... See Emma left today morning. So tomorrow let's go out and do all the stuff we used to do before. Just like old times."

Jade looked at him with a serious expression, "Nothing is like old times, Alec. Except for our faces everything has changed."

"Nothing ever changes between friends."

"But are we still friends? Really?"

That got Alec to keep quiet he sat across her thinking, while Kevin came and placed their order on the table.

He didn't stop to make any smart ass comment before leaving, sensing the tension between them.

"Yes we are. I know its been ages but you can't just undo a great friendship like ours." Alec said atlast.

"You can't?"

"No. We'll be friends forever."

Jade sighed and sipped her coffee without saying anything.

"You don't agree with me." Stated Alec flatly when Jade didn't say anything.

"No I don't. How do you expect me to? It's been 8 years since we last met or spoke. That's too long." Jade said.

"I know. And I'm sorry. But don't act like your the victim. You didn't try very hard either."

"I tried harder than you, Alec. But when the other person is not interested you give up after a point."

It was true. Jade had tried calling and mailing him for a year after he left.

But he had been so busy putting up the business that he had ignored them completely.

Till one day, she got fed up and stopped.

They sat in silence for sometime. Each lost in their thoughts.

"Let's give it another try. Please Jade not for my sake but atleast for our friendships sake. We have two days. Let's do all the stuff we used to. We'll go to the lake. Go to the old playground. Go drinking." Alec said breaking the silence.

He really didn't want to let the friendship they had go. It was their special thing and losing Jade as a friend would be too great a loss for him.

"I don't remember us going drinking very often earlier. Except for maybe the stunt after graduation."

"We would have if we were of age." Alec said, "So does that mean you agree to the plan?"

"I'll give it a try."

"That's great. I'll pick you up a 10?"

"10 will do."

Just as they shook their hands over it Kevin came and placed the bill between them.

Both Jade and Alec tried to pull the bill towards them.

"This will be interesting." Kevin mumbled with a smile and stood back to see what happens.

"I'm paying." Alec said.

"No ways." Jade pulled the bill towards her trying to read it.

"I asked you to meet me." Alec said pulling it to him.

"I agreed didn't I."

"Come on!"

"No ways! I'm paying. Otherwise tomorrow's deal is off." Jade said folding her arms over her chest. Clear triumph written all over her face.

"That's not fair."

"Who said life is fair?"

She pulled her wallet out of her bag and counted out the notes.

"Okay. You pay for your half I'll pay for mine."

"Okay."

They paid and walked out of the door. Alec was still sore about the fact that Jade had won so easily.

"Where's your car?"

He asked Jade. It had already become a little dark.

"Umm... Actually mom dropped me here. My car stopped working. So...." Jade said fidgeting with the strap of her bag.

"I'll drop you." Alec said like it was the most obvious thing.

Which it was, but Jade didn't want to agree.

"No it's okay. I'll get a lift from someone else."

Alec made a face and started pulling Jade towards his car, "Why? I'll drop you. Anyways I have to pick you up tomorrow so I should no where you stay."

Jade reluctantly sat in the passenger seat while Alec got into the car from the other side.....................

"You moved to the cool part of town?" Alec asked when Jade gave him her address.

Jade smirked, "When you sell enough books, you get enough money to buy a house in any place."

As kids Jade and Alec had always dreamed to become rich enough to buy an apartment in the southern part of Millbrooke, which was considered to be the cool part.

"And anyways I needed to get out of moms house. She was getting irritated by my habits."

Jade continued.

"What you brought too many guys home?"

"Yes actually. It may not seem so but finding a half naked guy early in the morning in the kitchen creeped out mom."

After Alec left Jade had gone through one night stands and boyfriends very fast. Much to the irritation of Amanda Tucker.

"Uh huh..."

Jade turned to see an uncomfortable expression on Alec's face.

"What? Uncomfortable to hear about my affairs?"

Alec turned around with a forced smile on his face, "Not really."

"I'm not uncomfortable speaking about it!" Jade shrugged, "And anyways it's not like when you and Emma are locked together in the guest room, you'll play scrabble."

She turned to see Alec actually blush while he drove the car.

"Well.... Actually I'm not staying in the guest bedroom. Only Emma is."

"What? Then where are you sleeping?"

"In my room." Alec gave a laugh, "You might be comfortable with the stuff Emma and I do, I don't think Mom is."

She wanted to tell him that even the thought of them sleeping innocently together made her get the creeps. But she just smiled and said, "So you'll are planning to marry?"

"What!? No!" Alec replied as fast as he could.

"Oh! I thought.... By the way Emma was speaking yesterday..." She let it hang in the middle.

"No... No... We have not even spoken about marriage."

"So still have the aversion towards marriage?" Jade asked half hopefully.

"Not really. I'm going to get married eventually and I know that at the back of my mind. But not anytime soon. You? Thinking of get married in the near future?" Alec asked thinking about the mysterious doctor she had been kissing in the parking lot.

"No ways. I'm happy without getting married." Jade scoffed.

"Why? What happened to the romantic girl who had decided her wedding dress when she was twelve?"

She laughed at the memory, "She grew up. I have no intentions of getting married now. If I want to stop having sex I'll start wearing crocs."

Alec burst out laughing.

The awkwardness which had been there in their conversation earlier had disappeared and now they were speaking freely. It was almost like old times.

Jade turned and just looked at Alec carefully.

The way his eyes crinkled when he smiled, the grip of his fingers on the steering wheel and the way his lips always tilted upwards even when he was not smiling.

Alec noticed Jade staring it him and asked, "What?"

"Nothing." She turned her head away from him quickly and saw that they had reached her apartment building. "This is me."

Alec stopped the car and she got down, "Thanks for the lift." She said poking her head into the car through the open window.

"No problem. Won't you ask me up for a cup of coffee?"

"You're anyways coming to pick me up tomorrow in the morning. Go home and get some sleep." Jade waved a good bye and walked towards the building.

"Hey! Which floor do you live on?"

Alec yelled from the car before Jade entered the building.

"Why?"

"I should know. Since I'm picking you up tomorrow." He replied.

"3rd."

"I hope you're not lying. I seriously don't want to disturb your neighbours by ringing their door bells. See you tomorrow."

Jade flashed a last smile and walked into her apartment building.

She sighed once she entered her room. She was going to spend the whole day with Alec and instead of the nervousness she expected to feel, she was excited.

And another surprise was that she actually felt like sitting down to write for sometime.

She changed into more comfortable clothes and sat on her table with the laptop in front of her.

Before she started writing she sent a quick message to Alec and then with a smile on her face got to work...........................

Alec had missed the feeling of coming home to find Mom sitting in the living room reading a book or Julia working on her laptop.

When he went home to his apartment in London, where he lived most of the time, only the empty apartment greeted him.

Or it was Emma who had recently shifted into his apartment.

He went into the room in which he had spent his childhood and teenage years and smiled. It still had the same decorations.

The navy blue bedcovers, white walls, posters of the band he had liked on the walls.

He sat on the bed and took out his phone to see if there were any messages.

There were two mails from Derek about some new scheme, which he decided to look at later.

And then there was a message from Jade.

Curious to know what she had to say so soon after he dropped her he opened the message and laughed when he read it.

It's the 4th floor.

It read.

Alec laughed and dropped his mobile thinking of the next day. If the car drive was anything to go by, tomorrow's meeting was sure to be a success.

Chapter 13

J ade woke up to the sound of someone banging the front door down. She picked her head up from the laptop cover.

She had fallen asleep while writing with her hand still poised on the keyboard. There was a long row of alphabets which didn't make any sense.

The doorbell started ringing again and Jade heard someone knock.

She got up groggily wiping her eyes with the back of her hand.

"Okay... I'm coming... I'm coming."

She dragged herself somehow to the door and pulled it open to see Alec standing on her doorstep with a bunch of roses.

"Good morning." She grumbled.

"Good morning? Good.. Morning? I've been standing here for the past 10 minutes ringing the doorbell and banging on the door with a bunch of flowers in my hand and you were sleeping?"

Alec said grumpily.

"You brought me flowers?"

"That's what registered in your head from all that I said?"

"Sorry... Come in."

He looked at Jade. She was dressed in shorts that left most of her long legs in display. Her black hair was ruffled and her eyes were bloodshot.

"Nice shorts."

"Ha!" Jade laughed sarcastically.

Jade moved aside so that Alec could come into the living room.

He was dressed casually in dark wash jeans and a plain white shirt.

It was really similar to the one Matt had been wearing the day they had met in Jo's.

"Here you go." Alec turned around once they were in the living room and handed her the bunch of roses.

She looked down and then looked back at Alec. Either her head was too clouded because of sleep- actually the lack of it- or finally Alec had lost his mind.

"You seriously got me flowers?" She asked in disbelief.

Alec shoved his hands in his pockets looking really uncomfortable.

"Well I saw them on the way here.... And I thought you'll like them."

"Yeah they are pretty."

She took the flowers to the kitchen filled a vase with water and put the flowers in it.

"Why were you still sleeping? Did you forget about the deal?" He said following her into the kitchen.

She looked up from the flowers, the colour was a deep pink which was so pretty, and said, "What time is it?"

"10:15. I've been at the door from 10."

"You were on time?"

"Yes. And you were not."

"I'm so sorry. I didn't sleep much last night." She said going out of the room carrying the vase with her.

"What were you doing?"

"Writing." She kept the vase down on the table and stood back to admire them, "They look lovely. Thanks."

"You're welcome."

"Look you sit, give me five minutes and I'll be ready." She said guiltily.

"Okay."

Jade flashed a guilty smile and ran into her room to get ready.

Meanwhile, Alec wandered around her living room.

The house had a cozy, laid back feel to it. None of the sofas matched, the cushions were all different colours. And there were too many of them everywhere.

There were huge waist high stacks of books everywhere, on the table, on the shelves. Even on the floor.

"Do you want anything to drink?" Asked Jade coming out of the washroom having cleaned up the best she could.

"No thanks. I'm good."

"Okay. Make yourself comfortable." She said going to her cupboard.

The first thing that came to her hand was a skirt which had small flowers on them.

"Hey Jade. Do you actually read all the books that you have here?"

Alec's voice from the living room reminded her that he was waiting for her.

This was not time to be choosy. Her only option was wearing the first thing she could find.

"Kind of.... Some of them are research for my books. And some of them are just light reads." She replied while putting on the skirt.

"Light read."

Alec looked at the book in his hand. It weighed more than a new born baby and was named, 'Medical Advances in the 70's.

Alec picked up a hard bound copy of her book and sat down to read it.

"You are reading my book?" Jade came out from her room and saw him reading her latest book.

"Yeah. I didn't get time to read this one though." Alec replied.

"This one?" Jade murmured pulling her hair into a loose bun, "You have read the others?"

"All of them."

Jade was surprised, she stopped in her tracks, "They are love stories."

"No shit, Einstein!" Alec laughed, turning the book so that Jade could see the cover of the book, which featured a couple in an embrace.

"That's... I don't even... I never thought you would read my books."

"They are your books, Jade. How could I not read them? And you are a good author."

Jade smiled and turned around.

This was the reason she had fallen in love with Alec. He did such sweet things without even realising what kind of effect he was having.

Though she was overjoyed that he had taken out the time to read her books, books that were not even the genre he liked, she didn't let it show.

Instead she looked back at him and said, "I'm ready!"

That was quick, thought Alec.

She was wearing a white skirt with small flowers on it, with a pink tank top.

He himself had dressed up very carefully that morning, putting on a shirt which was as close to what that 'Kissing in Parking lots' doctor had been wearing that day.

"What? Why are you staring at me?"

Alec quickly dropped his gaze, "I was just surprised that you got ready so fast."

Jade went to the shoe rack and started putting on ankle length sneakers.

"I told you five minutes. I don't take long to get ready."

"When Emma says five minutes she doesn't come out before 45 minutes. I was getting ready to spend a good half hour more."

"Are you already complaining about your girlfriend?" Jade smirked.

"I'm not complaining, I'm just saying."

"Of course you are!" She smiled while putting on her sneakers.

"Can we leave then? We are already late. Thanks to you." Alec stood up and walked to the door.

"Where are we going?"

"Being in the field that I am in I couldn't stop myself from making a small itinerary of all the places we should visit today. So first stop is the lake!" He cheered.

Jade laughed and followed Alec out of the apartment locking up behind them.

The Blue lake- as the local people called it- had always been their favourite place to hang out when they were in high school.

The lake was a bright blue colour even on downcast days, hence the name. And was surrounded with trees all around.

There was a certain calmness in just sitting there and thinking.

In the years just after Alec had gone, Jade had frequented the lake whenever she missed him. Which had been quite often.

They drove in silence to the lake.

Alec wondering how to start a conversation about the 'Doctor' while Jade tried to push down all the memories of them coming to the lake together threatened to pour out.

She should have realised earlier that agreeing to go to all their old haunts with Alec was not a good idea.

Atlast they reached their destination and Alec parked the car.

They got down and walked to the bridge on the lake.

Jade sighed, the silence and the beautiful lake. And all the million happy memories.

"It's been years since I last came here." Alec said, shoving his hands into the pockets of his jeans.

He could clearly remember the two of them sitting on this particular bridge after spending the whole day in school, doing their homework together.

Jade smiled, "I come here pretty often. You know whenever I'm stuck while writing. The silence helps me."

Alec stared at her. The Jade he remembered could not sit for a second without talking or doing something.

And now she craved the silence.

"You come here with Matt?" He asked.

"Matt? How do you know him?"

Jade was surprised. She was sure that she had not mentioned anything about her relationship with Matt.

Alec smirked, "Surprised?"

"I have no clue how you know Matt. So of course I'm surprised."

"I saw you'll kiss in the parking lot of Jo's that day. Quite a steamy kiss if I say so."

"You were there?"

"Yeah. I was taking Emma for an ice cream when I saw you'll kissing. I got quite a surprise. I didn't expect to meet you for the first time after so many years while you were sharing such an intimate moment with someone."

"Matt was my boyfriend. We had a breakup." Jade said walking away from Alec towards the bridge.

Alec moved towards her and stood next to her, "Didn't look like a kiss between someone who were not together any more."

"He wanted to get back together.... Why am I explaining myself to you? I don't ask you about explanations or how many times you have kissed Emma."

She seriously didn't need to explain her actions to anyone. Especially not Alec. She couldn't believe that he had been spying on her.

"Maybe you are explaining yourself because you still are doubtful about... You know... The 'break up.'"

The last two words were accompanied by sly smirk by Alec.

The smirk became even broader when Jade scowled at him.

"I can't believe you just said that."

"So was Dr Matt one of the half naked guys your mom saw?"

"Okay that's enough."

By this time both of them were standing right at the end of the bridge.

Jade went up to him and shoved him. And in a matter of seconds Alec found himself in the lake, drenched completely.

He came up sputtering water out of his mouth and breathing heavily to see Jade still standing on the bridge, completely dry and laughing her heart out.

"You're going to pay for this!"

In the midst of her uncontrollable laughter, Jade forgot to step back from the edge of the bridge.

Alec threw his hands around her thighs and pulled her into the water with him.

With an almighty splash, Jade was right beside him, wet and coughing out the lake water.

"What is wrong with you!?" She yelled coming out of the water.

"You started it!"

They glared at each other for a second before the burst out laughing.

It was just like old times. They were wet and laughing together.

They came out of the water, with their clothes dripping.

They sat at the edge of the bridge, still wet, talking and remembering all the old memories.

Jade's hair was stuck to her face and shoulders.

She was positive that she looked like a drowned rat, with mascara running down her face.

Her pink tank top was almost see through and her skirt was sticking to her thighs.

When Alec stared at her and started laughing she defiantly crossed her arms over her chest trying to cover a little of the damage.

"It's not funny!"

"Oh! It most definitely is funny. It might be the funniest thing I have seen in quite some time now."

They walked to the car, while Alec still laughed, clutching the side of his stomach.

His white shirt too had become transparent, giving a perfect view of stomach which had no flab only muscle.

It was taking a terribly high amount of self control on Jade's part to stop herself from staring at his body.

Once they reached the car instead of opening the door Alec went behind the car and opened the boot.

He pulled out a small back pack and started fidgeting in it.

"What is that?" Jade said coming to stand next to him.

"After so many years in the travel business the biggest lesson I have learnt is that, always carry a change of clothes." He shrugged and pulled out a dry shirt and a fresh pair of jeans.

"I'm cold!" Jade stated, trying to bring her situation to Alec's attention.

Alec looked up, halfway through opening his shirt, "Too bad for you."

Jade stomped her feet and got into the car, slamming the door in the process.

She tried to convince herself that she walked away from Alec because she was angry at him, and not because the prospect of seeing him without a shirt made her mouth dry and her cheeks flame up.

She sat over there with goosebumps on her arms, till finally Alec opened the door of the driver's side.

He threw a sweatshirt at her and sat down, "Put it on."

He was dressed in dry and fresh clothes. Jade picked up the sweatshirt which was surely going to be too huge for her.

"I don't need your help. Thank you very much!"

She threw the sweatshirt on the back seat, crossed her arms over her chest and stubbornly looked out of the window.

Alec looked at her and smirked.

Now this was more like the Jade he remembered.

He started the car and put on the air conditioner.

Jade heard the sound of the air conditioner and could feel the cool air on her already ice cold arms.

But she forced herself to ignore him.

Alec reduced the temperature.

Again no reaction.

Jade had become stronger at this game.

He reduced the temperature till it was the lowest and waited.

They sat over there in the stationary car. Jade stubbornly looking out of the window and Alec tapping his fingers on the steering wheel. Both of them waiting.

Suddenly Jade stretched her hand, took the sweatshirt and snuggled into it. Making a point not to look at Alec.

Alec grinned. He switched off the AC and put the car into gear, with a constant smile on his face.

Chapter 14

"Let's leave?"

Jade turned around to see Alec walk upto where she was sitting.

He had been attending a call from Emma who was still in Chicago, while she sat at the edge of the terrace and looked at the sun set.

"Why?"

Alec came and plopped down on his knees next to her.

After the lake, they went to Jo's for ice cream, then to town high school and atlast now they were sitting on the terrace of the Hopkins Villa.

"We still have to visit the kindergarten playground. How can we not go there?" Alec said.

She groaned, "Its so pretty here. And we can't do everything in one day!"

The view was really beautiful. From the terrace of the Hopkins Villa- which was situated on a small hill to the eastern part of town- the whole town could be seen.

The orangish red sun was setting and the sky had a pinkish hue to it.

There was a time when the Hopkins Villa had been the house to the most respected and richest family of the town.

The house itself was huge with French windows and elaborate gardens.

Amanda would always tell Jade stories about the huge parties that were held there. She even tried to describe the grandeur of the place in its full glory.

But years of neglect by the descendent of Reginald Hopkins who had originally built the Hopkins Villa, had left the Villa in a ruin.

The walls were crumbling, the gardens were filled with weeds and vines and the whole house had a ruined haunted feeling to it.

Jade and Alec had discovered the terrace of the in their senior year.

The grand view of the town and the almost haunted feel of the mansion somehow always drew them to the house.

They would sit on the terrace for hours on end and just talk.

This was the place they had tried and hated their first beers, which Alec had sneaked from a classmate.

"We can see everything in one day.... Wait!" Alec shoved his hand into his pockets and brought out a piece of paper.

He handed it to her. Jade saw that it was actually the itinerary he had been talking about.

"See only this is left." He said pointing at the kindergarten playground which was written at the end of the little page, "Then we will go to your apartment so that you can change, which you desperately need to do. And then go for drinks to Splendour."

Jade let the comment about her clothes slide. She was still wearing the skirt with Alec's sweatshirt on top.

The skirt had dried and become rough, paper like. And his sweatshirt, which had turned out to be really big for her, was till her thighs almost covering her skirt.

She had a good plan. Before Alec could take the paper from her hand and put it securely back into his pocket, she threw it out from the terrace and let the air carry it.

"Now it's not there." She said with a grin, "Sit down we aren't going anywhere."

Alec looked stunned for a minute but then gave in and sat down again. He knew very well that it was very difficult to convince Jade to do something when she had made up her mind to do something else.

"What if we don't have time to go to the kindergarten playground some other day?" He said after a few minutes.

"We'll take out time. Now shhh...."

Jade turned around to see in awe the million colours that were changing in the sky.

She always had loved seeing the sun set.

While Jade'a gaze was fixated on the sky, Alec looked at her.

The look amaze on her face was stunning. Her normally green eyes looked almost hazel in the reflection of the light from the sun.

She looked beautiful. If Alec had been a painter he would have made it a point to paint her like this.

With the rays from the setting sun reflecting on her black hair and adding an extra sparkle to her eyes.

He had seriously missed this about her in all the years he had been away. The awe, almost innocence with which she looked at things was amazing.

She found something inspiring in everything.

At last, Alec moved his gaze from Jade to the sky, to see the last few rays disappear at the horizon...................................Splendour was one of the oldest bars in the town of Millbrooke.

As kids Alec and Jade had always speculated how it must be like to be a grown up and walk into Splendour as casually as they saw the elders in the town did.

"It's our chance now, to walk into Splendour, glamorously and ask for two seats at the bar." Alec whispered into Jade's years as they walked to the door of the bar from where they had parked their car.

Jade laughed. This was definitely not the first time she was going to Splendour.

She had spent countless nights drinking in the bar with Nicole, Jason, and whoever she had been dating.

But this was the first time she felt excitement in her stomach.

They had stopped at her apartment so that she could change and get into a better state than she had been in.

After changing her clothes five times, while Alec waited for her, she decided on black jeans and a dark blue top.

The blue top brought out the green in her eyes according to Nicole. She managed to put her hair up in a messy bun and put on light make up, before Alec threatened to leave without her.

They went inside Splendour which was already moderately crowded.

Though it was not an Irish bar and the owner, Ned Jones, had never laid a step out of Millbrooke, the bar had a slight Irish feel to it.

People were sitting in the booths sipping their drinks, there was a small band of 4 people playing live music on the other side of the bar.

Jade smiled at the people she knew and walked to the bar.

Alec followed behind her.

So this was what it was like to grow up and continue living in the same small town for your whole life.

In the whole day that he had spent with her, Jade had stopped to speak to about 15 people she knew. She nodded and smiled at people on the road, asked about people's health and how was work.

It was unnerving for Alec who did not even know the name of his neighbour in London. Maybe because he rarely lived in his apartment for longer than 3 days at a stretch.

"What can I get you Miss Jade?" A gangly guy with freckles came up to them as they sat at the bar and asked.

"Hello Bob! I'll take my usual. Alec?" Jade said with another dazzling smile, which had Bob blushing under his wild mane of brown hair.

"A beer." Alec said.

Of course she knew the bar tender, she must know the name of his younger brother, what his parents did, where they lived, everything.

"Why the frown?" Jade looked up to see Alec with his eyebrows furrowed.

"Isn't it wierd to know everything about everyone?"

"What do you mean?"

Jade folded her hands on her lap and turned towards Alec, getting ready for a conversation which was surely going to be interesting.

"I mean living in a small town must be so exhausting. You know everyone, everyone knows you. And you, Jade, you seem to know everything about everyone."

Jade laughed, "It's not really a small town thing. Others just know each other. The reason that I know everything about everyone is because I like talking to people. I like knowing their stories."

Alec remembered, even as a kid, Jade had liked talking to people about their lives. She knew everything about the family members of the other people in their little circle of friends.

"Like see that lady over there?" Jade indicated towards a middle aged lady sitting alone in one of the booths, "That's Maurice Dawson. She had been married for 20 years when her husband died last year. Maurice and John, her husband, came to Splendour every Wednesday evening to have drinks after dinner for all the years that they were married. And now after John died she still keeps the tradition up. She comes every Wednesday, has a drink and then goes back to her kids. Her daughter is 17, in high school and her son is 14."

"That's difficult. Being alone with two teenage kids." Alec commented, still looking at the lady who, he realised now had a small, sad smile on her pretty face.

"Yes. She misses having John next to her, helping her with kids, seeing him every morning and spending time with him every minute of her life. And she works in the high school. She's a history teacher."

"How do you know such stuff?"

It was surprising how much Jade knew about the lady.

"I spoke to her."

"And she told you all this, about how difficult it is to have teenage kids and raising them alone?"

"Yes. Alec to know someone's story you just have to ask in the right way." Jade said, "It's not so difficult you know."

"But why? I mean... What do you get?"

"I like knowing the life stories of new people."

That was the reason she was a good author. She understood people and had a way of making people comfortable so that they told her about themselves without much encouragement or coaxing.

"It must be good to have the talent to do that." Said Alec just as the gangly Bob put down their drinks in front of them while sneaking a peek at Jade from the cover of his hair.

"To people. And the various stories they have to tell us." Jade cheered, holding up her glass.

Alec held up his glass of frothy beer, "To people. And those who listen to those various stories."

They clinked glasses and Alec took a sip of his beer. He placed the glass on the bar and looked up.

Jade had the glass of vodka still at her lips and she was drinking like she had been thirsty for years.

"Hey hey! Chill out." He took the glass from her hands and placed it next to his.

"That felt good!" She said smacking her lips.

Alec looked at the glass which was already half empty.

"Why the hurry?" He laughed.

"I don't remember the last time I had a proper drink. I have been so busy writing and Nicole has been busy with the twins. We have not got drunk for ages." Sighed Jade.

She could feel the warm liquid burn down her throat and spread the warmth throughout her body.

"So that's the plan, huh? Getting drunk?" Alec asked.

"Will that be a problem?"

"Nope... I like girls who can really drink!"

"So then Mr Alexander Carter, you're going to love me!" Said Jade enthusiastically before picking up the glass and taking another hearty sip of vodka.

This was one new side of Jade Tucker that Alec was seeing. And to tell the truth he actually loved it.

Chapter 15

Alec shoved the key into the lock to Jade's apartment.

This was the third key he was trying. As a reply to, "Unlock the door." a thoroughly drunk Jade had handed him a bunch of keys before sitting down on the floor.

Even as he struggled with the sheer number of keys, Jade was sitting and giggling away to glory.

"You know Jade, this will be faster if you get up and tell me which key it is!" Said Alec who was exasperated.

Jade laughed at that like it was a joke, "You know Alec your girlfriend has a horrible choice. I mean that green dress, who in their right mind spends money on a dress like that for themselves. It's horrible."

"Uh huh..." Alec replied still trying to unlock the door.

"And Julia was describing the beige suit she wore the day you'll came... Let me just say it sounds horrible!" Jade said and started laughing again.

Being drunk somehow reduced Jade's vocabulary to only a few adjectives.

The last few tequila shots had surely been a mistake, thought Alec as he finally opened the door. He pushed it and walked in.

He turned around to see Jade still sitting on the floor outside the apartment and talking to herself.

"Okay! Jade we have to go inside. We don't want to wake the neighbours..." He walked out and pulled her up onto her feet.

"Oops!"

Jade stumbled. Alec pulled her up just in time to stop her from falling.

"Oh! Alec just a last drink. I'm not even tipsy! Tipsy my foot! You'll learn your lesson when you wake up tomorrow... All the best with the hangover." Alec mumbled as he supported her till the bedroom, imitating her pleas from earlier that evening.

Jade just kept giggling. Drunk Jade reminded Alec of a five year old Jade.

"I'm drunk!" Jade stated as she plopped down on her bed.

Alec looked at her, "Now are you!" He said sarcastically. "You need to change."

Jade completely ignored him and started pulling at the covers.

"No... No... Change first. Okay. Jade change." He again pulled her up and made her stand on her feet, "I'm outside you change. Okay?"

Jade nodded her head, a pout playing on her lips.

Alec walked out.

It had been a mistake to let Jade drink so much.

She would have a horrible hangover the next morning.

But who was he to say anything to her about drinking too much. He had almost the same amount as her to drink. But all the tension of taking Jade back to her apartment and convincing her that calling her editor while she was drunk was not the best idea, had one good effect. It had drained out all the effect of the alcohol and he was no longer drunk.

He sat on the sofa and sighed.

Suddenly a loud noise came from the bedroom.

Alec jumped up and ran to Jade, images of her on the floor with a bleeding head playing on his mind.

Instead of all the horrible things that had gone through his mind, he found Jade sitting on the floor and laughing.

She had changed into a loose T-shirt which fell till get knees.

"What happened?" He said, picking her up from the floor.

When she had caught her breath, she said, "See what fell out of my cupboard."

That's when Alec noticed the dress in Jade's hand. It was the dress Emma had given to her the night of the homecoming party.

"Your girlfriend has a horrible choice!" Jade shrieked with laughter.

Tears of mirth were running down her cheek.

"Yes, that's very funny Jade. You need to go to bed now."

It took some time to control her laughter and coax her into bed, but finally Alec was successful.

He stood up once she was tucked in, "Okay now... I'm leaving! You go to sleep."

He started backing out of the room. He was almost out of the bedroom when Jade called out to him.

"Alec?"

"Yes Jade? What is it?" He came back inside and stood next to her bed.

Her eyes were drooping and Alec knew that it was only a matter of minutes till she would be fast asleep.

"Your girlfriend has a terrible choice." Jade slurred.

Atlast another word to describe Emma's choice!, thought Alec.

He smiled, "You might have mentioned that once or twice."

"Except you. Your not half bad..."

Jade flashed a smile at Alec.

"Thanks, I guess. Now sleep."

"Good night, Al!"

Jade turned around and closed her eyes, snuggling deep into the comfort of the blanket.

Alec walked to the door of the bedroom, switched of the lights and as he left the room he whispered, "Good night, Jady!"............ ....She woke up at 8 when her alarm started ringing.

Switching off the alarm, she got up, immediately groaning and clutching her head.

She felt like there were little and evil 'hangover dwarfs' in her head, hammering away to glory.

Jade somehow opened her eyes and got out of bed. All the events from last night filtered into her head.

She remembered the vodka which had been generously served by Bob and then the tequila shots she had ordered after that.

No wonder her head was on the verge of bursting.

But the events after that were pretty blurred. She remembered Alec refusing to let her have another drink and dragging her out of Splendour. She remembered being sick in some bushes. That was it!

How did she come home? How did she land up in her bed? Everything was a mystery.

She decided to think about all that a little later. Thinking made the headache worse.

She stumbled out of the bedroom and into the kitchen, thoughts of coffee flitting around her head.

Was she hallucinating or was that actually the smell of coffee?

She walked into the kitchen to find her coffee maker filled with strong black coffee. Someone had set a timer on the machine, since the coffee was still quite warm.

She almost moaned in delight while pouring herself a mug, the smell of the heavenly liquid wafting up.

She took a sip of the coffee, black, without any sugar and this time she really moaned.

After having a couple more sips she kept the mug and sat down on the kitchen chair.

There leaning on the fruit basket was a note.

She picked it up and recognised Alec's handwriting.

The note read,

Jade,

I knew you would wake up with a horrible hangover and decided to make it a little better.

I set the timing for 7:45 and I hope it's atleast lukewarm when you wake up.

You can thank me when we meet.

Alec!

That was so sweet of him. Jade smiled at the note and took another sip of coffee.

She made a mental note of thanking him in some special way.

She must have been a real pain in the ass last night. Like she always was when she got drunk.

Nicole was quite used to her drunk behaviour, whereas Alec must have gone crazy trying to handle her.

She would make it a point to make it up to him.

After finishing her coffee, she decided that the remnants of the hangover could be chased away with a couple of aspirins and a hot shower.

She swallowed the aspirin and went into her bedroom.

There on the floor near her bed lay the green dress that had been 'given' to her by Emma.

She picked it up.

What was it doing out here? She clearly remembered shoving it to the back of her cupboard.

That's when she noticed that the door of her cupboard was also wide open.

She went and put the dress back in.

After closing the door she saw herself in the full length mirror on her dresser.

She winced when she saw the state of her hair and her blood shot eyes.

The t- shirt she was wearing was all crinkled.

Wait! T- shirt?

She was surely not wearing a T- shirt last night, when they had gone to Splendour.

She remembered the blue top she had been wearing.

A look around the room, showed that the top and her jeans were lying on the other side of her bed, all crumpled.

Jade didn't remember changing out of her clothes.

So did that mean Alec......?

No way!

But then who else could have changed her clothes?

All the warm thoughts that had come into her head about Alec after reading the note quickly vanished.

He was going to pay for this!

Instead of going for the shower, as she had planned earlier, she changed into jeans and a hoodie, brushed her teeth in a hurry and left the house.

Alexander Carter had some very important questions to answer.....................Susan looked at the photo of Jade and Alec she was holding in her hands.

It really felt like Alec was back to Millbrooke to stay. And she couldn't pull the smile off her face.

She, Julia and Alec had eaten breakfast together earlier, chatting and laughing just like old times.

Even now as she cleaned her house she knew that Julia was up in her bedroom going over some mails while Alec was taking a shower in his room.

And that thought comforted her so much.

She really tried not to show it, but without her kids in the house she sometimes felt very lonely.

And this was the reason sometimes she was jealous of Amanda, though she was her best friend.

While her kids all had moved out of town and rarely met her, Jade still lived in Millbrooke and made it a point to meet her mother as often as possible.

But then Jade was as much a daughter to her as to Amanda.

She had never differentiated between her kids and Jade.

Never had it once crossed her mind that Jade was not her daughter, while lovingly feeding her as a child or taking her for shopping.

She still remembered, when Alec and Jade had been in high school, Jade used to come barging into the house. Most days without knocking or any other warning.

She would come into the living area, first hug Susan tightly and then stomp into Alec's room, either thoroughly pissed off at him or excited about something. Either way yelling on top her lungs.

Susan smiled at the memory and kept the photo she had been holding on the mantle.

The picture was of one such day, when Jade had come into the house yelling and screaming with joy.

She had come first in the essay competition in her school and had to tell all of them about it.

The photo had been taken by Susan, sneakily while, Jade had been giving the good news to Alec.

The absolute joy on Jade's face and the look of pride on Alec's made Susan feel like it was just yesterday when they had been teenagers, and not almost a decade ago.

Just as she was picking up the next photo to wipe it, she heard a loud noise come from outside.

It sounded like someone banging a car door.

Before she could look out of the window to see who it was, she heard the front door bang open and Jade walked in.

"Mrs Carter!" Jade came into the living room and hugged Susan.

"Jade… What are you doing here?"

"I need to meet Alec now!" Jade looked like she was going to kill Alec.

Susan looked at her with concern, "Is anything wrong?"

"Nothing's wrong… Where's he?"

Jade's expression softened a little as she spoke to Mrs Carter, there was no way she was scaring her because of something that Alec did.

"In his bedroom. I think he's taking a shower."

"Thanks Mrs Carter!" Jade flashed a smile and ran towards Alec's bedroom, leaving Susan stunned in the living room.

Once she got over the shock of seeing Jade, Susan laughed and sat down on the sofa.

A decade might have passed since the time Alec and Jade were in high school, but they still behaved just like teenagers. Or sometimes worse.

Chapter 16

A lec let the steaming hot water from the shower hit him right in the face.

There was something really soothing about taking a hot shower after having a perfect breakfast with your family. Something which he had missed for years.

He had woken up with a hangover, not a terrible one but still a pretty bad one.Most of which he chased away with the coffee he had with his breakfast.

He wondered how Jade was faring as he washed his hair.

She was sure to wake up with a raging headache and blood shot eyes.

Thinking about that, he had taken pity on her and set the coffee machine in her kitchen on a timer, before leaving the apartment last night.

His mind went back to all the events of the day. He had come to know so many things about the 'grown up' Jade in just one day.

Something's which had come as a surprise and the others not so much.

All said and done he had enjoyed spending the whole day with her and had more fun than he remembered having for years now.

Just as he was about to get out of the shower, he heard someone knock on his door.

Must be Julia, he thought, before picking up a towel and wrapping it tightly around his waist.

"Alexander Carter you better open the door right now, if you know what's good for you!"

He had just stepped out of the foggy bathroom when he heard Jade yell.

Jade?

What was she doing here?

As far as he knew she should have been at her apartment struggling with a horrible hangover.

He hurried to open the door, as the bangs and knocks became more insistent.

"Bloody hell! Chill out, Jade." He said pulling open the door.

Jade stood with her hands firmly fisted on her waist.

Her eyes were blurry and she looked like she was ready to strangle someone. Most probably him.

"Why weren't you opening the door?" She asked.

Alec raised an eyebrow, "Isn't it obvious? I was in the shower! Or do you think I'm wet because it was raining in my room?"

That's when Jade noticed that Alec was standing in front of her almost naked except for a white towel around his waist.

His sandy brown hair was dripping and stuck to his forehead.

"Uh...." The initial shock of actually seeing Alec's sculpted abs made Jade almost forget the real reason why she was there.

"Yes?" Alec shifted his weight from one foot to another.

Jade took a deep breath, "I need to speak to you. Let me come in!" She said trying hard to ignore Alec's bare and wet chest.

"Can't it wait? I do need to get changed."

"No it can't. Let me come in!"

Alec was about to say something more, but she ignored him and pushed into the room.

Alec's room was just as she remembered it from the sleepovers she had been for at his house as a child.

Sunlight poured into the room from the window on the other side of the bed.

His study table was cluttered like always and now had a few extra additions. His laptop, wallet and some other work related files.

"Close the door!" She said once she was inside.

She turned around and faced him. He was still standing near the door.

I hope his towel is tied tightly, thought Jade.

"You're scaring me now, Jade." But he still shut the door behind him.

"Did you change my clothes last night?" Jade blurted out as soon as the door was shut.

She didn't want to hold this particular conversation with any chance that Mrs Carter could be eavesdropping.

"What?"

"Alec did you change my clothes last night?"

"You don't remember?"

It didn't come as a surprise to Alec that the events of last night were a blur to her.

"Obviously I don't remember! I wouldn't ask you then!" Jade clutched her head as if the shouting was hurt, "I remember leaving Splendour and I remember puking last night. And the next thing I remember is waking up in my bed with a t- shirt on. A t- shirt I'm sure I didn't wear to Splendour. So who changed my clothes?"

This will be fun, thought Alec.

"It was me! I swear." He said picking up his hands in mock surrender.

When Jade narrowed her eyes to small slits and glared at him he backed away, "Oh! You mean....Jade I run my own business. I think I can change a girls clothes with my eyes closed."

Jade's tensed shoulders sagged a little.

"Not that I'm saying my eyes were closed." Alec added in the end.

The punch came out of nowhere and landed straight on the bridge of his nose.

The flash of pain made him take a few steps back.

Though Stuart was not even close to getting a 'Best Father' award, one thing he had taught Jade and that was to throw a mean punch.

And Jade had to agree, grudgingly thought that he had done a good job and she was grateful to him for the lessons.

"Sweet baby Jesus!" Alec gingerly touched his nose, his fingers came back bloody. "You punched me? My nose is bleeding! Have you completely lost it?"

"You deserved it!" Jade said crossing her hands over her chest and looking Alec straight into his eyes with a determined look.

"Ouch!" He exclaimed when he touched the bridge of his nose. "I think you broke my nose."

Jade smirked proudly, "I'm glad!"

Alec stared at the blood in his hand. He had been in his fair share of fist fights but this was the first time he had been punched by a girl as an adult. And it hurt like hell.

He sat down on the edge of his bed and shook his head, "Jade! You were drunk. You didn't pass out. You changed your clothes on your own without any help from anyone. Especially not me. I was waiting in the living room."

"Really? But you said.....?"

"I was teasing you. I didn't expect you to punch me." Alec laughed and then immediately winced when his nose hurt even more and blood spurted out.

"Oh! Shit!" Jade said guiltily.

She should have realised Alec was not serious. She should have listened him out before acting on her instincts and punching him.

"Yeah... Oh shit!" Repeated Alec before picking up the end of the towel to wipe his nose with it.

"No no no... Don't do that!" Jade realised his intentions and stopped him just in time.

She was already getting slightly breathless at the sight of his bare chest. Even the idea of seeing any other part of his body made her knees weak.

Even if it was just his shin.

"Lie down on you back and tilt your chin up. Stay like that. I'll just be back."

She left Alec, hoping he would listen to her and went into the bathroom which was still a little steamed up.

She took a deep breath to settle her nerves, before picking up all the things she needed.

"This is a very uncomfortable position." Stated Alec once she walked back into the room.

Jade kept the things on the table, "It will stop the bleeding."

She handed him the small towel in her hand, "Hold it to your nose."

Alec did as she asked and then looked at her expectantly without saying anything.

"Now don't get very angry but... You know this ring I wear everyday..." She pointed at the small silver ring on her index finger. "Well.... It has kind of cut your nose and so most of the blood is from the cut!" She said the last few words quickly.

Alec's eyes grew huge, "Are you serious? The least you could have done was punch me with the hand which does not have any ornaments on it!" His voice sounded wierd, a little nasal, as he was clutching his nose protectively.

"Look you shouldn't have teased me. Then you wouldn't have ended up with a bloody nose!" Shrugged Jade.

"Okay... So it's my fault now?"

"Let's play the 'blame game' later. I need to put this on the cut." Jade said holding up the bottle of antiseptic liquid in her hand.

Alec shook his head, "No ways! I'm not letting you touch my nose. It will sting."

"Are you seriously scared of a little sting? Really?"

"No it's not that." Alec said.

Jade smirked as a reply. Hurting his ego was an assured way of making Alec do everything she wanted him to do.

"Okay go ahead." He said at last, "You're just jealous that I have the royally handsome, Greek nose while you end up with the round stub as an excuse for a nose."

"Royally handsome? If you say so...." Jade put the antiseptic on a piece of cotton.

To get better access to his bleeding nose she bent over him while he lay still in anticipation on the bed.

Their faces were close and Jade could smell the soap he used. It had a woodsy smell which was quite pleasant.

"Ouch!" Alec yelled when she touched the cotton to the cut.

Jade just smiled and continued wiping the blood. Wiping a little extra hard than absolutely needed.

"Done!" She said, when she didn't have the heart to see him wince any more from the sting.

"Really? Why don't you pour the whole bottle on the cut?" Alec said sarcastically.

Once the pain subsided a little and became a small throb, he realised just how close their faces were.

He could feel her hair tickle his cheek where it fell out of the pony tail.

Had her eyes always been such a deep shade of green or was it because of the lighting in the room?

They stared at each other.

Each waiting for the other to say something.

"Alec?"

Jade and Alec were pulled out of the trance by the sound of someone opening the door and calling out to him.

They turned simultaneously to see Emma standing at the door with a shocked expression on her face.

Behind her stood Julia and Steve, with raised eyebrows and twin looks of amusement.

Jade immediately pulled back and tripped on the side table, almost falling.

"Emma! You're back?" Alec stuttered. His voice still a little funny.

His nose had stopped bleeding but there still were blood marks around it.

He had a startled expression on his face.

He looked like a kid caught with his hand stuck in a cookie jar.

Hell! He felt like a kid caught with his hand stuck in the cookie jar!

Chapter 17

"Oh God! I wish I was there!" Laughed Nicole, just like she had been doing for the past ten minutes while Jade recounted the events from earlier that morning. "What happened then?"

"Nothing much... Alec got up and started explaining what was going on. And then was interrupted midway through his speech by Steve who told him to put on a shirt or something...." Nicole started laughing again at that, "And I said that I had an important call to make, excused myself and ran from there." Jade finished.

"You ran?" Nicole asked once she had calmed down a little.

"Yes I ran." Jade spooned cereal into her mouth and then spoke through it, "You have no idea, Nicky! It had become so awkward. If looks could kill Emmaline's glares would have surely sent me to the Emergency Room."

"Alec didn't stop you?"

"No he was the only other person in the room who could see Emma's face. And he too was getting enough of those glares. So I ran."

One hour had passed since the time Emma had walked into Alec's bedroom to see Jade almost on top of her almost naked boyfriend.

But the redness had still not vanished from Jade's cheeks, the embarrassment still fresh in her memory.

She took a large swig of her coffee, which was her third cup of the day and continued, "Juliana tried to stop me. But then, I guess she saw the pleading look on my face and let me go."

What had happened once she had left?, thought Jade.

"But seriously, Jade you punched him? You made his nose bleed?"

This time Jade had to laugh along with Nicole.

"Yes I did. And I loved every minute of it." Jade replied.

After coming back home she had immediately jumped into the shower, to get rid of the massive headache which was partly due to the hangover and partly because of the awkwardness and tension from the Carter house.

Then she called Nicole and started telling her about her interesting morning while having cereal.

"In short you've had a terribly eventful morning. Now take it easy the rest of the day." Nicole said.

"Yeah... I'm planning to stay in the whole day. Watch some movies, get some writing done and rest. Nothing stressful."

They said their goodbyes and Jade kept the phone.

She picked up her empty bowl and mug and took it to the sink. As she washed them, she wondered what had happened to Alec after she had left.

The look on Emma's face had made it very clear that she was not going to let Alec off easily.

As she debated whether to give him a call or no, the bell to her apartment rang.

She walked to the door and pulled it open.

There on the threshold stood Amanda.

Jade could see that her mother had dressed up very carefully in grey slacks and a green sweater. Her grey streaked hair was pulled away from her face.

"Hi mom!"

Jade said moving aside to let her come into the house.

"Hello Jade! Did I disturb you?" Amanda asked sitting down on the sofa in the living room.

Jade came and sat beside her mother, "No... I just finished breakfast."

Amanda raised an eyebrow at her daughter, "Breakfast? What were you doing the whole morning?"

"I swear you don't want to know mom." Jade laughed, "Anyways what brings you here?"

"Actually... I got a call from Stuart this morning. He's in town."

The mention of her dad's name, made Jade sit a little straighter. Somehow any mention of Stuart Tucker managed to raise her hackles.

"What did he say?"

Her mother looked a little worried, "He said he's staying at The Inn."

'The Inn' was the most popular and ironically named inn of Millbrooke.

It was the place which housed most of the tourist crowd the little town got during the winter months.

"He's staying at The Inn?"

This was different.

Normally, Stuart always managed to meet Amanda on the day he arrived in town which meant that he always got invited to stay at her Mom's house.

He never had taken the initiative to book a room at the inn or any of the small motels in town.

Amanda crossed and uncrossed her legs, "I know. I was surprised too."

"Doesn't he want to 'meet' you, and 'apologise'?"

Jade knew that sarcasm was not what her mother needed at the moment but she couldn't help herself.

She just had a feeling that this was one of his new plans.

Amanda gave a stern look to Jade but answered normally, "He does. He requested to meet us at 'Beans' in an hour."

"By 'us' you mean 'you'."

As a rule, her dad had always wanted to meet only Amanda on the first day that he came back to town after one of his disappearances.

He knew that it was much harder to melt Jade than Amanda.

But she always managed to tag along with her mother for these meetings. Not that it made any difference.

If the meeting went according to her plans, she would send him packing on the first day itself.

"No. He especially told me to ask you to come too." Amanda said, "Will you come?"

If Jade was surprised she didn't let it show on her face, "Of course. Give me a minute. I'll just get changed."

What was her father upto this time?

Her plans of spending one drama free day were all history by the time she got ready and left the house to meet her father after 3 whole years.

Stuart Tucker had always been a handsome man, and age had not reduced the good looks in any way. Instead the years had just added to the dignified look he always had.

Maybe the good looks were the first thing that attracted, 18 year old Amanda to him.

His charm and crooked smile could soften even the hardest of souls and she had always been a romantic at heart.

So it had not taken long for her to fall head over heels in love with the town rogue.

Stuart too, fell in love with the sweet girl who was more often than not, hidden behind a pile of books.

This had always come as a surprise to Jade. Her dad had never liked life in a small town.

He wanted to travel the world live in different place, meet new people. Then why did he end up getting married to a girl who had no plans of ever stepping out of the town?

The happily married, blind in love couple had Jade just 2 years after the big wedding which had been held in the local church.

The first few years had been great for both Amanda and Stuart. But soon married life and family became like a prison for Stuart.

The family and the responsibilities that came with it were suffocating him.

Amanda and Jade were the only ones keeping him in Millbrooke and he started detesting them for that.

Finally, 10 years after their marriage, at 35 he couldn't take it any more. One night he packed his bags and left.

He knew he was causing a lot of pain to both his wife and his daughter but once he was out of the confining town, he could breathe again. He was free.

He kept coming back every few years to Millbrooke. Something always pulled him back.

But once he knew what life outside the small town was like, he kept going back for more.

Jade walked into'Beans' with it's strong smell of coffee and chocolate and immediately spotted her father looking uncomfortable in a booth, with a group of loud teenagers sitting next to him.

In the three years since Jade had last seen him, Stuart had lost a lot of weight and his hair had lost some of it's usual shine.

She squeezed her mothers hand and both of them walked to where he was sitting.

Stuart Tucker had the looks of an actor from the old black and white movies they showed on the TV. A sharp jaw, green eyes and a smile that had the power of getting him whatever he wanted.

He was tall and had a lean figure even at his age.

As soon as Stuart saw Amanda and Jade walk towards him he stood up and waited for them to come into hearing distance.

"Hello Amanda. How are you Jade?"

Jade noticed that his smile was just a little off.

"Hello Stuart. How are you?" Amanda asked as she took the seat next to Jade who sat down without even acknowledging his question.

"I'm fine. You look great, Amanda." Stuart said.

That was more like him.

Charm. Compliment. Lies. These things came naturally to Stuart Tucker.

"Thanks."

Before anyone else could continue the awkward conversation the waiter came to ask for their orders.

Jade gave her order and again sat quietly glaring at her father.

The silence continued even long after the waiter had served their drinks.

Stuart cleared his throat and finally broke the silence, "Congratulations on the success of your new book Jade."

Amanda had to nudge her daughter in the stomach till finally Jade spoke up, "Thanks."

Again the conversation came to a still.

Finally Jade couldn't take the silence anymore or bare the pleading looks her mom was sending her.

"So you're alone?" She asked.

Not exactly the conversation starter Amanda had hoped for when she had nudged her daughter.

"What do you mean?" If her dad was surprised at her question he didn't let it show on his face.

Jade smirked, "You know what I mean, 'Dad'." She emphasised the last word. "Where's Bianca?"

The name of his young secretary got the reaction, Jade had been hoping for.

Stuart's shoulders tensed and his lips formed a thin line. He in unclasped his fingers and held onto his cup of coffee.

"Bianca quit three months back. She's in London." He stated, he was clutching the handle of his cup so tight that his knuckles were white.

"So that's the reason you're here." Laughed Jade, "I should have guessed. Got bored of you did she?"

"Jade!" Gasped Amanda on the seat next to her.

"What? I'm just asking. I do have the right to ask don't I ?"

Jade knew that her words were hurting her mother more than Stuart who was her real target. But she couldn't help it.

One look at the man and all the bitter feelings she had for him came spilling out. Most of them because of all the pain he had caused her by leaving.

Bianca was a Mexican, stunning air head who had the attention span of a toddler and who also happened to be Stuart's secretary. Not to mention mistress.

"I came back here because I realised my mistake." Stuart replied.

"Like you do every 2 or 3 years." Jade scoffed, "Like you did 3 years back. Pity your 'visit' last time got cut short because of the business problems that you had to take care of. Everything's fine now?"

"Jade that's enough!" Amanda said.

There were tears in her eyes that Jade could see her mother was trying hard to stop.

"But mom...."

"Jade enough..."

For the first time in years Amanda raised her voice while speaking to Jade.

Silence fell again.

No one knew what to say.

"Amanda... Look about Bianca..." Stuart started.

Amanda started shaking her head. She didn't want to know.

"No... Let me explain. Yes. I was having an affair with her. She was young. Hell! She was younger than my daughter." Stuart let his head fall in his palms, "I won't say it was love. Because it was far from it. On my part as well as hers. For her, I was a way to get money and all the luxury that came with being my woman. She used me and I have to say.... I deserved it!"

"Stuart...." Amanda tried to stop him. She didn't want to hear all this.

During his last visit she had been introduced to Bianca, his secretary. And it had not taken her long to realise that a professional relationship was not the only kind of relationship they were having.

It had been clear by the way they would behaved around each other, talked to each other. Lingering touches. Secret looks.

Amanda had lived her whole life in a small town. But she knew the ways of the world. And she was not stupid.

She had been almost relieved when, Bianca had made up an excuse about some business emergency and had gone back to London. Taking Stuart along with her.

Knowing that her husband, ex- husband, had affairs was one thing. But seeing it so shamelessly portrayed in front of her eyes was another.

"No let me finish.... What happened three years back... I wish I could just completely erase all that."

Jade listened to her father speak. For the first time she believed his story.

With downcast eyes he recounted all that had happened in the past years.

Bianca had hatched a plan with her boyfriend before taking up the job as Stuart's secretary.

Stuart Tucker was famous for two things his wealth and his weakness for beautiful women.

Taking advantage of this weakness, the Mexican beauty had come into his life.

She fed him a pity story, about how she was on the run from a violent boyfriend, and Stuart had offered her a job.

For almost 4 years, she used him for money, to live the life she wanted.

Now Stuart knew that she used to squirrel away some of the money to her boyfriend.

But soon they became more ambitious they wanted money for themselves, without going through all the trouble of acting in front of Stuart.

She had had all the access she needed to Stuart's accounts and file.

So they came up with another plan. Stuart didn't go into all the details but from what he said, Jade understood that they stole more than a million pounds from him.

"There was no way I could frame them. Bianca might have been an air head but that boyfriend of hers was sharper than nails." Stuart sighed, "When I confronted her, she said one thing that I will never forget. She said that what they did to me was million times better than what I had done to you'll. If they deserved to go to jail, I deserved to rot in hell."

By this time Amanda was crying. Jade took her mother's hand and squeezed it.

"And you know what Amanda?" Her father continued, "I completely agree with her."

There was water in his eyes too. This was the first time Jade saw her dad cry.

"So why are you here?" Amanda words were almost inaudible.

"I'm here because I hope that you both will forgive me. Though I would not have forgiven myself if I had been in you place." He turned to look at Jade. "I know what you think. You think that I'm here because of all that happened with Bianca. But more than stealing from me. She taught me a lesson. A lesson I should have learnt years back. Let me make amends."

Jade didn't know what to say, he sounded so genuine, so like the father she remembered.

"I'll stay at the Inn. But I wanted to say this, I'm here to stay. I'm not going back."

They sat at the table each lost in their own thoughts.

"We should leave." Amanda stated once she had composed herself.

"Okay." Both Stuart and Jade said together.

They got up and as Jade started following her mom out of the cafe, suddenly Amanda turned around to face Stuart again.

She took a deep breath, "Jade I hope you don't have a problem with this." She said to Jade then continued, "Come for lunch to my place tomorrow."

Jade looked at the hopeful smile in her dad's face. He nodded and they walked out of the cafe again leaving him at the both.

"Say something Jade." Amanda said once they were outside.

She shrugged, "I don't have a problem."

"You don't need to come you know."

Jade could see the hope flare in Amanda's eyes. The hope of getting her Stuart back.

And for the first time in years, Jade didn't want to crush the hope.

"I don't know if I'm making a huge mistake. But no I won't come."

She was gifted with a huge smile from her mother for that.

This time even she hoped that her dad was here to stay. That doesn't mean she would forgive him. Far from it.

But it would mean not seeing Amanda get hurt. At least for some time.

You better not hurt my mom again, Stuart. This is your last chance.

These words kept playing on a repeat in Jade's mind as they walked to the parking lot where Amanda's car was parked.

Chapter 18

J ust as Jade was getting into her mom's car, her cell phone started to ring.

She pulled it out of her purse and saw that it was Julia.

"I need to take this call." She told Amanda who was getting into the driver's seat.

Amanda nodded, "Want me to wait?"

"No it's okay. I'll walk. I'll call you later, okay?"

Jade gave one last parting smile to her mom and started walking.

"Hi, Julia!" She said after picking up the phone.

"Hello Jade! So what have you been up to after your major escape?"

Jade laughed at Julia's teasing tone, "Look the great escape had been necessary. You could not see Emma's face. She looked like she wanted to kill me. Like really!"

"Well... She almost killed Alec!" Julia chuckled, "So I guess it was good you ran."

"What happened after I left?"

"Nothing much... At least nothing that I know about. She started throwing questions at him. And well we- Steve and me- excused ourselves. I was reluctant but my dear husband forced me. I was scared that the Emma would eat my little brother alive."

Jade laughed at that, "Then...?"

"Then there were in Alec's room for like an hour. At first we could hear her yell and then suddenly everything went quiet. I have no clue what happened."

"You're not at home are you? If anyone hears you speaking like that about Emma...."

Julia interrupted her, "Ofcourse I'm not at home. I don't have a death wish. I had actually gone to invite Nicole and Jason."

Jade frowned, "Invite?"

"That's the reason I called. See since you and Emma started off in such a good manner..." They laughed at that, "I was thinking let's sort out all the tension. We'll go for drinks and dancing. Maybe have dinner."

"But..."

This was what she had been dreading. Jade didn't want to go, not for any other reason but because she would be like the third wheel, or the seventh wheel in this situation.

Without a boyfriend she would just feel awkward.

"No... Don't say no. Look it's all sorted out. Emma and Alec are game. Nicole is calling her mom to take care of the twins. Please Jady!" Begged Julia.

By this time Jade had reached the Main Street. She looked around aimlessly, trying to find some some excuse so that she could avoid going.

"Jules..." Suddenly she saw something that made her smile.

She had an idea.

"Okay..." She continued, "But I'll be getting a date!"................
....."That was the last patient for now, Matt."

Matt picked up his head from the file he had been concentrating on, to see Mrs Lloyd standing at the door to his office.

Mrs Lloyd was a middle aged, sweet lady who worked as the receptionist at his clinic. But was more like a substitute mother to him in the absence of his own mom.

"Thanks Mrs Lloyd! Why don't you take a break? Go get some lunch." Matt said with a smile, before returning to his file.

Instead of taking him up on his offer, Mrs Lloyd walked into his office.

Agatha Lloyd had seen many young men in the town of Millbrooke. Some of them ambitious, others just lazy.

But Matt Damon was the most hard working guy she had met. He worked day and night. Sometimes missing meals to see a patient.

"You should take a break too." She said, taking the seat opposite him.

Matt looked up again, surprised to see her still in the room.

"Yeah maybe after sometime."

"You know what you need in your life? A woman. Yeah that's what you need." She continued even after the surprised look Matt gave her. "A woman who will take care of you when you don't. You'll find a girl very easily. A handsome lad like you."

Matt laughed. This was not the first time he was having the conversation with Mrs Lloyd. In the four years since he opened his clinic in Millbrooke and the woman, who surely must have been quite a looker in her youth, this conversation had taken place twice every week.

Sometimes more.

"You broke my heart Mrs Lloyd. And you know I can never love again. What's the use of even trying?"

"Rubbish!" She flapped her hands at his words. But Matt could see the rosy flush come onto her pretty face.

"It's true! Ralph Lloyd is the luckiest man I know!" Insisted Matt.

She ignored him and continued, "What happened between you and Jade? She looked good with you. Got all her looks from her beautiful mamma after all! Amanda, pretty but unlucky in love! Poor Amanda!"

Agatha was proud of herself for knowing all the gossip in town. And even the most ignorant person knew about Amanda and her husband.

"We broke up." Stated Matt, not liking the turn which the conversation had taken.

Mrs Lloyd frowned, "Why did you do that?"

"I didn't do anything." Shrugged Matt, "She dumped me."

"Hmm... Well you'll find someone for yourself too. Better find her fast. Before you work yourself to the bone."

Matt laughed at that and waved his hand when she bustled out of the door.

He suspected that she was going to come up with atleast 4 girls he should take for dinner by the end of the day.

Agatha Lloyd had tried to patch him up with almost all the girls of his age in town.

Sometimes girls who were younger than him.

Much younger than him.

He could relate with the disappointment that had flashed on her face on hearing that he was no longer with Jade.

It was a feeling he himself got most days.

His relation with Jade had been some of the best days of his life. She was interesting, intelligent, kind and stunning. Qualities which were difficult to find in one girl.

So it had been a natural step for him to ask if he could move in with her. If only he had known that she would react to that by breaking up with him, he would kept quiet.

He was startled out of his thoughts of Jade when Mrs Lloyd poked her head back into his office.

There was a huge smirk on her face.

"Someone's here for you." She said, the smile still stuck on her face. Like a kid who was going to play a prank.

"A patient?" He asked.

"She doesn't look ill. I'll send her in." She winked, "All the best!"

Matt was confused.

Mrs Lloyd winked at him. Something was up.

Before he could speculate any longer there was a knock on the door to his office.

Jade was standing over there with a small smile on her lips.

She was dressed in jeans and a light green shirt. Her hair was pulled into a pony tail. No wonder he had fallen so hard for her. She looked beautiful.

"Jade?"

Jade was not surprised to see the look of shock on Matt's face.

She had seen his clinic while talking to Julia and had decided to go meet him immediately.

"Hello Dr Damon!" She said, "Can I come in?"

"Yeah... Please sit!" Matt stuttered offering her the seat opposite him.

"Was I interrupting something?" Jade asked once she had taken her seat.

He shook his head, "Not really. It seems that the citizens of Millbrooke are all healthy today! I just told Mrs Lloyd to take a break herself."

"That's good."

"So what brings you here?" Matt asked.

Jade took a deep breath, "Actually this is going to sound a little wierd or absurd."

"Go ahead." Grinned Matt, "I love wierd and absurd stuff."

Well, here goes, thought Jade. After all what could be the worse that could happen? He would say no? But then what would she do...? She would cross that bridge when she came to it.

"I was invited to this thing tomorrow. Just dancing, drinking... Maybe dinner. You know Nicole and Jason... Alec, my friend who's just back from London, his girlfriend, Julia another friend and her husband from Chicago.... Well couples... So I told them I would get a date too...." She ended awkwardly.

While talking to Julia she had said the first thing that came to her mind when she saw his clinic right there in front if her. It had seemed like a sign. The idea that Matt might say no, or he might have other plans had not struck her.

But waiting for Mrs Lloyd to tell Matt that she wanted to meet him, Jade had been stressing out that maybe it had been a mistake.

"So you want me to come? As your date?" Matt asked at last.

"Well... Kind of.." Jade clasped her hands in her lap. "It's okay if you have other plans."

He's going to say no. It's obvious. She had dumped him. Then said no to him again a few days back. Why would he help her?

"I'll come."

"What?" Jade asked, surprised that he had agreed.

Matt shrugged, "I don't have plans. And it will be nice to meet your friends."

"Thanks." Jade smiled, still surprised.

"I'll pick you up at 7?" He asked.

"Yeah... That'll be good."

Just as Matt started saying something, Mrs Lloyd poked her head into the room again.

"Matt, Noelle Jones is here for her appointment." She said, her face splitting into a grin again.

"Okay.. Just a second." Matt said to her.

He saw the woman wink at him again and walk out.

"See you tomorrow then." Jade said getting up.

"Yeah..." He smiled, "see you!"

As Jade left the office Mrs Lloyd walked in again, almost immediately.

"What happened?" She asked all excited.

"Ahh.. Nothing."

"Tell me! You have to tell me!"

He laughed at the way Mrs Lloyd looked at him, almost begging.

"We're just going out tomorrow evening with a few of her friends." Matt said giving in.

Mrs Lloyd smiled and clapped her hands, "That's good. That's perfect. You'll look so good together.... Ahh... Young love. Reminds me of when Ralph was courting me!"

Though Matt wanted to laugh at Mrs Lloyd's reaction, he fisted his hands on his waist and said, "I thought Mrs Noelle is waiting out there."

"Spoil sport. Act all you want. I know you want to dance with joy." When Matt frowned at her she smiled and backed out, "Okay okay! I'll send her in. But love is in the air!" She went out humming to herself.

Once she was out of the room, Matt grinned.

She was right. He really wanted to dance.

There must be some reason that Jade had thought about him and not anyone else. He would convince her to give their relationship another chance.

And maybe this time she will realise that they were meant to be together.

Chapter 19

"What were you up to Alec?" Said Emma once Julia and Steve left the room, her voice so cold that it could freeze water.

Only five minutes had passed since the time Emma had walked into his room to see Jade and him in an, admittedly suspicious pose.

But already he could feel the start of the headache which was soon going to accompany the throb in his nose.

This conversation was not going to be enjoyable.

"Emma... Look it was nothing."

Emma laughed sarcastically, "It didn't look like nothing. So this was the reason you didn't have a problem when I left? You got a chance to spend time with your beloved Jade."

The way she spit out Jade's name made him want to defend her. But he knew that wouldn't be such a good idea.

Especially in the fix that he already was in.

Alec groaned, "Emma I know it looks bad. But..."

She didn't let him finish, instead she walked up to the cupboard in his room and started rummaging in it.

"Looks bad? You know how embarrassing it was for me? First of all I walk into the house and don't see you anywhere. And then your mom says that Jade's in your room. Then we see that the door is closed. And the cherry on the cake was that I pull the door open and there the black haired, arrogant girl, who thinks no end of herself is, on top of my boyfriend. Who by the way is naked." She took out a shirt from the cupboard and threw it at him.

"Em..."

"Don't you dare, Em me..." Emma sat down clutching her head, "I was so embarrassed."

"Emma, Julia and Steve are family. They understand... And anyways it was nothing."

"You call this nothing! And is Jade also family?" Emma's voice had escalated so much that Alec was sure everyone in the house could hear her yell. "And what do you mean they understand? They understand that there might be a possibility that you're cheating on me?"

And as far as he knew his sister, even though Julia had agreed to leave the room, she was surely standing just outside the closed door and eavesdropping.

"Cheating? Where did that come from? It was nothing like that. Look Emma... She came to my house because of a misunderstanding. And she punched me... And it started bleeding... Well she was just putting antiseptic." He said, his voice muffled as he put on the shirt.

"And what was the misunderstanding?" Emma asked.

There was a smug look on her face. Almost like she knew that his answer was going to give her more ammunition to use in the argument.

Okay this was going to get him into more trouble.

"Umm..Jade thought that I changed her clothes." He said quickly.

Alec had this rule. If a bad thing had to be done, he did it fast. Like ripping of a band aid.

She raised her eyebrows, "And why would she think that?"

"Well...Actually...We had gone to the bar together last night and she got drunk and she didn't remember what happened last night. So when she woke up with different clothes on she thought that I...."

Emma stood up, "She doesn't remember? How convenient for you!" She said accusingly. "And I'm glad to know you've been having fun in my absence. No wonder you weren't there to meet me when I came back."

How was he supposed to know that she would come back a day earlier? What did she expect him to do stand at the door, moping the whole day waiting for her to come back?

"You weren't even supposed to be back till tomorrow."

As soon as the words were out of his mouth, he regretted them.

If Emma had looked angry till then now she looked furious. Her face was slowly becoming red.

There was a glint in her eyes that almost scared him.

"Emma..."

"So that's the thing. You got a chance to have all the fun you want to. Without me around. And there I was in Chicago feeling all guilty about leaving you here and going to work."

Alec winced at her words, and that made his nose sting.

Emma had always had this way of glaring when she was angry.

Like she was throwing imaginary daggers at you.

Suddenly Emma sat down on the bed. Like all the energy had left her body.

It was so sudden that for a second Alec thought that she had tripped.

She let her head fall into her open palms.

Alec waited for her to say something.

"Emma..."

"Are you serious about us?" Emma picked her head up and Alec saw the tears on her cheeks.

The waterworks. Why did every argument with her end in tears?

"Ofcourse I am!" He said quickly, as he bent down in front of her.

"You never behave that way!"

"I brought you to the place which means the most to me in the world. Because I wanted you to meet my family and see the place I really belong to. Emma how else do I prove it to you?"

Her next words made Alec sit down.

"Ask me to marry you." Whispered Emma.

What just happened?

He looked carefully at her, waiting for her to start laughing.

But something in her face made him realise that she was serious.

"Uh... Em..."

"I want to get married. We've been in this relationship for so long. You are serious. I am. We've met each other's families. What else do you need?" She said, her face crumpling.

Alec raised his hand to his face and tried to press the bridge of his nose, like he did whenever he was stressed, forgetting about the cut.

His regretted it as soon as his finger touched the cut on his nose.

"Emma I have never thought of marriage." He stated, letting his hands fall back into his lap.

"Then think about it."

This was not what he had expected when the argument had started. Emma got angry fast but she just normally yelled at him till she finally was tired and she cooled down.

Before now, there had been no indication that she was on any other track about marriage than him.

Nothing she had ever said had made him think that she wanted to get married.

But now when he thought back, all the shenanigans about meeting the parents, moving in together and all the talk about how her Cousin Nancy who was marrying though she was two years younger than her.

And even all the talking about marriage with Jade.

How had he missed all the hints!

Alec got up and walked to the window of his room and looked out.

"Give me some time to think about it." He said, atlast breaking the silence.

"Take all the time you need. But Alec, please tell me if that's not what you want." Replied Emma.

He didn't turn around. He heard her leave the room, closing the door behind her.

He exhaled loudly.

This trip back home was becoming more difficult than what he had thought it would be.

First the feelings that had surfaced when Jade had been putting the antiseptic and then the conversation with Emma.

He had to get out of the house, before he went mad.

He remembered the stuff which he had thought he would do that day, originally. Before all his plans had been dashed by the women in his life.

He got dressed quickly and left the house without telling any-one.

Chapter 20

Alec always considered Jason to be one of his good friends, because of whom he survived the 4 years of high school, without going mad.

But once he left for Thailand and then went to London it had become impossible to stay in contact with anyone.

He had got quite a surprise when Jo told him that he got married to Nicole.

Relationships very rarely survived from high school till getting married.

Alec remembered Nicole as the pretty blonde girl who always sported band aids, and managed to get hurt atleast 10 times in a day.

It was a rare occasion when Nicole was completely injury- free.

Jason had been the football captain in high school and also the swim team captain. Completely in control, Jason had a way of moving that was careless yet confident.

On the other hand, Nicole was clumsy. They were like chalk and cheese, and Alec was sure they were perfect for each other.

Nicole had moved into town midway through high school and had joined the school where, Jason, Jade and he studied.

They never were very good friends, but somehow, mostly through swim team Nicole and Jason became friends and soon much more than that.

Jade and Nicole became really good friends in college, just around the time when she started drifting away from him.

He rang the bell on the door of the pretty house, which his mom had told belonged to the Bradshaw's.

"Coming!" Someone yelled from within.

Alec heard something fall to the ground and break.

The twins! How could he forget?

"I'm so sorry!"

The door was opened and Alec saw Nicole standing at the door with a tired look on her face.

She looked just like he remembered her, petite and thin.

With a heart shaped face and a smile which was too big for it.

The smile which flashed on her face as soon as Nicole noticed who was at the the door.

"Alec!" She exclaimed. "I'm sorry I don't think I should hug you."

That's when he noticed that the front of her shirt was splashed with something which looked like milk.

He couldn't stop the smile from coming onto his face, "Hey Nicky! I hope that's milk."

Nicole laughed, "Still the Alec I remember. Come in!"

She led him inside. The house that looked serene and calm from outside looked like a bomb sight from inside.

There were cushions on the floor. Toys were strewn everywhere along with shoes, clothes and books.

And right in the middle of the living room was the source of the noise from earlier and the milk on her shirt.

"So Nicky, you're still as clumsy as before."

"Unfortunately yes, but this time it wasn't my fault. My twins decided that the right time to come and hug my knees was when I'm carrying a glass of milk." She smiled while picking up some of the clothes from the floor. "Sorry for the state of the house."

"No problem. There are two kids living here. Two really energetic kids as I hear." He said helping her pick up some of the cushions.

"Oh yes! They are as energetic as possible."

"I'll just take out that car from under the table. I don't like the twins going under there." She said bending down to pick up the bright orange toy car.

"Where are they anyways? And where is Jason?" Alec asked looking around.

"Jason took them to get cleaned up. Believe it or not, they were in a worse state than I am right now."

Alec laughed.

"Nicole who was at the door?" The sound of Jason coming into the room startled Nicole. "Hi Alec!"

"Hey Jase!"

Alec started saying something else, but Nicole's yelp stopped him.

At the sound of her husband coming into the room, Nicole quickly tried to get up and in the process placed her hand on a piece of glass.

"Ouch!"

Alec saw the blood prickle out of the cut on her hand and immediately went to pick her up.

Jason who was coming into the room with one twin on each arm, on the other hand said calmly, "Of course you would do that. The antiseptic is in the kitchen, I'll go get it."

Jason put down the kids on the sofa and with a warning to not get down, he went into the kitchen.

"Why is the antiseptic in the kitchen?" Alec asked once Nicole was on the sofa with a hand pressed tightly on the cut.

"Well... The twins get into so many scrapes and then there is me... So there is someone who is bleeding all the time. Jason came up with the idea of keeping a first aid box in all rooms." Nicole replied.

"Except for the living room. I'm so stupid that I thought that it would be difficult to get hurt in the living room. I guess I was wrong."

Jason came back with a first aid kit in his hand and a rueful smile.

"It's a good thing you're back home early today. I don't know what I would have done." Nicole hissed as Jason placed the cotton with the antiseptic liquid on it right on the cut.

Alec winced. He still remembered the sting of the antiseptic. His nose still a fresh reminder.

"Thinking of your nose are you?" Nicole asked, when she saw the grimace on Alec's face.

"How do you know?"

The cut was still there on his nose, and the bridge of his nose had become bluish- black.

"Jade told me what happened." She chuckled.

Ofcourse she did.

By the time the cut was bandaged and Jason had packed up the first aid box, the twins were squealing and fidgeting on the sofa, where they had been told to sit.

"Mom!"Noah yelled out atlast, unable to tolerate the punishment of sitting still.

Nicole turned around, "Yes Noah?"

"Who is he?" The little guy pointed a fat finger straight at Alec with a grin on his chubby face.

"Haven't I told you that pointing is rude?" When Noah's hand dropped with a guilty smile, Nicole continued, "Alec why don't you introduce yourself?"

Alec bent down in front of the doge till he was at their eye level, careful to stay away from the broken glass shards.

"Hello! I'm Alec, I'm a friend of your parents." He said.

Nadia, who had been looking at him suspiciously the whole while spoke then, "No. Moms friend is Jady! Our godmother!"

"Yes. Well Jade is my friend too. We all were in school together."

That interested the twins. They looked at each other and shared identical looks.

"So where's Jady?" Noah asked.

"At her home I guess." Alec replied.

"Nadia Noah did the two of you introduce yourselves?" Asked Nicole saving Alec from the interrogation ceremony that was sure to follow.

The twins had many questions. Questions about every single thing. And they just needed one opening to start asking them.

Huge grins split their similar round faces. While Noah had inherited Nicole's hazel eyes, Nadia had got Jason's sharp blue ones.

"I'm Nadia."

"And I'm Noah!"

The kids said together with toothy grins.

Alec smiled and ruffled their hair, "That's nice!"

"Alec why don't you and Jason sit and get talking. I'll go and change and I'm sure the kids would like to go watch some TV."

Nicole spoke up.

At the sound of the word TV the twins exclaimed with joy.

"I'll clean up the glass then." Jason said, "We can talk while I clean up."

Nicole lead the twins out carefully avoiding the broken glass.

"So Alec... How's life been?" Jason asked as he started sweeping the glass.

"Life has been great! But not as good as yours ofcourse. Married and twins. You have been busy."

Jason laughed, "Yeah... I got lucky. And what about you? Wanderlust is going great and I heard about Emma."

The mention of Emma's name brought thoughts of the earlier conversation in his mind.

He shook his head and grinned, "We should all meet up one day."

"Yes absolutely."

They spoke for some more time, remembering the old days and catching up with each other's lives.

"I had to talk to you about something more." Alec said once Jason had finished cleaning up and was sitting next to him.

"What?"

Alec told him about the idea he had been thinking about for some time now.

An idea which would make a huge difference in the life that he lead now.

"That's awesome, Alec." Jason said once he heard about it, "I can give you number of people who can help you out. I really hope it works out."

"So do I." Alec said.

Jason was the first person he had told about the idea he had been brooding over for almost a year now.

Just as they were discussing the rest of the details, the door bell rang again.

Nicole who had been in the kitchen the whole while, beat Jason to the door, which she opened to see Julia standing out there.

"Both the Carter siblings had the thought of dropping by on the same day." Nicole said as she lead, Julia into the living room.

"Alec!" Julia looked at her brother who was sitting on the sofa with a surprised look on her face, "But your car was at home."

"I walked. What are you doing here?"

Alec had decided to leave the car home and walk the little distance to Jason's house.

Julia sat down and said, "I'm here to invite Nicole and Jason."

"Invite?" Jason asked.

"Yeah... We were planning to go out tomorrow night. Just drinks, dancing and stuff."

"And how do I not know about this?" Alec asked his elder sister.

"Well I did speak to Emma and she's in." Julia shrugged.

"What do you say Nicky?" Jason looked at his wife.

"I can call mom, to look after the kids. I'm in."

Nicole seemed very excited at the prospect of going out.

"So it's decided even you'll are coming! That's great!"

Alec smiled at the enthusiasm of the women. Then a thought came to his head.

"Who all are going?" He asked Julia.

"Well Steve and I, you and Emma and now Nicole and Jason. I'm going to ask Jade after this."

So Jade was coming. Would she bring the doctor with her? Or was she being honest when she said that they had broken?

"That'll be good. You know since Jade and Emma had started out on the wrong foot." Nicole said sheepishly.

How did she know everything?, thought Alec.

"So it's decided." Jason said.

"Where are the twins? I want to meet them." Julia said changing the topic.

Nicole took her to meet the twins who were in the other room, with a promise of getting something to drink for the men.

Alec sat silently, lost in his thoughts for sometime. He was thinking about what Emma had told him that morning and about what had happened with Jade.

Atlast he started speaking.

"I know this is going to sound weird and.... It's not something you would expect Alec Carter would ask. But... When.. Or actually how.. How did you realise you were in love Nicole? That she was the one." Alec realised that he was stuttering and decided to shut up.

Jason had been expecting a question like this. He had been where Alec was right now. Confused and frankly a little scared of finding that special 'the one' people keep talking about.

And to make it worse for him, Alec also had Jade in his life.

He smiled, "It's not weird at all. You know we both had been dating since junior year when she moved into town. But I was still shit scared. I still remember that day clearly. I was having breakfast and Sam walked into the kitchen. You remember Sam?"

Alec nodded. Sam was Jason's younger brother, who was now in Paris where he was living his dream of being an artist.

"Well he walked into the kitchen and I still don't know what happened but he tripped and before I knew it he was on the floor. Well... Instead of seeing if he was okay, the only thing that was going around in my head was that, this was something Nicky would do. I closed my eyes and clearly imagine how she would look. Sitting on the floor ruffled, with an almost fed up smile on her face." A smile formed on his face, "Long story short, my mom used to always tell me and Sam, when you can picture her reactions and the way she would look in situation that are not even connected to her, then she's the one."

Just as Jason finished speaking, Nicole walked in carrying a tray of coffee in her hand followed by Julia.

"I didn't know what to get so I decided on coffee." She shrugged and placed the tray on the table.

Julia came and took the seat next to Alec and asked, "What have you guys been talking about?"

"Uh... Nothing." Alec replied a little too quickly, the result was that he got a suspicious look from Julia.

Before she could voice her suspicions there was a loud noise from inside.

"The twins!" Nicole exclaimed.

She started walking out of the door at the sound and tripped over the end of the sofa.

"Oh" she said once she found herself on the floor. "I'm fine! I'm fine!" She said before anyone could get up to help her.

Alec closed her eyes. He could see her reaction. The huge grin on her pretty face and sparkle in her eyes. He could imagine how she would get up and pick Nicole up before sitting down and laughing till she almost wet her pants.

With his eyes closed he could see the way her hair swayed. The graceful way she had of carrying herself.

It almost felt like she was sitting right opposite him. It felt like it was real.

He opened his eyes with a jerk.

Jason had noticed the expression on his face, he raised his eyebrows at Alec.

Alec just shook his head glad that none of the others had noticed him.

Jason's mom had to be wrong.

He felt shaken up.

It was not Emma's face or Emma's smile that had flashed in his head.

It had been Jade.

Chapter 21

S TEVE

Sometimes some events change the perspective you have of where you are in life, or what you want from it. One decision. One moment. That's all that is needed.

For Alec it had always been his decision to leave his family, friends and gather the courage to go to Thailand to start Wanderlust from scratch.

But now...

The realisation that maybe he had feelings for Jade, the same Jade who he had grown up with and who was his best friend, completely unnerved him. Feelings that were more than just friendship.

He had never thought of falling for Jade. Never had it occurred to him that maybe the love he had for her was not strictly the innocent feelings one had for their best friends.

Jason's mom had to be wrong.

He had brought Emma to meet his family. He was dating her.

Emma, who wanted to get married, thought Alec.

He was not ready to take the plunge, even though marriage had never scared him. He had seen his mom and dad have a lovely married life, for whatever few years they had together before the accident. And now Steve and Julia seemed to be happily married themselves.

But the thought that he would have to make a decision about whether or not he should propose to Emma, so early in his life, had never occurred to him.

It was not like he was in love with Jade. Love had never been something Alec believed was possible for him. Yes, people fell in love and found the Mr or Miss 'Right' of their life. But he had always thought that he would never be that kind of person.

Alec had a firm belief that when the right time came he would find a girl he really cared for. And maybe he would make the big commitment and get married.

But that commitment was a big decision and he didn't want to take it

"My life's a mess!" He sighed and let his head drop into his open palms.

He was sitting on the front porch of his house while all the others were inside chatting over glasses of wine.

He could hear the voices even from the place where he was sitting.

For some reason he had the sudden urge to go talk to Jade and tell her everything.

But what would he say to her? That he was thinking about her when he should have been thinking about the biggest decision he would ever have to make in his life.

And what if she had been lying about that doctor and they still were dating. Alec didn't want to end up making a fool of himself, when Jade just thought of him as a friend.

And then of course there was the matter of Emma. She didn't want him to meet Jade. She was already thoroughly pissed off at him and Alec didn't want to make it worse.

He didn't know what to do.

Steve excused himself from the living room and went in search of his brother- in- law.

Alec had been missing ever since he had walked into the house with Julia after coming back from Jason's house.

And though he loved his wife and mother- in- law, being the only guy in the room with three women was a role he didn't really like to play.

Especially since one of the said women was the uptight Emma.

He still wondered how the free natured and fun loving Alec had fallen for a girl like her.

He didn't have anything against her but she couldn't be anything like , a girl who would be good for Alec.

He walked onto the porch and saw Alec sitting on it with his head in his hand.

"What are you doing here?" He asked walking up to where Alec was sitting.

Alec picked up his head at the sound of Steve's words.

He found his brother- in- law standing right next to him with his usual cocky smile.

"Nothing." He shrugged and turned back.

He heard Steve take a seat next to him on the edge of the porch.

"Are you thinking of the fight from this morning?" Steve asked with a concerned look.

What harm would it cause if he told Steve everything?, Alec wondered.

He needed to tell someone about everything in his life. Before he went completely crazy from all the stress.

"You want to know what's wrong? So listen... Emma catches me in a suspicious pose with Jade and picks up a fight with me. I cover everything up the best as I can so that she's happy, but the truth is that in that moment the only thing I wanted to do was kiss her. I mean Jade. And then she says that she wants to get married. Now I mean Emma. Emma wants me to propose to her. And I don't have a clue what to do! So I come up with the plan that maybe talking to Jason will make my decision easier. But guess what? He made it worse. Now I don't know what to do!" Alec exhaled loudly once he finished speaking and then looked at Steve with an expectant expression.

"Okay..... That's a lot of problems. What do you want me to say to that?" Steve said atlast.

There was a glint of amusement in his blue eyes as he looked at Alec.

"Give me a solution! Why do you thing I told you all this?" Alec exclaimed.

Steve somehow managed to control the hysteric laughter that was bubbling within him.

How had Alec managed to get himself in such a fix?, he wondered.

He made his face into a grim mask and said, "I have no right to make a decision for you. But I think that you should talk to Jade."

"Oh really? Like that didn't strike me!" Alec said sarcastically, "And what about Emma?"

"Let me first get over the shock. She really told you that she wants to get married?"

"No she told me that she wants me to propose."

On hearing this, Steve could no longer hold his laughter and he burst out.

Alec patiently waited for Steve to compose himself and then glared at him.

Steve sobered up as soon as he saw the disgusted look Alec was giving him, "Look that's your decision to make. And I'm nobody to say anything in it. But first talk to Jade."

Alec exhaled loudly, "But that's the problem. Emma will blow her top if she knows I've gone to meet Jade."

"I've got an idea! I'll tell Julia to convince Emma to go shopping tomorrow. So while they are gone you can go speak to Jade."

"You would do that?" Alec asked, surprised and weirdly touched.

"Of course. Though it will be harder for Julia."

"Thanks!"

"You don't need to thank me Alec." Steve smiled.

He got up to go back into the house when Alec suddenly called out to him.

"Steve?"

"Yeah?" He turned back and looked at Alec again. The troubled look in his face made Steve feel bad himself.

"How did you decide that it was the right time to propose to Julia?"

"You're her brother I can't possibly tell you that without receiving a bad trashing in return."

Alec smirked at that, "I won't do anything. I promise. Tell me."

"Okay." Steve shoved his hands into his pockets, looked his brother- in- law straight in his eyes and said simply, "I tossed a coin."

For a second the words didn't register in Alec's head. He kept looking at Steve waiting for him to start laughing. But Steve just kept looking straight back at him with a smirk on his face.

"You're kidding, right?" He asked at last.

"No. Those were the days when I was working in London. And Julia was still in Chicago. We were trying out the long distance thing."

"So you tossed a coin? It's my sister you're talking about not a stupid game of cricket." Alec said enraged, and forgetting his promise.

At that moment he really felt like fisting his hand and teaching Steve a lesson.

Steve smirked, "Cricket... I never really understood that game." When Alec glared at him, he continued, "Okay... Look.... I was drunk."

"That's no excuse."

"Of course it's not. I didn't even mean it as an excuse. Let me tell the whole story."

He waited for Alec to give his consent. Once Alec nodded his head reluctantly he started speaking.

"I was drunk and confused much like you are now. I decided to toss the coin. Just so I got an easy answer. If it was heads I would propose to Julia the next day and if tails, I would wait for a few months. I had the ring and everything. It was heads and I took a flight the next day to Chicago and proposed to her."

Alec looked up once Steve was done with his story, "Does Julia know about this?"

"Yes. I told her as soon as she said yes."

"And what was her reaction?"

Steve chuckled remembering the events if that day, "That's her story to tell."

"Okay."

Convinced that there was no chance that Alec's protective brother side would wake up at night and come to strangle him. Or do a Jade, as they had started referring to the punch on his nose.

"You coming?" Steve asked from the door.

"Yeah... Give me a second." Then Alec thought for a second, "Actually, do you have a coin?"

Steve laughed at that, "Alec there's one difference between your situation and mine. I was sure that I wanted to marry Julia. I knew that I wanted to spend the rest of my life with her. But you.... Decide whether it's going to be Emma or Jade... Or anyone else."

"Can I toss between Emma and Jade?" Alec asked only half-joking.

"Now you're making me want to punch you."

"Just kidding! Just kidding!" Said Alec holding up his hands in mock surrender.

Steve smiled, the poor guy was thoroughly confused and he didn't know what to do about it.

"I'll be inside. Come in when you're ready." Steve opened the door and was half inside when he turned around and said, "One more thing Alec, if it's not Emma then tell her. She deserves to know."

Saying this Steve walked into the house and went back to the living room where the three ladies were still talking.

"I should know myself before I tell anyone!" Alec whispered and dropped his head again in his palms, just like he had been sitting before Steve came out.

Tomorrow he would talk to Jade and hopefully he would get some clue as to whether Jade had any- any at all- feelings for him. Let everything go smoothly!

Chapter 22

"Hey Jade.... It's me... Uh.. Alec."

Emma was in the kitchen having breakfast while Alec stood in his room and called Jade.

"Alec! Hi!"

Jade sounded groggy and half asleep. Alec could hear the ruffling of the bed covers as Jade sat.

"Hi! Yeah... What are you doing today?" Alec asked, he ran his fingers through his hair and shifted his weight from one foot to the other.

There was a minute before Jade replied, "We are going out in the evening right? I mean Jules called last evening..."

"Yeah... Yeah not in the evening. I mean in the morning, I want to meet you."

"Okay...." Alec heard her yawn, "Come over, but Emma...?"

"She's going out shopping with Julia. I'll be there around 10?"

It had all been planned. Julia had convinced a reluctant Emma, after a lot of arguments.

"Yeah... 10 will be fine."

As Jade was speaking Alec heard someone walk to his room.

Thinking it must be Emma he quickly whispered, "I got to go now. See you at 10."

Just when he kept the phone the door to his room opened and instead of Emma, Steve stood in a white t- shirt and jeans.

"Hey, they are leaving. Come on!" He said.

Alec pulled on his shirt jacket style over the plain t- shirt and followed Steve out of the room.

"One thing, Al. Julia told me to warn you. You better be home when they come back. She'll give you a call when they are nearby."

"Yeah... That's fine." Alec said as they entered the living room.

The three women were dressed and at the door ready to leave.

"Bye Em!" He said, hugging his girl friend who looked terribly reluctant to go.

The expression on her face was more she was being abducted against her wishes rather than going for a fun day of shopping.

"You sure you won't get bored?" She asked, trying to find some excuse to not go.

Julia and Susan were taking her to the nearest mall to shop for some dress to wear to the club that evening.

Alec smiled holding her by her shoulders, "No I won't get bored. I have some mails to answer and then I thought I'll got out with Jason and Steve. You go have fun!"

Emma gave him a painful smile, but a smile none the less, and followed Susan out of the house.

Once Julia and Steve parted from their own embrace, Alec received one last warning glare from his sister.

"I mean it Alec!"

"I know... I know. I'll be home I promise!" He said and lead her out.

The women sat in the car and Julia drove away.

Steve turned to him once they were out of sight, "Ready to talk to Jade?"

"No. Not at all!" Steve laughed while Alec ruffled his hair again in agitation.

After waking up to a call from Alec, which sounded suspiciously like they were planning an illegal meeting, Jade had pulled herself up from bed and had walked straight into the shower.

After a shower and a cup of coffee, she went to get ready.

She dressed carefully in a white summer dress with short sleeves and pulled her brownish black hair into a loose braid.

Since when had she started getting ready so carefully for Alec, she thought shaking her head.

It was 10 by the time she got ready. Alec was late again.

She went into the kitchen and made herself another cup of coffee.

Just when she took the first sip of coffee and sat on the bed, the door bell rang.

Thinking it must be Alec she opened the door.

But instead of Alec's tall and lean frame, she was face to face with her father.

"Hi Jade." Stuart Tucker said.

"Hello." Once she was over her initial shock she took a step back and let him get into the house.

"Can I get you some coffee or tea?"

Her face was grim as she asked him. It was highly unusual for him to come to meet her in the absence of her mother.

This was the first time he had come to her apartment and seeing him amidst the familiar background, made her uncomfortable in a way.

He sat on the sofa, "Tea or coffee? How mature has my Little Blade become! You know you're just like your mother. There's very little of me in you... You must be glad about that." He paused, "Whatever you're having will be fine."

Jade went to the kitchen and poured another cup of coffee.

She took the time to compose herself. The use of her dad's old nickname for her always crumbled her resolve of being mature and formal.

It reminded her of the old days when he was only her dad, who she loved with all her heart. And who loved her back and was always there for her.

She rubbed a palm across her face and walked out of the kitchen.

She handed him the cup and took the seat opposite him, waiting for him to speak.

"I came here to apologise." Stuart said after taking the first sip of his coffee and taking a deep breath.

"Apologise for what?" Jade asked with narrowed eyes.

"For all that I've done over the years, the amount of time I hurt you and Amanda. And though I know sorry is not a word which will make anything better. I just wanted to say I'm sorry!"

"I know."

Stuart looked his daughter into her eyes that were the identical to the eyes of the woman he had fallen in love with. Amanda.

"I meant what I said that day... I really am here to stay this time."

Jade just nodded before asking, "Are you still staying at The Inn?"

"Yes. Though I'm meeting Amanda for lunch and dinner. We have a lot to talk about." He paused, "That brings me to the other reason I'm here today. Your mother and I, we think we all should meet for dinner one day. She told me to invite you for dinner tonight."

There was a hopeful look in Stuart's eyes.

"I have other plans."

"Oh!" His face fell. "That's okay then."

That's when Jade realised that he thought she was lying to avoid going for dinner.

"No really... I was invited by a few of my friends to go out tonight. Will tomorrow be okay?"

For the first time she was agreeing to meet him not for her mom but for herself.

The smile which her sentence brought to his face almost hurt her eyes, it was so dazzling.

"Tomorrow will be great." He said placing his empty cup on the table. "I'll get going."

He got up and Jade followed him to the door of her apartment.

"Uh... Wait." Jade said as he started going away with a nod of his head.

He turned around with a small smile on his face and looked at her expectantly.

Stuart knew that this was as difficult for Jade as it was for him. Maybe more.

"I want to forgive you. I don't know why but I actually believe you." Jade took a deep breath, "But even if I forgive you... When I do... It's going to take me time to forget."

"I know... I understand and I'll wait."

Stuart looked at his daughter who had grown up so fast and walked away suppressing his urge to go and hug her.

But he knew that hugging her would make the situation worse than making it better.

He was making progress. And he would be happy with whatever little he got.

Jade was still sitting where she had plopped down after her dad had left, when the door bell rang again.

This time when she opened it, it was Alec standing on the doorstep.

"Hi!" He said awkwardly after seeing the expression on her face.

It was not exactly tired, it was sad and the smile which she gave him was stressed.

"Come in."

He went in and sat on the sofa, "I saw Stuart leaving from here just now. What was he doing here?"

Alec had been there to comfort Jade all those years when her dad would come back before leaving them with broken hearts again.

He had seen everything happen and it always made him so angry.

But he had been to young to do anything about it. Now he was much older and if that man was still hurting Jade and Amanda he was going to make him regret it.

"He came here to meet me." Jade said simply, sitting opposite him.

"Meet you?"

Was that the reason behind the sad look on Jade's face?

"What is he doing here in town?" Alec's voice was rising.

"Look it's a long story. It's okay." Jade said trying to calm him down.

"How is it okay?"

The stress of the last few days caught up with her, "Alec you've not been here for many years. You have no clue what's happening in my life. You were not there when so many important things happened in my life."

Alec looked at her, surprised at her sudden outburst, "Why are we going back to that? I thought we sorted it all out."

"It's not so easy, Alec" she ran her fingers through her hair, ruffling her braid. "How am I supposed to forget all these years? And act like they never happened. I'm supposed to forget everything and act like everything's hunky dory. Guess what? They're not! Things suck in my life right now and you coming back are not making them any better."

She no longer knew whether she was talking about Alec or her dad. And she didn't care. She needed to rant out all her anger and frustration.

"Do you have any clue how many times I've missed you in these years? How many times I wanted to meet you, talk to you.... Just see you for Gods sake!"

She buried her face in her hands and inhaled.

There was no use in yelling at Alec.

She composed herself and looked up. Alec was sitting, stunned on the sofa with an almost pained expression on his face.

"I'm sorry... I just... I'm sorry!" Jade said.

They sat in silence for some time. Both lost in their own thoughts.

Finally Alec got up and went to her, he bent down and held her hands, "It's okay. I'll go get some water for you and then we'll talk. Okay?"

Jade nodded. She didn't have the energy to say anything else.

As she waited for Alec to come back with a glass of water she wondered how much of what she said was meant for Alec and how much for her dad.

Chapter 23

"So what brings you here?" Jade asked Alec.

They were sitting together on the little terrace attached to her apartment.

She was a little more composed.

She could see the bruise on his nose which had now become a blue colour.

"I wanted to meet you." Alec stalled.

He didn't know how to start the topic. He didn't even know what he wanted to say to her.

"We are meeting in the evening anyways."

"About that what time exactly are we meeting?" Alec knew his question was stupid and had no relevance to what he actually wanted to talk about but he couldn't help it.

Jade gave him a quizzical look, "I'm not sure... 7:30 I guess. Matt's picking me up at 7." She shrugged.

Alec's ears pricked at Matt's name, "Matt?"

"Yeah... I invited him as my date. I didn't want to come alone."

"But I thought you'll broke up?" A million thoughts were going around in his head while Jade sat there nonchalantly.

"We did break up,but that doesn't mean we're not friends. He's a close friend of mine and he agreed to come."

Alec thought that he saw a dreamy look in her eyes.

"Why did you'll break up?" He asked.

Jade snapped out of her thoughts, "He wanted different things from life and I wanted different things. But we had a great relationship. You know he's such a great guy. We were really happy when we were together...."

Before Jade could complete whatever she was saying Alec blurted out, "Emma wants to get married!"

"What?" She just stared at him with a bewildered look on her face.

"After you left yesterday she told me to ask her to get married."

Alec didn't even know why he was telling Jade all this. He was supposed to break the news to her more calmly and maybe after some time.

"And what did you say?" Jade said at once.

"I said I needed time to think."

"You had time. Almost one whole day. What did you think?"

She could feel her heart sink. This was not how this was supposed to go. She had been trying to make him a little jealous by talking about her relationship with Matt.

The plan had backfired horrifically.

"I don't know, Jade." He rubbed his face, "I really don't know!"

"Do you want to get married to Emma, or no? How difficult is this question?"

"It's a big decision. I don't want to end up getting a divorce. What do you think I should do?"

Jade looked up at Alec. Her best friend looked like he was on the verge of going mad.

"You know what I think of marriage. And yeah... Marriage is the reason for 100% of divorces."

Was this the time to make jokes?, thought Alec.

"That's bullshit, Jade!" He said.

"No it's not. If you don't get married you won't get divorced as simple as that!" Jade shrugged nonchalantly, though she could feel the tears pricking her eyes.

"Why are you so against marriage?"

"I'm not against marriage! I just think it's not for every one." She got up and walked to the railing of the terrace.

"Yeah right! You hate the word marriage... And I guess I know why."

She turned around and looked Alec in his eyes with a daring look.

"And may I know what's the reason?" She snapped.

"What happened with your parents does not happen to everyone." Alec said as an explanation.

"I can't believe you just said that!" Jade gasped.

This had nothing to do with her parents and everything to do with her feeling for Alec.

"It's true."

"No it's not! And I want you to leave right now!" She yelled.

"Jade..."

"I don't care what you think of me. You're not some psychologist. You can't say stuff like that out of nowhere and get away with it."

"I didn't mean it that way. It came out the wrong way. I'm stressed." Alec stood up next to her.

"And you think I'm not. Go get married! Go live happily. I don't want to know. Just get out of my house right now!" Her voice had gone up to dangerous level.

"Let me explain."

"Now! Get out of my house!" She went into the house and pulled the door wide open for him to leave. "I've had enough of your explanations. Go get married to the woman who you're so scared of that you have to lie to, to meet your friends."

She could feel the anger and tears bubble up and wanted Alec to be far away from her when she burst.

"Listen to me..."

Jade interrupted Alec, "No you listen to me.... I don't care whether you marry that.... That arrogant, stupid and rude girl. I don't care if you spoil your whole life. I don't care." Her voice broke, "I just need you to leave right now."

Alec's shoulders slumped as he walked out of the apartment. He turned around to say something to Jade, but she had already slammed the door shut.

Inside Jade stood with her back pressed against the door which she had just shut.

Atlast she let the tears, she had been controlling, go.

After years she let herself really cry.

It was like her heart was breaking into a million pieces. And though she had always known that Alec could never be hers, she had hoped for it.

And now...

She fell to pieces and curled up on the floor where she had been standing.

The mobile in his pocket rang as he took the first sip of the drink the bar tender had placed in front of him.

Alec took it out of his pocket and saw that the call was from Julia.

"Hey Al, we're 15 minutes away from home. I hope you're back." His sisters voice came on as soon as he picked up the call.

"No I'm not."

Alec realised he was slurring a little. He had come directly to the bar after being kicked out of Jade's house. He was already on his third whiskey .

"What!? Go home right now, Alec!" Julia screamed.

"Give your phone to Emma." Alec said ignoring Julia's yells.

"Why do you want to talk to Emma? She's gone to buy Mom a bottle of water. Alec are you drunk?" To say Julia sounded surprised would have been an underestimation.

"I need to talk to Emma. Just give her the phone."

"I don't know what you're up to. I really...." Alec heard the car door slam close. There was a pause for sometime.

"Alec?" Alec heard Emma say.

"Hi Emma! You had fun?" Alec asked gulping the remnants of his third whiskey before signalling for another.

"Yes. Is something wrong?" She sounded cautious.

Alec took a sip from his new whiskey before replying, "No. Nothing's wrong. But I won't be home when you'll come back. I have a little shopping to do."

"Shopping?"

"Yeah.... I thought about what you said yesterday. And...."

He was interrupted by Emma who sounded very excited, "Oh really? Sure! Take your time!"

"Thanks! I'll talk to you later, okay?"

Emma kept the phone immediately.

Alec knew his plan had worked. She would not be upset if he was not at home.

But the thing was he had not been lying. As soon as Emma kept the phone he called up Jason.

If he was really going ring shopping he needed all the support he could get.

Jason and Steve were confused when Alec told them to meet him at the bar in Main Street but they agreed.

Alec had decided to go buy the ring and propose to Emma as he was leaving Jade's house.

It was pretty clear that she harboured no feelings for him. She was desperately in love with that doctor!

And by her last words it was pretty clear she didn't care what he did with his life, so he might as well make Emma happy.

He was buying a ring. He was going to propose to Emma.

But first he needed liquid courage. He gulped his whole whiskey in one shot.

She was going to be cheerful. She was going to smile and have fun.

Jade looked into her eyes in the mirror and swore to herself. She was going to smile and laugh the whole evening, even if it killed her to see Alec. That too, with Emma next to him.

She was not going to let him see that what happened in the morning had affected her in any way at all.

She was going to enjoy herself.

She picked up the glass of red wine she had placed next to her table and took a big sip.

She eyed herself in the mirror. She had taken time in getting ready very carefully.

She was wearing a dark red colour dress, which left her hand bare and fell till her knees. The dress was tight at the waist so it looked slim and then flowed out.

Her hair sat at the nape of her neck in small knot and she had forced her feet into sky high silver heels.

Her make up was perfect and she was going to try her best to make the evening just as perfect.

If the smile on her face faltered a little it would go unnoticed.

She gulped the rest of the wine.

The door bell rang.

Matt stood outside the door to Jade's house at sharp 7 just like he had told her.

He was dressed in a black button down shirt and black pants.

The door was pulled open and Jade stood with a huge smile on her face.

"Hi Matt! Come in!"

Matt followed Jade inside, "Hey Jade! You look beautiful."

And she really did. The red dress made her skin glow.

Since her hair was pulled back her neck was left bare. She looked beautiful and charming.

"You don't look bad either. Let's have a glass of wine before leaving."

Jade went into the kitchen. Before Matt could protest she poured the wine from the bottle into a glass and held it out to him.

"Jade, I'll be driving. So I don't think I should be drinking." He said.

"Oh! Since I've already poured it!" She held the glass to her own lips and gulped the whole wine in one sip, while Matt stared at her with wide eyes.

After dating Jade for a long time, Matt knew that Jade was a light weight.

She acted like she could handle her drink but always ended up getting drunk.

"Slowly!" He said in reflex.

Jade just laughed as she kept the glass on the table.

"Chill out, Matt! It's party time!"

She was smiling and laughing even all the while as they left and drove to the club where they all had agreed to meet.

She became a little quiet as they were about to reach the club but very cleverly covered it up by starting a new conversation the next minute.

It was almost like she was putting up an act. But for who.....

Matt kept wondering why she had to put up an act for anyone they were meeting today.

He was not going to let such thoughts come into his head. Today was the day he was going to convince her that they were good together.

And he would accomplish his task no matter what!

Chapter 24

Jade entered the noisy and dimly lit club with her hips swaying to the music and her hair flowing behind her.

All around, people were grinding against each other, drinks were being passed around.

Matt could hear pieces of conversations that other people were having while following Jade to where she had spotted Nicole and Jason.

"Hey guys!" Jade squealed as soon as she was in their ear shot.

She hugged both of them and stood back with a grin still plastered to her face.

"You'll know Matt. Matt you know Nicole and Jason." She said.

Matt smiled at the couple sitting on the sofa.

Millbrooke was a small town so it was not very difficult to be faintly acquainted with most of the people living there.

When Matt had been dating Jade they had often gone on dinners together. Jason was among the first friends he had made after just shifting to town.

"Hey Matt!" Nicole said from her place on the sofa while Jason got up to give him a half hug.

Before the conversation could be continued any further Matt heard Jade speak, "They're here!"

Her smile had become a little more forced.

Matt turned around to see who had come.

Pushing through the grinding, sweating bodies of the people on the dance floor were four people who Matt had never meet before.

But he recognised two people, from all the photos in Jade's apartment.

It was Julia and Alec her friends.

But why did their arrival change Jade's mood for the worse instead of the other way round?

Emma followed Julia and Steve into the lights and loud music of the club. Alec had his hand on her waist.

She couldn't be more out of place. And there was no way that she could feel more happy.

The day had been great. She had picked up a great dress for herself with help from Julia and Susan. And the aquamarine colour looked stunning on her.

She had gelled quite well with her soon to be in- laws if she said so herself.

And to make everything even better, Alec had said that he was going to go ring shopping.

She felt like breaking out into a victory dance.

Everything was falling into place. Just like her mother had told her it would.

They found Jade standing near a table which was a little away from the dance floor.

"Hello!" Julia exclaimed as they reached the table. She hugged both the women and the taller man before holding her hand out to the other guy.

"Hi, I'm Julia. Well Juliana Ashby. You must be Matthew Damon." Julia said.

"Yes. But please call me Matt."

The guy was handsome and spoke in a friendly way. Emma immediately took a liking to him.

Jade did all the introductions and all of them sat down. Matt had been introduced as her date for tonight, much to Emma's surprise.

"Emma you look lovely today." Jade said with a genuine smile once all of them had settled down.

Emma wanted to narrow her eyes. Why was she being so sweet? But instead she smiled, "Thanks! And so are you."

"Oh! Thank you!" Jade smiled back.

Jason took everyone's drink orders and headed towards the bar. Julia and Matt declined since they were driving while Jade ordered a martini for herself.

After the orders were placed, Jason and Steve excused themselves with their respective wives to join the other couples on the dance floor.

Emma was laughing at something Matt said when Jade got up and tapped her on her shoulder.

"Can I talk to you for a second?" She whispered into Emma's ears.

Emma was confused but still nodded.

They walked out of the club away from all of the noise leaving Alec to wonder what was going on, with only Matt for company.

Jade had been avoiding looking straight at him ever since they had come. But she didn't look disturbed or unhappy in any way.

He smiled awkwardly at Matt once but not a word was exchanged.

Once they reached outside, the cool air a stark contrast as compared to the heat inside the club, Jade spoke up, "Look Emma I know we got off on the wrong foot. And I just wanted to say sorry incase I was rude that day."

"I should say sorry too." Emma said.

Emma had been taught from a very young age that it was important to be polite and sweet to everyone.

Her mother would have been horrified if she had been there to witness the way she had behaved with Jade both the days they had met.

Paula Burns had one rule, Be good with your friends but be better with your enemies.

"And if there was any misunderstanding on your part because of yesterday let me clarify, there's nothing going on between me and Alec. I promise."

Atleast nothing from his side, thought Jade.

It hurt her to lie but Jade still faced Emma with a bright smile on her face.

"Oh that's okay! Alec explained it to me." Emma said a little gleeful at the thought of the ring Alec had bought for her.

"I'm glad we could sort it out."

They started heading back in when Emma stopped and turned to Jade, "Are you dating Matt?" She asked.

"Uh... Not really. We were in a relationship but we broke up some days back. We still are really close friends."

"Just so you know, I think he's a great guy." Emma said, "And I got that impression pretty loud and clear even in the few minutes I spent in his company."

"I know." Jade's smile was genuine this time.

By the look on her face, it was clear to Emma that there was something more than friendship going on between Matt and Jade.

But she didn't comment on it.

This meant that there was really nothing between her and Alec. He had not been lying.

No that she thought about it she could be friends with Jade. She was not so bad.

They walked back into the club together.

And Emma was a happier than before, if that was possible.

Jade was whisked away by Steve for a dance as soon as she came back into the club.

One dance lead to another and soon she was dancing with Jason.

Alec and Matt who had got fed up with the awkwardness were out of their seats themselves and on the dance floor.

Before long Jade was completely winded from all the dancing and moving.

A slow song came on just then. And in the midst of the confusion, Jade found herself in Alec's arms both of them swaying to the music.

"Hi!" He said.

"Hey!"

They drifted along with the music.

"I'm sorry about this afternoon." Alec said atlast.

"I'm sorry too." Jade replied. "I shouldn't have thrown you out like that."

"And I shouldn't have said those things. I didn't mean them."

They smiled at each other and for a second Jade almost felt like everything was back to normal.

She smiled and let her head fall into his shoulder.

"You look stunning." Alec said.

Jade's smile became bigger, "You don't look bad either. You clean up well Carter."

Jade couldn't see Alec's face but she could feel him smile.

Just as she was really drifting away with the music her mind went back to the conversation from that morning.

She straightened up a little and asked a surprised Alec, "What about Emma? Did you decide anything?"

Alec had been dreading this question ever since he walked into to the club to see Jade looking absolutely beautiful. Looking at her sit over there had brought up all his feelings for her again.

Even while dancing for a second it had almost been like they were a normal couple in love on a date. No baggage. No complication.

And if there had been no feelings in Jade's eyes for him when she had been smiling at him, he was surely hallucinating.

But one answer was going to spoil the whole thing.

"About that..." He started saying.

Jade had grown up with Alec. She knew when he was stalling and when he was lying.

And that moment his expression said pretty loud and clear that he was preparing himself to lie to her.

"Don't lie to me Alec. Just say it."

They had almost stopped moving.

"I.... Uh... I bought a ring." He said quickly.

Jade stopped moving completely. Her eyes became emotionless as he looked at him.

If there had been a flash of hurt on her face she covered it up too quickly, "I guess congratulations are in order."

"I've not yet proposed."

"You bought the ring that means you want to propose."

"Jade... I don't know." Alec said.

"I hope you'll have a happy life."

The song was over. Jade moved away from him and with one forced smile she walked back to the table leaving Alec alone on the dance floor.

She went to the bar and ordered herself tequila shots.

The two martinis since she had arrived had not done anything to numb her feelings.

He had bought the ring.

But he had not proposed.

He had bought the ring.

She kept chanting this in her head till the bartender placed the tray of small shot glasses filled with clear liquid.

She picked up the first one and gulped it down.

And waited for the alcohol to kick in.

He had bought the ring.

But he has not proposed as yet.

Chapter 25

"**I**s this seat taken?" Matt asked her standing next to her.

"Of course not!" Jade said cheerfully with a big smile on her face, before bursting into a fit of giggles.

Her pupils were dilated and Matt could smell the sweet smell of tequila coming from her.

Danger!

He knew from experience that Jade had a habit of becoming a giggly, cheerful person only when she was extremely drunk.

He jumped on to the bar stool and looked at her.

"Are you okay?" He asked.

"Yes. I'm perfectly fine."

There was the too cheerful smile.

The bartender placed another tray of tequila shots in front of her.

"Tequila?"

"Yes!" Jade said picking up the first one, "Cheers to life. Which might I say sucks!"

She gulped the first one down in a hurry.

"I love tequila. Right now I would love to hug the person who invented it!" She said after banging the glass down.

She could feel the fiery trail of the liquid down her throat.

"I think he must be dead Jade." Matt said.

"Then I'll take him out of his grave and kiss him."

"That's hygienic!" Matt shrugged.

He was rewarded with loud laughter from Jade, followed by another shot.

After the two glasses of wine and the drinks she had had since coming to the club it was pretty clear that Jade was not far from being completely drunk.

When she was on her third shot, Matt spoke up, "I think you should slow down."

She was already on her 8th shot.

"I guess I'll take a break." She said much to Matt's relief.

Jade was already feeling very woozy. But that was what she needed. To feel numb. To not feel the pain.

She turned around in her seat so that she had a clear vision of the dance floor.

There in the middle of all the people Alec was dancing with Emma, who was almost clinging onto him for life.

"You love him don't you?" Matt asked suddenly.

"What?"

"You love Alec."

Matt had seen the exchange between them even if he couldn't hear the words.

It was clear from the way she looked at Alec when he wasn't looking.

And she was hurting. Matt could see that too.

"Where did you get that idea?" Jade asked, her eyes were still on Emma and Alec dancing.

"I see the way you look at him."

The way I look at you when you're not looking, thought Matt.

"The expression on your face when you're with him. It's pretty clear. He must be blind to not see it."

Jade turned to him atlast. He could see the tears in her eyes.

"He's going to ask her to get married. He has a ring."

Jade looked defeated. Like all the life from her body had been sucked out.

Matt knew how she felt. He was feeling the same way.

"Why don't you tell him?"

"Because he thinks we're just friends. That's what he wants to be."

She controlled the tears that were fighting to roll down her cheek.

She had cried enough that morning.

By the time she had stopped crying her eyes had been red her face had been completely blotchy with tear tracks.

She tried to stand up, thinking of going out in the cool air to compose herself, but as soon as she stood she felt herself stumble.

Matt caught her just in time.

The alcohol was catching up. She was drunk. Really, terribly drunk.

"I think I should take you home. You're really drunk Jade." Matt said throwing his hand around her shoulder and giving her support.

"I think I am." Jade slurred, "I feel sick."

Of course she did. She had been knocking down her drinks like she had a train to catch.

And then all the emotional wreckage Alec was causing.

"Let's go home."

He half carried her half supported her till the car after telling Nicole that he was taking her home.

Nicole had flashed him a worried look but she knew better than to comment.

She knew what Jade had been doing.

Drinking herself to oblivion.

And she also knew that Matt cared for her enough and was capable enough to see her home safely.

Nicole helped Matt put Jade into the car and let them leave without a word.

"Drive safe!" She said to Matt as he got into the drivers seat.

She walked back into the noisy club and sat at the table.

She would give Jade a good talking to when she next met her that much was for sure.

Nicole saw Alec and Emma still dancing.

Alec was trying to steal glances around the bar, over Emma's head.

Looking for Jade?

Nicole felt horrible for what her best friend was going through, but she was so helpless.

She couldn't do anything about it.

"I've loved him since high school. I never stopped loving him."

Matt turned towards the passenger seat, surprised to hear Jade speak.

She had been sitting quietly for the past 5 minutes. So quietly that he had almost thought she had fallen asleep.

Matt wanted to ask her why she hadn't told him then. But he knew she would tell him stuff only when she wanted to.

No amount of questions would get her to talk if she didn't want to.

"I was so stupid. I waited... Looking for the right time to tell him. But I was too late. He left. And now that he's back it's even more impossible."

He voice was so soft that it was almost inaudible.

Matt had to strain his ears to hear what she was saying.

"He's getting married to Emma." She turned to face Matt. There were tears on her face, "It's over."

"Jade...." He started saying something but was interrupted.

"No... Don't say anything." Jade whispered.

The rest of the drive went by in silence till the reached her apartment building.

Matt got out of the car and went to her side to help her out.

After some struggles and getting rid of her heels she was on her feet.

"Matt, it hurts so bad... It really does."

It hurt Matt too. To see Jade in this state. Drunk. Crying.

Being a doctor he had a tendency of always trying to reduce the pain of anyone he met.

And it made him feel so useless that he could not help Jade in any way.

She was vulnerable and hurting.

And he couldn't do anything.

They took one step towards the door of the building.

Maybe it was the quick movement. Or finally all the events of the evening caught up with Jade.

But before Matt could help it, she was violently sick all over the pavement and over his shirt.

"Oh shit! Oh God! I'm so sorry!" Jade started saying.

"Jade it's okay."

"No... No... I'm so sorry. I'm such a fool."

She didn't know what to do. She had never been so embarrassed in her life.

No words from Matt stopped her. She kept apologising and trying to wipe his shirt till finally he held her firmly by her shoulders.

"Jade!"

She stopped muttering and looked at him.

"It's fine. There's no problem."

"You wash the shirt at my place and then go home." Jade said.

"I'll go home and...."

"No... Please."

Matt could see that tears were threatening to spill from her eyes again.

"Okay... Okay. Let's go up."

They walked up to her apartment where Matt expertly opened the door.

"Give me your shirt. I'll put it in the washing machine."

Jade said once they were inside.

"I'll do it." Matt said leading her into the bedroom, "You get into the bed."

"Take off your shirt and put it into the washing machine. I'm not sleeping till you don't!" Jade said stubbornly as he put her under the covers and kept her heels on the floor.

Matt chuckled. This was more like the Jade he knew.

Stubborn.

She was drunk but she knew exactly what she wanted.

"Here you go mom!" He opened the buttons of his shirt and walked into the washroom to put it in the machine.

He came out once he had started it, to find Jade fast asleep in her bed.

He walked closer to her and bent down.

She looked so peaceful.

Her eyes were shut and her eyelashes were making shadows on her cheeks.

Her hair was fanned out on the pillow with one single strand on her face.

Matt took the strand of hair, twirled it around his finger and placed it behind her ear.

"Good night, Jade." He whispered. "Where's Jade and Matt?" Alec asked Nicole as soon as the song was over and he was back at the table with Emma.

"Jade was not feeling very well. So Matt offered to take her home." Nicole said in between sips of her drink.

Ofcourse she was not feeling well, after the amount she had had to drink it would have come as a surprise if she was not drunk and sick, thought Alec.

He had seen her at the bar gulping down tequila shots like her life depended on it, while dancing with Emma.

Emma sat down panting, from all the dancing, "I hope she's okay."

There had been an obvious change in Emma's behaviour toward Jade ever since they had their little talk and Alec was dying to know what the reason behind it.

"We should also leave shouldn't we?" Julia asked.

She was red in the cheeks from all the dancing and laughing. Her eyes were glinting.

Even though she had not had a single drop of alcohol to drink she looked high on much more than life.

"Yes I think we should. My wife here's a little too excited." Steve said throwing a hand over her.

Nicole placed the empty glass on the table and looked at her watch, "Oh it's late! Jase we should go home too."

All of them agreed that it was time to go home. Each tired and a little tipsy.

But the only thing going on Alec's mind was concern for Jade.

"Alec why are you standing there?" Emma asked when she was inside the car while Alec was still standing and wondering what to do.

He hoped she wouldn't get angry at him for what he was about to say, "Em I was thinking I'll go check out if Jade's okay. I'm kind of worried about her."

"Oh!" Her eyebrows furrowed for a second, "But Matt did drop her home right? And he's a doctor. He would know if anything was really wrong with her."

"I know but.... I want to make sure for myself."

He waited for her to refuse to let him go and get angry but instead Emma very calmly replied, "Okay. Come in, Julia can drop you at her apartment and then you can come back on your own."

Alec was surprised.

What had Jade told Emma?

He nodded his head, worried that any questions might lead to Emma changing her mind and sat in the car.

Julia who had been sitting in the car and listening to their conversation all the while started the car immediately and drove to Jade's apartment building.

She stopped the car in front of it and he got down.

"Don't get too late!" Julia said when he was out.

He turned towards the back seat where he saw that Emma was already fast asleep.

Steve gave him a grin and they left.

He went up to her apartment and rang the bell.

No one answered.

He rang the bell again.

There was no answer.

Worried now, he knocked on the door.

Immediately the door was pulled open.

But it was not Jade standing behind it as he had expected it to be.

It was Matt. A shirtless, bare chested Matt.

"I'm so sorry. I was in the washroom so I couldn't open the door."

Alec just nodded at him, too stunned to say anything.

What was he still doing at Jade's house? And where was his shirt?

But Alec didn't ask the questions that were going around in his head, "Where's Jade?" He asked instead.

"Oh she's asleep. She just fell asleep." Matt said pulling up his pants a little while saying it. "Is there something I should tell her?"

"No.... No.... I just wanted to know if she's okay. I mean you'll left in such a hurry."

"Oh yeah... Sorry about that. She got a little too drunk. So I thought that bed would be the best thing for her."

We'll is that so? Bed would be the best thing for her.

"Anyways I'll tell her you were here." Matt shrugged.

Alec fisted his hands stopping himself from doing something he might regret, "No that's not really necessary. I'll tell her myself when I meet her."

"Okay. G'night then!"

So he was planning to spend the night there. This was how it was. Their breakup was a lie all along.

Alec controlled his anger, "Yeah Good night."

He turned around and ran out of the building. He started running blindly.

Whatever little hint of emotions Jade had shown while dancing had surely been acting on her part.

She was still very much dating Matt.

Bed will be the best thing for her!

He kept running in the direction of his house, though his feet and calves were burning and he could barely take a breath.

The distance from Jade's apartment to his house was not much but it still took some time to cover it.

But Alec found himself at his gate within minutes. He was panting and coughing from the exertion, but he didn't stop.

He pushed open the door which had been kept unlocked for him and ran up the stairs to Emma's room.

He knocked on the door three times loudly. When no one answered, he banged on it a couple more times.

"Emma, open the door." He yelled between gasps and pants.

Emma opened a door to see a completely winded Alec standing there.

"Alec? What wrong with you? You're sweating and…. You need to sit." She said.

Alec saw her standing over there in a dressing robe which had been quickly thrown on and her hair falling around her face.

He didn't care if he was making a mistake or no. He was going to do this.

He needed to do this.

He held his knees and took deep breathes for a minute.

"Alec... Are you okay?" This time it was Julia.

The bangs and the yells had woken up Steve and Julia who were staying in the room next to Emma's.

Alec stood straight, he was breathing a little normal now. He looked straight at Emma and said, "Will you marry me?"

No preamble. No explanation.

"Alec... Are you...?" Steve started saying from behind.

Alec didn't listen to him. He thrust his hand in his pocket and pulled out the box.

He held it out to Emma and asked again, "Emma will you marry me?"

Emma cast one look at the diamond ring took a deep breath and yelled, "Yes! Yes I will!"

She threw herself at him.

Steve who was standing next to his wife looked at the scene stunned.

What about all the doubts? What about Jade?

While Julia went up to her brother and soon to be sister- in- law and have them hugs.

He shook his head, as long as Alec was happy with his decision who was he to say anything.

"Well... Congratulations!" He too joined his wife.

Hugs were passed around. Julia and Emma squealed over the ring. Steve patted him on his back. Emma kissed him.

But all the while Alec just stood in the midst of everything wondering what he was doing.

And thinking what would be Jade's reaction to his decision.

Why should he care? She was happy with Matt! She didn't need him.

So he was going to prove it to her that he didn't need her either.

She could be with Matt. And live her own life.

Bed will be the best thing.

He excused himself from the excited group on the pretext that he needed to sleep and went to his room.

He was asleep before his head hit the pillow.

Bed will be the best thing for her.

Chapter 26

B LAKE

This time when Jade woke up with a horrible headache and blood shot eyes, there was no comforting smell of coffee wafting from the kitchen.

She was still wearing the dress from last night, which was completely ruined. All stained and crinkled.

Her heels were lying at the foot of her bed.

As the events of last night came flooding into her head, she just got a strong urge to bury herself under the bed covers again. And not wake up for the next 10 years.

But she still had to face the day, she put her feet on the cold floor and somehow dragged herself out.

Just as she was about to leave the room, dreaming about the coffee she would make, she spotted a piece of paper on her night table.

She picked it up.

Jade had to blink her eyes twice to remove the blurriness from it before she could read the words.

Jade, You fell asleep before I could come out of the washroom and I didn't want to wake you upJust so you know I did wash the shirt before leaving, even though I have a fully working washing machine back home.Anyways I hope the hangover (I'm sure you have one) is not very bad. Take two aspirins if it is. I'm a doctor can't resist it.I had a great time last night. Thanks for taking me with you.PS:-Alec had come. But you were already asleep. He didn't leave a message though, he said he'll tell you when you'll meet.

The smile that had been on her face while reading the note from Matt disappeared when she read the postscript.

Why had Alec come home? What did he have to say to her?

He had got the ring. He was going to marry Emma.

But a small voice in Jade's head kept repeating the words,But he has not proposed as yet.He has not told her about the ring.

She shook her head. If she kept thinking about Alec and Emma she would end up spending the whole day sitting on her bed.

He had got the ring. But she had only one chance now, and she could only hope and pray that he didn't propose to her.

"Hi mom!"Jade said into the speaker of the phone while washing the utensils in the sink.

The mobile was wedged in between her ear and shoulder.

She had decided to do all the house work instead of sitting and thinking about Alec.

She had showered out the remnants of her hangover and then got down to work.

Just as she had started making some progress with the mobile had started ringing.

"Hello Jade! Good morning. How was last night? Was it good?"

Her dad coming back had had a good effect on her mom. She sounded cheerful and happy.

Peaceful in a way. Like her life was perfect for the first time.

"I can't say whether it was good or bad... All I can say is that it was quite eventful." Jade replied to her mom's question.

"Why does that sound like you had a terrible time?" Amanda asked.

Jade laughed and washed the soap of her hand, "No mom. It's okay. You tell me, what have you been up to?"

"Nothing much. I've been meeting up with Stuart everyday. Talking to him. Jade you know something....?"

Amanda's words intrigued her she propped her hip on the kitchen table and asked, "What?"

"I think I found my old Stuart."

"I'm glad mom... I'm happy for you."

And she really was. The way things were going she had a feeling that maybe she too would be able to forgive her dad.

"You're coming today evening for dinner right?"

"Yes I am."

She looked around the room. She had washed all the dishes, dusted the whole apartment, vacuumed and sorted out her cupboard.

She didn't have any other thing to do.

She had to do something to stop herself from stressing over Alec. And God knew she was not in the state of mind to write.

"Mom you know what? I'll get the dessert for tonight."

Jade very rarely cooked but when she did her dessert were to die for.

"There's no need..." Amanda started to say.

"Please mom." Jade whined, "Imagine my chocolate and coffee mousse! Imagine..."

"Okay okay... My mouth is watering. And your dad will love it."

Jade laughed.

The rest of the conversation went quickly and before long Jade kept the mobile down.

She would have to go to the store to get all the ingredients for her famous chocolate coffee mousse!

Alec loved her mousse. It had been a habit for her to always make it for him on his birthday without fail ever since she had learnt the recipe in middle school.

She shook her head. She was not going to think about Alec.

She went to get ready.

Jade put on a pair of khaki shorts and a light blue shirt.

While she was putting her hair into a braid the cell phone she had placed on her bed started ringing.

She picked it up and was surprised to see the name on the caller id.

"Hi Blake!"

"Don't you 'Hi Blake' me." Said Blake Hastings who was Jade's editor and also one of her best friends. "You were supposed to call me yesterday to give me the update on the new novel. I've been evading calls from the publishing house since yesterday."

Blake Hastings, was an otherwise care free and free spirited person, but she took her job as Jade's editor very seriously.

She made it a point to work hard at everything related to her job.

And her hard work and determination was one of the major contributing factors to Jade's quick climb up the ladder of fame.

"Blake you need to breathe." Jade said once she was done with her yelling.

She heard the other girl laugh slightly on the other line, but she quickly covered it, "Why didn't you call me yesterday?"

"I've been busy, Blake. Really!" Jade said guiltily. "I'm so sorry."

Ever since Alec had come back to town she was neglecting her writing, she had been ignoring calls from Blake and missing her appointments.

He was affecting her professional life as well as her personal life.

Blake had grown up with her father, in Chicago, after the death of her mother.

She knew what sadness and defeat sounded like. And that was exactly what she heard in Jade's voice.

"Is something up?" She asked.

Jade say down on the bed, "I've not written anything much in the past 5 days. With all that is going on in my life I'm not really in the mood to write ideal love stories for my heroine."

"Boy trouble?"

"Oh you could say that!"

Jade filled Blake in on all that was going on in her life.

As a rule, new and fresh authors were always appointed to experienced editors, who were capable enough to advice them about what was good and what was bad.

But unlike others Jade had got Blake as her editor. Fresh out of college both of them had barely any clue of how the industry worked.

Jade just knew that she wanted to do what she loved. Write. And Blake wanted to follow in her fathers footsteps and become a renowned editor like him.

Their friendship had bloomed over late, sleepless nights, scratching their heads over the stories and promotions and over a mutual love of coffee and chocolate.

Once Jade was done updating her editor on all the events of her life she sat back and waited for the reaction.

"Okay!" Blake breathed, "That's a lot to take in. Let me just say you're mad to be in love with him. Alec's a fool. A complete idiot. Why are you in love with him?"

"I've asked myself that question a 100 times already." Jade let out a breathy laugh, "I don't know."

"You know what? I'll call the publishing house and stall them. You sort out everything in your life first. There's no need to add the tension of writing into all this."

Blames words brought tears of gratitude to Jade's eyes.

The girl who never cried was now crying over stupid things. She sniffed and controlled the tears.

"You're the best Blake!" She said.

"Say that during my funeral while giving my eulogy. Martins is going to kill me. But I'll do it for you."

They laughed together.

Martins was the owner of the publishing house and he was known for two things, his short temper and ginger hair.

"I'm sure you'll survive."

"Jade, I hope you don't get more hurt." Blake said on a more serious tone once they had finished their usual anger filled rant on Martins.

"I think I've had my share of hurt. I guess it could only get better now." Jade said trying to cheerful.

How much more wrong could she be?

For a Saturday afternoon the supermarket was surprisingly emp-ty. There were few people, idly walking through the aisles. Even the baggers standing at the billing counters seemed bored as they played video games on their cell phones and gossiped in whispers.

But the lack of crowd was a good thing for Jade as she walked past the shelves and picked up the stuff she would need to make dessert.

She didn't want to meet people. She didn't want to talk to anyone.

Her ear phones were stuffed into her ears and were belting out rock music as she dropped the packet of unsalted butter into her trolley.

One of the fondest memories Jade had of her grandmother, was that of Nana teaching her to make the mousse.

A recipe which had been passed on for generation in Amanda's family.

She had prepared it so many times over the years, Alec's birthdays, Amanda's birthdays and other special occasions, that she knew the recipe by heart.

She no longer needed a piece of paper to tell her how much dark chocolate she had to add.

As Jade was looking at the cartons of eggs kept on the shelve she felt someone tap her shoulder.

She turned around and was surprised to see a smiling Julia standing behind her.

She pulled out the earphones and smiled, "Hey Jules!"

"Hi Jade! How are you feeling today?"

"Much better than yesterday." Laughed Jade, "I think I had a little too much to drink last night. That's a lot of stuff in the cart."

Julia was carting her own trolley which was filled with loads of normal household stuff.

She glanced at the stuff and chuckled, "Mom needed some stuff so she sent me. By the way did you hear?"

"Hear about what?"

"Didn't Alec call you?" Julia asked, with a frown on her face.

Jade shook her head, "No."

"Well I'm sure he'll call you soon to tell you."

Now it was Jade's turn to frown.

"To tell me what exactly?"

All the hope she had managed to gather before getting out of the house that morning, hopes that Alec wouldn't propose to Emma, hopes that he would realise she loved him, all of them were broken into a million pieces by one small sentence.

"Alec proposed to Emma." Julia said.

Chapter 27

"What do you mean he proposed?"

Jade was so shocked that she almost dropped the carton of eggs she had in her hand.

Julia looked at her with a smile, "He asked her to get married. Last night I was getting into bed, Steve was already in bed and we heard shouts and bangs coming from Emma's room. We ran out to see, Alec standing with his hands on his knees panting while Emma stood with the door open as confused as us. Alec didn't answered any of our questions and instead proposed to Emma as soon as he got his breath back. To say she was overjoyed would be an understatement."

So he had asked her to get married. He has given her the ring. Even after talking to her in the club. And being so awkward about the whole scenario. As if he didn't really want to marry Emma.

She wanted to move and run away from there. But her feet were stuck to the floor. She gripped the carton in her hand till her knuckles were white.

"Jade? Are you okay? You look sick."

She was startled out of her thoughts at the sound of Julia's voice.

Tears were stinging her eyes but she swallowed them and trying to force a smile on her face.

"No I'm okay. It's a hangover from yesterday night I guess." She tried to make her smile a little more convincing before continuing, "That's very good news. I'm very happy for both of them."

"I know. I wonder why Alec didn't call you"

Jade knew why he had not called. And she didn't think that she would actually pick up the phone if her even did.

"No. He must be busy."

"He's a fool. Emma's been jumping around the whole house since morning. She's already planning the engagement party."

She had to get out of there before she broke down in front of Julia. It would not be a good idea if Julia came to know what was happening.

"Julia I should get going. I just remembered that I had to make a important phone call."

"I was thinking we could have coffee together. Can't you stay for one cup of coffee?"

Julia actually looked disappointed. Whether it was because Jade was cancelling the coffee plan or because she would have to go back home and face the overexcited Emma, Jade didn't know.

"We'll take a rain check on it? Sorry!"

"Okay. But next time we have to go."

Jade smiled, doing her best to ignore the heavy feeling in her chest.

"Sure."

She said bye and went to the billing counter on auto.

The only thing going on in her her head were Julia's words from earlier and Alec's words from last night.

"Alec proposed to Emma."

The last thing Jade wanted was to breakdown in front of the guy who was billing her stuff.

She paid for the stuff took the bags and went to her car.

The sky had become darker than it had been when she had entered the store.

A storm was on its way.

She put all the stuff in the trunk and stood up.

This was how it had felt 8 years back when Alec had told her that he was going to Thailand. Only this was a million times worse.

Now she understood why people kept talking about broken hearts. Her heart felt like it had been broken into tiny small pieces, only Alec could fix.

She shut the trunk and started walking.

If there was just one way to delete all the feeling she had for him she would have done it without a second thought.

If he had not come back and if she had just heard about the engagement from Susan maybe it wouldn't hurt so bad.

Who was she kidding? It would have hurt just as bad.

Till now she had a hope of Alec coming back into her life. But now....

The diamond ring on Emma's finger was the end to all her hope.

Alec will go back to London with his fiancé. And here she would be alone and desperately in love with a guy she will never have.

Before she knew it tears were running down her face.

Jade never cried. But ever since Alec came back to Millbrooke she found herself crying ever day.

She had no clue where she was headed. She just kept putting one foot in front of the other.

There was thunder in the sky and it started raining. Her tears mixed with the raindrops.

She knew that she would get drenched in a matter of minutes and she was not even dressed for such weather.

But it made no difference to her. She kept walking. Alec's words going on and on in her head.

There were no people on the streets everyone had taken shelter to stay away from the cold rain.

"Alec proposed to Emma."

"You remember this picture?"

Amanda placed a picture of Jade in front Stuart.

They had been doing this for an hour now.

They were sitting with all the photo albums in the house and going through them with a bottle of red wine to keep them company.

"Of course! It had taken you more than an hour to finally put her into that dress."

Amanda laughed. Jade had always hated anything with ruffles on it, even at the age of three.

And the dress that she had on in the photo was pink with more ruffles on it than any other dress in the world.

It had been a 3rd birthday gift from her Aunt Martha, and Amanda had hated it almost as much as the Jade.

She didn't remember the last time she had just sat with Stuart going over old memories and laughing with any inhibitions.

It was a new experience and she was enjoying it thoroughly.

The old Stuart, the Stuart she had been waiting for was sitting next to her and she could not have been more happy.

She looked at him, the blue eyes still sparkled with humour, the black hair was now streaked with white. But that give him a more dignified look.

"Stuart..."

Amanda was interrupted by the sound of the doorbell ringing.

"I'll get it."

He pushed himself up and walked towards the door.

It had been raining very heavily out there for sometime now. Whoever had come in the middle of such a storm sure was gutsy.

He pulled open the door, and there on the doorstep stood, Jade. She was absolutely drenched.

Her black hair was sticking to her pale face.

Her clothes were soaked through and her eyes were bloodshot. She had been crying.

"Jade?"

At the sound of her dad's worried voice, Jade looked up.

"Dad." She sobbed.

Her knees were weak. It was a miracle that she was standing and had not fallen to the floor yet.

"Come in! Come in! You're drenched.... Come... Amanda!"

He was so surprised at the state in which his normally cool and composed daughter was in that he practically didn't know what to do.

He pulled her inside away from the rain.

"What?... Oh!"

Amanda came up behind Stuart and saw the state in which Jade was.

"Amanda... Jade..."

Stuart stuttered.

"Mom!"

When Jade had started walking aimlessly from the grocery store, somewhere in the back of her mind she had known where she was headed.

The one place where she was the most comforted. Her mom's house.

"Stuart, go get some towels first and then please make a cup of tea for her." Amanda said taking charge of the situation.

"Okay."

Stuart was only too happy to go out of there. He had never been good with crying women.

They made him feel helpless and weak.

And now that it was his daughter it made him feel even more helpless. Helpless that he could not prevent anything from hurting her.

He was surprised at the protective feeling he got for his daughter.

He hurried of to get dry towels for Jade.

"Jady, come with me."

Amanda guided Jade into the living, while she still sobbed.

The centre table was covered with photos.

She made her sit on the sofa and sat beside her.

"Sweetie?"

Jade looked up at her mom's kind face and burst out.

"Alec asked Emma to marry him. Last night. And mom it hurts so bad. I never meant to fall in love. And Alexander Carter was the last person I had thought I'd ever fall I love with. But he made me fall him love with him twice. Twice mom!"

Amanda had always known this would be how the friendship between her daughter and Alec would end. With a broken heart. Either hers or his.

No one can have such a strong bond with another person without falling for them.

"Jady..."

Jade interrupted her, "When dad left, I said that's it. I won't trust any other man. I will not give any guy the power to break my heart. But then Alec... He earned my trust along with my friendship. He taught me how to love and it don't know when friendship turned into love. And then... And then... He went away. Went away to follow his dreams. He didn't fall in love with me. Again I said over no more falling in love. No more... And then he came back. And he made me fall for him again. I know he has a girlfriend and I know it is wrong. But I couldn't help it. I hoped.... But then he... He proposed to her. And it hurts so bad Mom!"

Amanda pulled her daughter into her arms and let her cry as she used to do when she had been small.

"I understand, sweetie. I understand."

She patted her back. There was only one thing worse than going through a heart break. It was seeing your child go through a heart break and not having the power to do anything about it.

She held her tightly while Jade's body shook.

"I got the.... Towels" Stuart came into the room with two white fluffy towels in his hand.

She took the towels from his hand and put them on Jade.

"I'll go get the tea."

He went out of the room again. His blood was almost boiling.

He had heard what Jade had said, and at that moment he wanted to kill that boy.

How could he happily get married, after breaking Jade's heart? How could he do this to someone who was so in love with him?

And then it dawned on him. What Alec had done was not so different from what he himself had done.

Only he made a even bigger mistake. He had broken Amanda's heart more times.

He had made her cry many more times.

In the living room, Amanda took hold of Jade by her shoulders and made her sit upright.

"I know how you feel, baby. Believe me. There's no one else who understands how you feel right now more than me. But you have to be strong. You have to go on. And you have to believe that everything will become better."

She had been through this. All this. And she wouldn't let her daughter lead the life she had been living, waiting for Stuart to come back. She had got him back, maybe Jade wouldn't be as lucky.

"How? How do I do that?"

"When your dad left I had only you. Only you to comfort me. Nothing else. I did it didn't I? And you have me, your friends, your work. You have a great life in front of you. I know it seems silly what I'm saying. And you've no interest in listening to me. Right now, you just want to cry and yell. But there will be a time, sooner or later, when you will have to wipe your tears, get up and get on with life."

"What if I don't want to?"

"You have to sweetie. It will take time. But the pain will become less at some point. I promise."

Amanda held her again.

After Jade's tears slowed down a little, Amanda sent her to have a hot bath, before she caught a cold.

The hot tea had helped a little but she was still drenched.

She sank down on the sofa and put her head in her palms.

"Amanda?"

She looked up to see Stuart, standing near the door leading to the kitchen.

"She's gone to have a bath."

"I know." He walked up to the sofa and sat down beside her. "I'm sorry."

"What?"

"I'm sorry. I'm the biggest biggest jerk on this earth and I don't deserve to have you at all."

Amanda looked at Stuart to find tears in his eyes.

"No...."

"Yes, today I felt like killing Alec for what he did to our girl. But then I realised that it was not as bad as what I did to you. I don't deserve you."

Amanda hugged him and they sat like that with their arms around each other for a long time.

"I love you, that's all that matters." Said Amanda breaking the silence.

"I love you too. And I won't leave you ever again even if God himself asks me too. Never again."

Jade came down after the bath to find her parents hugging each other on the sofa.

And even though thoughts of Alec were still in her head. She smiled through the constant ache in her chest.

She didn't get her love, but her mom did. And she was happy for that.

Chapter 28

1 5 years ago

Jade walked up to where, Alec and Julia were standing on the playground.

She was angry, extremely angry on Alec. So angry that she had not spoken to him, for the past 4 days, which was her personal record.

"Why did you'll call me over here?" She said crossing her hands over her flat chest when she reached them.

Sh glared at Alec who was standing behind his elder sister with an uncomfortable look on his face.

Good he deserved to be uncomfortable, thought Jade.

"Hi, Jade!" Julia was the first one to speak up.

Jade had got a call from Julia that morning requesting her to come to the kindergarten playground in the afternoon.

Jade had come but now that she thought of it she shouldn't have.

She didn't reply to Julia but stood and continued glaring at Alec, who was slowly turning a embarrassing shade of red.

She could feel the anger rise again.

Their school had organised a story writing competition for all the students in the age group of 10- 15.

12 year old Jade, who had already discovered her talent of writing had been very excited to participate in the competition.

Days were spent thinking up the story and then a few more days had been used to write it up in her best handwriting.

She had done her absolute best, trying to make it the best entry.

But on the day of the submission, Alec had taken the papers she had lovingly filled and completely spoilt them by spilling water on them.

There was no way Jade was going to forgive him for doing that. She hadn't been able to submit a story and instead of her, her biggest nemesis in school, Bella Hawthorne won the competition.

And to make it worse, he had not even apologised.

"Alec wants to say something to you." The elder girl said when Jade didn't say anything.

"What?" Jade asked.

"Say!" Julia nudged her younger brother.

"I'm not going to say any thing." Alec said stubbornly.

"Chicken!"

"Nerd!" Alec retorted.

The two of them started throwing names at each other.

"Guys can you'll do this sibling rivalry thing later?" Jade spoke up interrupting their argument.

Julia and Alec looked at her guiltily.

Julia spoke up again, "Alec wants to apologise to you."

"I'll believe it when he says it." Saying this Jade turned around and started walking out of the playground.

"Jade!" She turned around to see Alec run up behind her.

"What?"

"I really am sorry. I hate it when you're angry with me." Alec said when he reached her.

"Then why do you do stuff that makes me angry on you?" Jade asked.

Alec smiled guiltily, "I'm sorry. Actually I got jealous."

When Jade looked at him shocked he continued speaking, "Really I got jealous of you. Even I wanted to participate in the competition but I can't write even a half decent story. And you're so good at it."

He looked down at his sneaker clad feet.

"But that's the only thing I'm good at!" Jade said.

"No you're good at everything. You always end up coming first in school. You're even good in sports. It's not fair sometimes."

"But you are the one who answers all the questions in school. You know so much stuff about so many different places."

"That's nothing." Alec said shaking his head.

"It is!" Jade insisted, "That's you're talent. Like writing is mine. I really wanted to participate in that competition you know."

"I really am sorry. I even got something for you to make up for it." Alec scrambled in his pocket and came up with something, "You remember the ring Mrs Watson's husband gave her? The red one which you liked so much..."

Mrs Watson was their home room teacher, who had been given an ornate ruby ring by her husband for their anniversary. A ring which Jade had fallen in love with.

Alec handed her a ring which looked just like that ring and said, "Well this is not the real thing. I asked mom how much the real one would cost and let me just tell you it was way out of my budget. So mom helped me get this for you. It's not as good but..."

"It's perfect!" Jade explained and hugged Alec.

It had fake stones set into a silver ring. There were many small clear stones surrounding a big shiny red stone.

"Really?"

"I love it!" She put it on her finger and held her hand out to observe the effect.

"So I'm forgiven?" Alec asked with a cocky smile.

"Yes you are." Jade smiled back.

Dinner was a subdued matter. Though she tried to plaster a smile on her face and kept up a conversation with her dad, Jade knew that her parents could see right through her facade.

She knew by the wary looks they were giving her and concerned looks they were exchanging.

Her mother had made her favourite lasagna for dinner, but the cheese and tomato sauce was completely tasteless to to her.

Jade just wanted to go back into her room and snuggle into the bed she had grown up sleeping in.

Her mom had convinced her to stay back that night. Not that Jade had put up much of an argument.

"Mom, I'm really sleepy." Jade said once dinner was done while helping her mom clear the dishes.

"Of course sweetie." Amanda went to her daughter and placed a light kiss on her forehead, "Go to sleep. I'll clear up the rest of the dishes."

"You sure?"

"Yeah."

She smiled at her mom. A smile that was a silent thanks. She knew her mom understood.

She said good night to both her parents and went up to the room.

Fortunately, she was fast asleep as soon as her body hit the bed, giving her no time to think about and cry over all that had happened today.

When Jade woke up the next morning, she was completely disoriented for some time.

It took her few minutes to realise where she was.

And then everything came flooding in. She groaned and held her head.

If this was going to be the way her day was going to start always, then she might as well stop writing, abandon her life and go live in the Himalayas.

She pulled herself up and actually looked around. Her room looked the same as it did when she had moved out.

Her mom hadn't touch any of her things.

She pulled herself up from her bed atlast and went into the washroom to splash water on her face.

As she was coming out with the towel still in her hand, she stumbled over something lying near her bed.

She bent to pick up the box on the floor.

It was an old wooden box with stars and flowers stuck on it.

Jade remembered the box clearly, as if it had been yesterday, when she had made it with some help from Alec.

They used to call the box, 'Friendship Box' and it had all the things they associated with their friendship in it.

She opened the box and started going through everything.

There were cards and notes, Alec had given her at different points, there was a friendship bracelet, some photos.

It had been ages since she had last seen the box and it brought back so many happy memories.

She picked up the photos from the box to take a better look at them, but something fell to the ground.

Jade bent down again and found something she had not laid eyes on for 8 years.

A fake ruby ring, which still sparkled like it had been given to her just now.

She picked it up and looked at it with a wistful smile playing on her lips.

She remembered the day Alec had given the ring to her.

She had worn it every day since that day. No matter how many other rings she had got she had worn it everyday faithfully.

Till the day Alec told her that he was going to Thailand.

On that day she had come back home, taken it off of her finger and put it in the box.

She quickly opened the clasp of the plain silver chain she had around her neck. She put the ring in the chain and then put the clasp again wearing it like a locket.

She let the chain fall.

Now the ring would stay close to her heart forever even if the person who had given it to her didn't.

She held her hand over where it lay before getting to get ready. She sneaked out of the house without waking her mom.

She half ran, half walked to the place where she wanted to go.

Within a few minutes Jade found herself in the kindergarten playground. The place where she had met Alec for the first time.

It was still early in the morning and there were very few people on the road.

The ground was a little wet still from all the ran from yesterday, but Jade found a dry spot under a tree.

She sat over there and opened the small notebook she had taken from the desk in her room.

She lost herself in writing, while the ring lay nestled under her tree. When Alec had gone to Jason's house to talk to him about his plans, he had not thought that things would happen so fast.

Less than four days, and he had already decided on a place.

His plan was working.

Around the time when Wanderlust had become more famous than Alec had ever expected it to become he had come up with a plan to do something he had always wanted to do.

Open up a Wanderlust office in Millbrooke and move back to town.

He didn't want to stay away from home, his mom any longer.

And Jade.

He shook his head once and looked around the place he had chosen for the office.

It was spacious with plenty of light and many windows.

He could see how it would look once the office was made completely.

He could almost feel the energy coursing through the place.

The office was very close to the kindergarten. Once he had finished looking around the place he decided to go to the playground and take a breath of air before going home.

Emma had been on a high ever since she woke up that morning.

Just as she had been the day before.He had stayed in his room the whole day yesterday, pretending to be ill. But he had to get out today. Her excitement was tangible and so was his moms.

So much so, that he and Julia had not been able to take it any longer. They both had made excuses and left the house.

He had come to the site to talk to the contractors who told him that they would start working from the next day.

As soon as he entered the playground he saw something that made his heart beat louder.

Under the shade of the tree Jade sat with a notebook on her lap. She was scribbling as fast as she could into it.

Her long hair was flowing around her face with the morning wind. Her tongue was out in concentration as she turned a page and continued writing with fervour.

He walked closer to her but she didn't even look up, she was so lost in the story.

"Writing something?" He asked once he was in hearing distance.

Jade immediately picked up her head to see who had spoken. Once she noticed him, her face got a steely expression on it.

"What are you doing here?" She asked.

"I was right around the corner from here for some work. Thought I'd take a walk." He replied.

Jade looked at her wrist, but there was no watch there.

"It 10:30. If you want to know." He said sitting down next to her.

Jade scowled, "I didn't. Alec why are you sitting here?"

"The last time I checked, this was a free country." He said, simply.

"Do whatever you want to do." Jade said getting up.

She couldn't handle being so close to him.

She couldn't handle seeing him. He looked so handsome in a full sleeved blue t- shirt and black jeans.

She picked up her notebook and the pen.

Alec realised her intentions of walking away and so he stood up himself.

"Jade… Wait!" He said.

"What?" She turned around to face him. It was taking a lot of energy to keep her face blank of any emotions, "Look Julia told me yesterday. That you.... You... Proposed! So congratulations! Now let me go."

He caught her wrist before she could leave.

"Wait Jade let me..." He started to say.

"Let me what? Explain myself? There's no need of that. You want to get married to Emma its your choice. Completely yours! But you shouldn't have lied to me. About not knowing what to do!" Jade yelled.

"You're acting like I'm the only one who lied. What did you do huh? Telling me that you and Matt broke up. I came to your apartment after you left. I know what was happening." Alec said equally loudly.

"What...?" Jade was confused. What was Alec saying?

"I saw him without a shirt. Shamelessly pulling up his pants. I remember what you said about half naked guys...."

Before Alec could complete his sentence Jade picked up her free hand and slapped him on his cheek with a satisfying sound.

He looked shocked for a second.

"I don't owe you an explanation for anything. Why don't we just make it a point to not meet each other or talk to each other?" She said, trying to free her wrist.

"Jade..." Alec tightened his hold on her wrist, "Will you listen to me?"

"You're hurting me Alec!" Jade lied through gritted teeth.

Alec immediately left her wrist, "I'm sorry. I didn't mean to..."

"Bye Alec!" Jade turned around and started walking out.

"Jade I don't know why I proposed to Emma. I don't know what got into me when I saw Matt. I was angry and drunk....."

"That's no excuse." Jade said, she had stopped walking when Alec had started speaking. "And I know why you proposed to Emma. Because she is 'The One' for you."

"Maybe she's not... Maybe 'The One' for me had been right in front of me all along and I didn't notice."

Jade's heart was beating so loudly that she wondered why Alec couldn't hear it.

"Maybe I was wrong all along."

Alec had been taking steps towards where Jade was standing while speaking.

Just as he finished talking he reached her and laid a hand over her shoulder.

She turned around to look at him. Her green eyes were shining with unshed tears.

"Alec..."

"Don't." Alec said and bent down to place his lips on hers.

Jade had always thought that her first kiss with Alec would be magical, sweet, soft and promising.

This kiss was magical, but nothing closed to slow.

It was like he was trying to tell her all the things he had not said through a kiss.

She found herself kissing him back. She wound her hands around his neck and Alec pulled her closer to him.

She wondered what it would be like if this worked out. If they ended up together.

What if Alec was really in love with her?

She could almost see the future. How it would be all perfect for them.

She poured all her love into the kiss.

But that would not happen would it? He was engaged. He was going to get married to Emma.

Emma who had been so sweet about Matt yesterday. Emma who was so excited about the wedding. Who was already planning the engagement party.

Jade broke the kiss and pulled back. Alec looked at her confused. The look on his face made her want to give in and kiss him again.

But thoughts of Emma stopped her.

"Bye Alec." She said and walked away.

"Jade..." Alec called out and she made the biggest mistake of the day, she turned around.

Well, the second biggest. The kiss definitely deserved first place.

It took her a lot of strength to turn her back on his pleading face and run back home.

Chapter 29

The house looked good. It was big, and was in an area which was surely rich.

Emma will be happy over here, thought Paula when the car stopped in front of the Carter house.

They got down of the rental car. As Mark paid the driver Paula looked at and observed the house more carefully.

"Isn't the house really beautiful?" She asked when her husband came and stood next to her.

When no reply came she looked up to see that Mark was busy typing something into his mobile.

"Are you even listening to me? Or are you to engrossed in that mobile?"

"I heard you Paula. You think the house is beautiful and I agree. Now this is an important mail and I need to reply to it. Would you rather that I finish it while we're outside, or do you want me to be engrossed in my mobile inside in front of everyone?" All the while as he spoke his eyes were trained on his mobile.

Paula just huffed and waited for the driver to take out their carry-on bags from the trunk.

It had been their decision to take a rental from the Chicago airport. Alec had offered to come pick them up.

But Mark didn't like the idea of imposing that way.

"Let's go." Mark said atlast when he was satisfied with the mail.

Paula rolled her eyes but still followed him.

They walked up the stairs and rang the door bell.

"They're here!" Emma said running into the kitchen where Susan was talking to the caterers.

Over the three days she had spent with Susan they had come quite close while doing all the preparations for the party.

She had been standing near the window waiting for her parents to come since morning, poking her head out every two seconds.

And now that they were here, she had a sick feeling in her stomach.

She hoped that they didn't say anything wrong or do anything to hurt any of the members in Alec's family.

"Are they? Why don't I open the door while you go call Alec, okay?" Susan said, dismissing the caterers and walking out.

Emma ran up the stairs. She found Alec in his room just sitting on his bed and staring at the wall.

"Alec, they're here!" She said when she entered his room.

Alec looked up and for a second his eyes were blurred, as if he had been thinking about something very serious and Emma had interrupted him.

"Is something wrong?" Emma asked when Alec didn't reply.

He cleared his throat, "No no... I'm fine. They're here? Good. Let's go down." He said as he raked his fingers through his hair.

Emma was still concerned but just then the door bell rang.

Alec and she walked down the stairs quickly to see that Susan had already opened the door and she was ushering them into the living room.

"Hi mother!" Emma said, she brought on a smile on her face even though she felt sick and kissed her mother on her powdered cheeks.

Paula Burns was as usual immaculately dressed in grey trousers and an off white sweater. Her platinum bold hair, which was chin length surrounded her pretty but sharp face.

"Hello, Emma. How have you been?" She said. Her accent sounded stronger and more pronounced, since Emma had gotten used to hearing the American accent for the past few days.

"I have been great." She moved to her dad and kissed him on his cheek too. "Hello father."

Mark Burns was a tall man, with broad shoulder and a body he had maintained with great pride.

His brown eyes were covered with glasses and his hair was swept back.

He too was wearing a grey pants and a dark green sweater.

He smelt faintly of nicotine when Emma went close to him. Surely from the cigarette he smoked when her mother was not around.

"Hello doll." Mark said.

"Was the journey fine?" Susan asked as she stood behind them.

She felt completely underdressed in her jeans and plaid shirt.

"The journey was good. You must be Susanne Carter." Paula said, before giving her the air kisses which were so famous.

Susan had seen people exchange air kisses a million times on TV but this was the first time she was in their place.

She stood awkwardly while Paula blew kisses and then stood back.

"It's umm... Susan. But that's fine, I'm glad to meet you Paula." Susan said.

"Hello I'm Mark!" Emma's father extended a hand to her.

Susan timidly shook the big hand and smiled, "Hello, I'm Susan, Alec's mom."

"Hello Ma'am. Hello sir." Alec nodded his head at Paula and then was subjected to a hand squeeze by Mark.

Just then Steve and Julia entered the living room.

Both of them were sweating and looked ruffled.

Emma closed her eyes. It was not very difficult to guess what they had been doing before being interrupted by the door bell and what would her parents say about it.

She could see the smile Paula tried to hide her frown behind when Emma introduced them.

Mark didn't even take the efforts to hide the disgust with a smile.

After all the introductions were made, Susan got in cups of coffee for everyone and handed them around.

They all sat on the sofa. There was an awkward silence. While everyone quietly sipped their coffees.

This was going to be bad, thought Emma.

This was going to be horrible.

These people didn't have anything in common.

Susan started talking about the preparations for the party. But is was only so long that someone could talk about hors d'oeuvres and the guest list.

Before long they were sitting in silence again.

"This is really awkward." Emma heard Steve whisper to Julia before Julia shushed him.

She couldn't agree less with him. This was the mother of all awkward meetings!

This was a horrible idea. "Mom, Alec... Can we talk to you for a second?" Julia asked coming into the room after she had gone to the kitchen to keep her cup.

"Yeah sure sweetie."

Susan and Alec excused themselves and followed Julia to the kitchen where Steve was already standing.

He had another cup of coffee in his hand and a smug smile.

"Is something going on?" Alec asked suspiciously.

Julia shook her head, "No."

While at the same time Steve nodded from behind, the smile now a full blown grin.

"Julia what is it? It's not right to leave the Burns alone over there." Susan said.

Steve took another sip of his coffee, "Yes Julia.... Do tell." He encouraged his wife.

"You shut up! This is all because of you!" She yelled.

But the smile on Steve's face somehow just became bigger.

"Mom and Alec... See I wanted you'll to be the first people to know...Well ofcourse after me and Steve and the doctor...But that's not counted." She said while wringing her hand.

"You're stalling,Julia ." Steve interrupted.

Julia glared at him, "So why don't you say it?"

"Okay..." He shrugged.

Steve came and stood next to her and looked at Alec and Susan who were both standing with confusion visible on their faces.

"Mom, Alec.... Julia is pregnant." Steve said simply. "Ouch! What was that for?"

Julia had hit him on his shoulder with all her might, "We are pregnant. We! That's how you say it.... You idiot!"

"What difference does it make? And anyways I'm not pregnant. At least I wasn't the last time I checked. Want me to check......?"

But Steve didn't get to continue what he was going to say because Susan had started squealing.

"That's such great news! Oh my God!" She exclaimed hugging both Steve and Julia, her eyes were damp with tears but there was a smile on her face, "I'm going to be a grandmother!"

Once Susan had asked about everything. All the medical details. Julia's diet plan. The due date. The doctor.

The three of them stood back and just grinned at each other.

That's when Steve noticed that Alec had not uttered a word. He was still standing right where he had been with a shocked look on his face and his mouth open.

"So what's your reaction, uncle Alec? Or did the cat get your tongue?" Steve asked, emphasising the uncle.

Alec blinked, "You'll are giving me a niece."

Julia laughed and shrugged, "It can be a nephew. We're not checking though. We want it to be a surprise."

"You are giving me a niece. A niece?" His expression was blank but he went and hugged his sister and Steve.

He kept repeating the words, "A niece?"

This came as a complete shock to Alec, but then when he thought about it, it shouldn't have.

Julia had been away from alcohol ever since she had come to Millbrooke.

Alec had noticed Steve exchanging secret, love eyed looks with his sister and had passed it of as normal couple behaviour.

Julia explained that she had suspected it since before coming to Millbrooke, but she had not told anyone except Steve because she didn't want to disappoint anyone.

The doctor had called that morning to confirm her suspicions.

"And I wanted you'll to be the first ones to know." Julia said, "Mom, to keep up with the bracelet theme I got a charm. Will you put it on my bracelet for me?"

There was a tradition in their family. On the wedding day the oldest Sheridan woman- Susan's maiden name- gave the soon to be bride a charm bracelet with a single charm on it.

And over the years that girl collected charms and put them on the bracelet to mark every special occasion.

Julia took out the charm and the bracelet from her pocket and handed it to her mother.

Susan took a closer look at the small silver charm and saw that it was a small cradle.

She smiled and with tears blurring her vision she put the new charm onto the bracelet and secured it around Julia's wrist.

"So you got a bed... Because that's where you'll did it... And that's the reason you're pregnant?" Alec asked. He was finally over the shock that her sister and brother- in - law were going to have a baby.

"Alec! It's a cradle. Not a bed." Julia said.

"I think it's a bed too." Steve whispered to Alec soft enough that Julia wouldn't hear it.

Susan looked at the bracelet one last time, "It's beautiful." She said.

The bracelet already had a key and an 'S' on it.

Now the cradle was added.

Charm.

Oh no! How could she forget?

Susan stepped back and pressed her hand to her mouth.

"Charm!" She exclaimed.

"Mom?" Julia looked at her mother with concern.

"I've got to... Charm! I'll be right back okay? I'm very happy for you. You don't know how happy! But I have to go! Charm!" Susan said all flustered and then she sped out of the room.

Alec looked at Julia with a confused expression, "What was that?"

"I think our mother finally has gone mad." Julia replied, as the three of them looked at the door through which Susan had left muttering all the while. "What do you mean she left? Where did she go? She has to talk to the caterers! They don't trust me... And my accent!" Emma snarled when Alec told her about Susan sudden exit.

Alec shrugged, "I really don't know where she went. I'm as confused as you are."

"But the caterers!"

"I'll help you. Come." Alec took her hand and walked to the kitchen.

All the preparations for the engagement party were almost done. It was being held at the Carter house itself. Only the few last minute adjustments were to be made.

With all the confusion of Julia's news and the talk of hors d'oeuvres Alec had not got one chance all day to think about Jade or what he was going to do.

The kiss.

He could still close his eyes and find himself in the playground. He replayed the whole scene.

But the hurt that had been in her eyes before she ran away was enough for him to feel the guilt and confusion come back.

He would have to talk to her tonight, her thought to himself as he out the last buttons of his shirt.

The party was going to start in an hour and he had been strictly warned by the women in the house to not come down till he was completely ready.

Susan had entered the house half am hour back with no signs that would give away clues as to where she had disappeared.

The guests would start arriving any time now.

Jade would come. Would she?

Even the thought of Jade and what he was going to tell her made Alec feel like he was going to hurl.

He didn't know what to do... But he knew that whatever happened he had to talk to Jade.

Chapter 30

Jade straightened her dress once again and ran her fingers through her open hair.

"Jade you look perfect!" Exclaimed Nicole who had entered the party with her.

Jade had been fidgeting with her dress and hair every two seconds.

She looked nervous and she kept wringing her hands.

"I know. Sorry. I'm just....." Jade started saying.

"Extremely nervous." Nicole finished the sentence for her.

"Yes."

Nicole laughed at the pained look on Jade's face.

She was looking beautiful in the black sleeveless dress.

"Nicky... Come here. Steve wants to talk to you." Jason said coming towards where they both were standing.

He had been pulled away by an excited and kind of nervous Steve as soon as the three of them walked into the party.

Nicole turned to Jade with a questioning glance.

"Go. I'll be fine! Don't worry." Jade said.

"You sure?"

Jade smiled, "I'll be fine! Go! Jason take her."

Nicole walked away with Jason while Jade went deeper into the room.

The room was crowded with people standing in groups chatting while sipping from their glasses.

She noticed Emma talking to someone. She looked beautiful in a blue dress.

She looked relaxed and laid back, completely unlike what she looked the first day they met.

Where was Alec?

She did not want to meet Alec today.

It was his party. His house. But she was going to do all she could to avoid coming face to face with him.

She started looking at people around her, smiling at the people she knew.

Suddenly she heard someone clear their throat from behind her.

She turned around, to see Matt standing opposite her.

Matt was standing behind her, a smile on his face and his hands shoved in the pockets of his dark blue trousers.

"Hi! What are you doing here?" Then she realised how she sounded, "Sorry that sounded rude."

Matt laughed, "No it didn't. Emma called me and invited me to the party."

"Emma? How does she have your number?"

Why had Emma called Matt for the engagement party even though they barely knew each other?

"Well you gave her the number." He replied simply, "You look gorgeous by the way."

But the compliment didn't register in Jade's mind, "I didn't give her your number. I would remember if I had."

"Well you gave my number to Nicole, didn't you?"

Jade nodded, "Yes but that was ages back."

"Yeah... So Nicole gave the number to Jason, Jason gave it to Steve. Then Steve gave my number to Julia, she gave it to Mrs Carter and then Mrs Carter gave it to Emma. That's how she got my number."

"So how does that mean I gave her your number?" Jade asked with a confused look.

"Transitivity!"

"What's that?"

"It's a geometry thing. A is equal to B. B is equal to C. Then A is equal to C." Matt grinned.

"You're such a nerd!" Jade laughed.

"But the nerd got a smile to your face." He said.

Jade smiled, "Yes he did."

"So you came?" He asked.

"So I came."

"So did you speak to Alec?"

"So... No I've been a coward."

"So you're going to ignore him?"

"So.... Well yes kind of." Jade said laughing at her own stupidity.

How did she expect to ignore someone in their own house, during their engagement party.

"That's going to be tough." Matt said with a grin.

"You can say that again."

They both looked at each other and started laughing. So she had come.

And she had got that doctor with her again.

Alec was supposed to be talking to Sheriff Preston. But instead of paying attention to what he was saying Alec was busy trying to catch glimpses of Jade.

The room was crowded and people kept coming in the way.

She was standing near the back of the room with Matt and they were talking and exchanging huge smiles.

"Alec... Sorry Sheriff can I borrow my fiancé for a minute?" Emma came from nowhere and stood next to Alec.

"Sure! Sure!" The jolly man guffawed.

Emma pulled Alec by his arm and started walking across the room with her hand tightly wound around his arm.

"Susan is introducing my parents to Amanda and her husband... It's Stuart right? So I thought we should introduce Jade too." She started saying while she dragged him in the general direction of where Jade was standing.

"She looks busy. Later maybe." Alec tried to make excuses.

Emma turned her face to him with a grin on it, "They look so cute, don't they?"

"They?"

"Matt and Jade! I invited Matt myself. I think they really look good together."

So Emma had invited Matt and not Jade.

Was Emma trying to act matchmaker with those two?

By the time Alec digested the fact that Emma was trying to get them together, they reached the place where they were standing.

"Jade!" Emma exclaimed and hugged her.

This was the girl who somedays back had spilled wine on Jade's dress.

"I'm so glad you could make it." Emma continued once they pulled back from the hug.

"I had to come. And anyways… Congratulation! I have to see the ring."

"Thanks! Here…" Emma held out her hand with a smile and Jade saw the ring which Alec had given her.

It was a traditional ring with a square cut diamond set in a platinum ring.

"It beautiful." Jade said, "Not bad Alec."

Alec who had been staring at Jade till then managed to bring a small smile on his face.

"Congrats to both of you!" Matt spoke up.

"Thank you Matt! I'm so glad you could make it too." Emma said, "Now I want both of you to meet my parents. Come."

"Mother this is Jade Tucker, Alec's best friend from when they were children. And Jade these are my parents."

Emma had almost dragged all three of them to the other side of the crowded room to make the introductions.

"Hello Ma'am. Nice to meet you Sir." Jade smiled at the couple standing in front of her.

Looking at Paula Burns gave her a glimpse of what Emma will look like 30 years from now.

She had the same face structure as her daughter and though Emma was a little taller than her mother they looked really similar.

"Hello Jade." Paula smiled.

Best friends is it? Then why was Alexander look at this girl with those glimmering eyes, she thought.

"Isn't Jade a lovely name!" Mark said while shaking Jade's hand.

"And this is Matthew Damon. He's a doctor and he's also Jade's boyfriend." Emma said cheerfully.

At her words, both Alec and Jade started coughing loudly. While Matt stood there with a grin on his face.

"Well actually..." Jade started saying when she recovered from her coughing fit. "We are not...."

"They broke up some days back." Alec completed for her.

Mark smiled, "Well Matthew I would love to have a chat with you sometime. You see our company deals with pharmaceuticals."

With this both Mark and Matt stepped away from the group and soon were busy talking about common acquaintances and experiences in the field of medicine.

"So Alexander and Jade, how did you both come to be such good friends?" Paula asked.

If Emma noticed the smirk and sarcasm on her mother's face she didn't let it bother her.

"Well we met in kindergarten." Alec started.

Jade followed him, "Yes and we became friends. Our moms are really good friends, too."

"Oh yes. I just met her. Amanda Tucker and Stuart Tucker." The older lady said. "But I always found it surprising when people from opposite sexes became good friends."

Where exactly was this conversation heading?, wondered Jade.

"They never had that problem, did you'll?" Emma spoke up.

Before either of them could say anything they were saved by Julia who walked upto where they were standing.

"Jade I need to talk to you. Hi Paula, Emma and Alec!" She said nodding at the others and then tugging at Jade's hand.

Julia was looking really pretty in a silver cocktail dress with black gladiator sandals. Her golden curls were pulled into a casual up do.

"Okay. Please excuse me." Jade followed Julia to the dining room which was empty and quite. "So what's the matter?"

"I've got to give you some news!"

There was a glimmer of excitement in her eyes and she couldn't bring the smile off of her face.

"News? What's going on exactly Julia?" Jade asked propping her hip on the dining table and making herself comfortable.

Julia clasped her hands and said, "I'm pregnant!"

"What!? Really? Oh that's such great news! Congrats!" Jade hugged Julia.

"Thanks! I'm so happy."

"And I'm so happy for you. When's the baby due?" Jade asked.

"Somewhere near Christmas."

"That is so cool. A Christmas baby!"

It's surprising how talk of babies and kids makes all the other matters in your life seem small.

Giving birth to a baby. Bringing a new life to this world is just a magical thing.

Jade forgot about all the problem in her life as she listened to Julia tell her about all their plans and preparations.

"I'm so happy for you. I can't wait for the baby to get here. And I have to talk to Steve." Jade said.

There was a knock on the door to the dining room both the women turned around to see Alec standing at the door.

He somehow looked tired while looking handsome in the black trousers and dark grey shirt he was wearing.

"Hello!" He said.

He was looking straight at Jade.

"Hi Alec! I was just giving Jade the good news. But what are you doing here? People outside are waiting to talk to you." Julia said, walking up to him.

"I know. But I need to talk to Jade for a few minutes." Alec replied, his eyes were still trained on Jade.

Jade frowned, "Me?"

"Yes."

Jade knew what he wanted to talk about. The kiss.

And she was not interested in talking about it.

"You should seriously wait… I mean… It's your party and you need to meet people." Jade tried to make excuses.

Alec turned to Julia, "Will you handle things outside? It will take us a few minutes."

"Okay. But you have a time limit. And if Emma asks about you I'm coming to get you." She agreed and left the room.

"We'll be on the front porch." Alec called out behind her and then motioned for Jade to walk through the door of the front porch.

Reluctantly Jade agreed and she walked out into the starry night.

Chapter 31

"What did you want to talk about?" Jade turned around and asked Alec once they were on the porch.

"You've been avoiding me, right?" He asked.

Jade turned her back on Alec, "Yes, I have."

"Why?"

"Why do you think Alec?" She replied.

He walked around her and came to face her, "We need to talk."

"No we don't." Jade snapped, "What do you want to talk about?"

"About.... About what is happening. You.... Me..."

"Emma?" Jade finished for him. "Look this is your engagement party. You're engaged. With Emma. So I'm sorry, but we don't have anything to say."

"We have the kiss to talk about."

Jade's heart sank at the mention of the kiss.

She had avoided any thoughts of it for the past few days.

And now.

"Alec that's the.... That's the last thing I want to talk about." She said.

"So we just forget it happened?"

"Yes. That's what we should do. And right now we both should go back inside."

Jade started walking towards the door off the porch, but before she could take more than a couple of steps before Alec caught her hand.

"Don't go, Jade. You remember what I said that day...."

How could she forget?

She could still hear those words clearly.

Maybe she's not... Maybe 'The One' for me had been right in front of me all along and I didn't notice.

"I remember and that what hurts the most. But nothing can be done. Nothing." Jade said, she tried to control the tears that were about to spill out of her eyes.

"We can...."

"No we can't. No. So just let me go!" She shrugged her hand and removed her wrist.

That's when the door to the porch opened and Julia walked out.

There was shock clearly seen on her face when she saw the way they were standing and the expressions on their faces. "What is going on over here?" Julia asked as she stood at the door to the porch. Her hands were fisted on her hips and there was a confused look on her face.

"Nothing, Julia." Jade snapped.

She felt like pulling at her hair or maybe punching someone.

"It's not nothing. I can see that something is going on over here. Every one is looking for you out there Alec and you're still here." Julia was not going to let it go.

She could see that Jade had been crying recently and Alec looked stressed out and tensed.

"Don't you'll get it that maybe I don't want to talk?" Jade glared at both the Carter siblings.

Alec looked at her with a pained expression, "Jade just listen to what I have to say...."

"Alec there's nothing more left to say. This is your engagement party for God's sake!" Jade interrupted Alec, "It's over. The kiss was a mistake! A horrible and terrible mistake. More on your part than mine. Now just leave me alone! Go back to Emma."

"Kiss? Will someone please tell me what is happening?" Julia asked again coming onto the porch and closing the door behind her so no one could hear the conversation.

"Jade, the kiss was not a mistake. How can you even say that something so special was a mistake?" Alec said ignoring Julia completely.

Jade looked at him with her eyes shining with anger and hurt, "I can say that because you, Alexander Carter, you are engaged. You were engaged when you kissed me. And you didn't have any right to."

"Like you didn't respond. Wasn't that cheating on Matt?"

Before any other word could be said, Jade raised her hand and slapped him across his face with a satisfying noise.

Alec held his hand to his cheek more out of shock than hurt.

"You are no one to comment on my personal life." Jade hissed out.

"And you have all the right to comment on mine?" Alec asked.

Julia came to stand between the two of them before Jade could hit him again. The bruise from his nose had still not disappeared completely. And the slap was surely going to leave behind a mark.

"Guys! Stop behaving like kids. If there is a problem then deal with it. Like adults. Stop fighting." She said.

"Why are you coming in between?" Jade snarled. She was still glaring at Alec.

"Someone needs to." Julia said, "Now please talk it out. Without shouting or hitting."

"I don't want to talk about all this anymore. It's over. Everything is done. Alec is engaged to Emma. And they will get married. Live a happy life, Alec."

She started walked back into the house but she didn't go any-where near the party.

Instead she went into the dining room and stood with her hands pressed to the table top, trying to control her emotions.

She was not going to cry. Suck it up, Jade!

"Alec what the hell is going on? Kiss? You and Jade?" Julia asked Alec, who was standing with his eyes stuck to the door through which Jade had left a few seconds back.

"I love her." Alec stated simply without even thinking for once what kind of confusion that would cause for his elder sister.

"What!?" Exclaimed Julia, "You love Jade... But Emma! I'm con-fused Alec."

"You're confused? Seriously? And what do you think I'm going through?" Alec yelled, raking his fingers through his hair.

"If you're in love with Jade then why did you propose to Emma? And if you know now, then break up with Emma. Tell her the truth."

Alec turned around to look at his sister, "You think that didn't occur to me? Do you think I'm that dense? I don't want to hurt her like that."

Julia raised an eyebrow, "And you're okay with hurting Jade?"

"Jesus, Julia! I don't want to hurt either of them. What do you want me to do? If I break the engagement then I'm hurting Emma. And if I don't then I'm breaking Jade's heart."

"You're going to end up hurting both of them if you continue to do this!" Julia couldn't believe that her brother was being so obtuse. "Emma will understand. Whether you tell her or no. She is bound to understand that you're not in love with her. You don't want to spend your life with her. And then you're going to end up hurting her anyways."

"What do you want me to do?" Alec was frustrated. "I don't want to hurt them."

"You made a mistake. Accept it! Take responsibility for it! Grow up! What are you doing with your life Alec? What do you want to do?"

Alec sat down on the porch and let his head fall into his hand.

"Go speak to Jade. Now!" Julia continued.

Alec looked at her and saw that she meant what she was saying.

He got up and went in search of Jade. Julia was right, it was time that he really spoke to Jade. Just as Jade had almost composed herself, there was a knock on the door. She turned to see Alec standing.

And all her feelings and emotions came rushing back in.

It was like every time she controlled herself, Alec came in front of her and everything broke down.

"Alec please!" She said. She felt tired. Hell, she was tired.

Alec walked into the room, his head hung low, "Can we talk normally Jade? Julia was right. We need to deal with this like adults."

"That's what we tried to earlier. Didn't go very well. Let's just...." She sighed, "Let's just stay away from each other. It's the best for both of us."

"But.... I need to explain."

"Don't you get it that talking to you is more painful than seeing you with Emma? Can't you see that this very difficult for me? Or don't you want to see?"

Till then both of them had been speaking in low voices, but Jade couldn't hold it in any longer. She burst out.

She took a deep breath, turned away from Alec and closed her eyes, "Just go Alec. Leave me alone for few minutes. Just.... Go..."

"I'm sorry...." She heard him leave the room, and she let go the breath she was holding.

She needed time to think to compose herself. When the knock on the door came again Jade didn't even bother to turn.

"Just leave me alone, will you! I don't want to talk to you right now. Don't you get that?" On her last words she turned around to face the door, her hair swinging around her.

"Expecting someone else were you?"

Instead of Alec at the door, as Jade had been expecting it was Matt. He had a concerned look on his face.

Jade let her tensed shoulders fall and she turned around again.

"I'm sorry." She muttered.

She heard Matt's shoes tap on the floor as he walked into the room and came to stand next to her.

"Are you okay, Jade? You look- for lack of a better word- disturbed."

It was true. Her face was pale and Matt could see the tension and stress that was flowing out of her body in waves.

Along with handfuls of hurt and pain.

"You could say that again. My life is very disturbing at the moment." Jade scoffed.

"Alec?"

The question was a simple one. It had to be answered with a simple yes or no. Even a shake of her head would have worked.

Then why was there a lump in a throat stopping her from answering.

She took deep gulps of air. Put all her mind in releasing the tension in her body and looked at Matt.

"I'm fine." She even managed to put on a small smile on her face.

But Matt saw right through her facade. He raised one eyebrow and repeated his question, "Alec?"

"Matt."

"Alec?"

Jade had to laugh. At the sound of her laughter Matt let a grin come on his face too.

"Yes. Alec. Who else will it be? I'm going to go mad. You know what I should do? Take a long holiday." Jade said.

Matt looked at her. Her shoulders had fallen and though she was trying to cover up her pain with a smile and silly behaviour, it was clearly visible in her eyes.

"You really need to take a break. That's all you need." He said. "All this has stressed you out and you're tired."

"Are you gay?" Jade asked.

"You should know... I was your boyfriend." Matt replied playing along.

She laughed, "It's just that how do you understand me so well. Know what I need. It's like you're not a guy. Atleast not like the guys I know."

"I'm a guy and you know me."

"You know what I mean."

He smiled, "Yes I do know what you mean. And to answer your question, no I'm not gay. I would have dressed a little better if I was."

"Yeah that's there."

"As for understanding you... It's partly because I'm a doctor it's kind of my job to understand what's wrong with people. And partly because I know you Jade."

Jade's face softened.

"Yes you do." She sighed, "It would have been so much easier if I would have fallen in love with you rather than that idiot."

"I like to think that." Matt replied.

"I should go back to the party. And I also need to apologise to Julia. I kind of snapped at her. Took out Alec's anger on her."

"That's harsh." He smirked.

Jade gave a breathy laugh and started walking out of the room. When she reached the door she turned around, "Matt you remember what I told you that day... The girl you will end up with will be really lucky."

"You bet." He grinned smugly.

Jade walked out of the room leaving Matt alone.

The smile slowly fell from his face.

"I wish you were the one." He sighed.

Jade walked back into the party. It was still in full swing.

She found Julia talking to Steve at the other side of the room. She walked up to her and pulled her into a hug.

"I'm sorry." She whispered into Julia's ear.

"It's okay... But Jade..." Julia pulled back with a concerned look on her face.

Jade shook her head, "No.. I'm fine. Let's leave all that."

She smiled and started a conversation with Steve, congratulating him about the good news.

She spent the rest of the night trying to avoid Alec and she was glad that she was successful.

Chapter 32

It was the morning after the engagement party and Emma could feel all the stress and fatigue of the last few days catch up with her.

She groaned, moaned and stretched before getting up.

It was a good thing that her parents had decided against staying back in Millbrooke and instead they had gone back to Chicago last night.

If either of the prim and proper Burns would have seen Emma still in her pyjamas at 9 in the morning they would have surely thrown a fit.

She went into the washroom and got about her usual morning routine.

While brushing her teeth, she wondered about all that she had heard last night about the childhood Alec, Jade, Julia all of them had spent here.

Everyone she had been introduced to had recollected stories about the absolutely notorious kids that Alec and Jade had been.

It sounded so much different than what her days growing up in London had been like.

She had attended tea parties with her mom, she had been dressed in perfect dresses and her mom had perfected her posture ever since she was 2.

As a kid she had never known what it was like to play pranks on her teachers, she had never had ice cream eating competitions.

No midnight snacks. No picnics at the bottom of the backyard.

She sighed. Her childhood had been controlled and thought out. Hell, her adulthood was also planned by her parents.

She splashed water on her face.

What was the use of thinking all this?

She showered and changed into a fresh pair of pants and a shirt.

Even her dressing sense was influenced by how her mom liked her to dress.

She went down with hopes of breakfast and a cup of tea. With all the stress from last night, she had ended up skipping dinner.

"Good morning, Emma!" Susan said cheerfully when she entered the kitchen.

As per her daily morning routine, Susan was making breakfast for all of them.

Even though it was almost 10 in the morning, except for Emma and Susan no one else was up as yet.

"Good morning, Susan!" Emma said and took a seat on one of the chairs near the kitchen island.

Susan flashed a smile at her, "What do you want for breakfast?"

"It's okay... You don't...." But before she could complete her refusal, her stomach gave a loud growl of hunger.

"I can hear." Laughed Susan, "I'm making eggs. Want some?"

"Sure." Laughed Emma, and she poured herself a glass of orange juice.

Susan scrambled some eggs and put them in front of her on a plate with a slice of toast.

"Thank you, Susan." Emma said and started gobbling the eggs.

Susan sat opposite her and took a sip of her coffee.

"Emma, I wanted to talk to you." She said.

Emma looked up, "Yes?"

"Well come with me to my room once you're done with break-fast."

Emma's curiosity was piqued she quickly finished her breakfast chasing the last bite with a large gulp of orange juice.

"In the Sheridan family, Sheridan is my maiden name, there had always been a tradition." Susan said as they walked together towards her room. "When a girl is going to become a bride, the eldest the mother or mother- in- law gives her a bracelet."

They entered the room. It was decorated beautifully in light colours of peach and beige. The room was neat and had loads of sunlight pouring in through the windows.

"A bracelet?" Emma asked.

"Yes a bracelet. A charm bracelet to be precise. You must have noticed me wearing mine." Susan went to her cupboard and took out a box from inside.

"Yes I did actually."

Emma took a seat on the edge if Susan's bed. She remembered the pretty bracelet on Susan's hand.

The charm bracelet she had been wearing had about 10 different charms on it and was jiggling while she worked.

Susan sat next to Emma and opened the box she had taken out of the cupboard, "So to keep along with the tradition I got something for you."

She took out a small box from inside the bigger one and handed it to Emma.

Emma opened it. There was a delicate, silver bracelet lying inside it. It shone against the blue velvet background.

"It's beautiful!" She gasped taking it out.

There was one small charm hanging from it. On closer inspection Emma noticed that it was a bird. It too was silver in colour with small blue gems instead of eyes.

"When my mom had given me my bracelet two days after I said yes to Jackson, it had only one charm. A dog."

Emma furrowed her eyebrows and gave a laugh.

"I know. It doesn't sound very sentimental and canines don't have as much emotional meaning as maybe a butterfly or a he art.... But mom used to always say it is necessary to be as faithful and loyal to whoever you have relationships with. Whether it's a relationship with a friend, spouse, family, everybody. So a dog."

Emma laughed, "That's sounds sensible."

She had a smile on her face but there was a terrible feeling of jealousy in her stomach.

She envied this relationship girls had with their mothers.

The little tips and lessons mothers gave their daughters. She had never been lucky enough to get any of those.

The only tips her mother had ever given her were about how she could get married to someone rich and get settled.

No special bracelets. No marital tips.

"I filled my bracelet up in the years to come. One charm for every significant event in my life." Susan continued, bringing Emma out of her thoughts. "When Julia was born it was a small doll. For Alec it was a little car. When Jackson died I put a J so he would always be close to me. I kept adding to it till now my bracelet is so clustered that you can't see one charm properly."

"It's your whole life in one charm bracelet." Emma said with a smile. She wished she could be like Susan. Spend her whole life and not regret a thing.

"Yes. Like a personal scrap book. Maybe that's what the Sheridan women wanted when they started the tradition."

Emma looked at the bracelet in her palm, "It's beautiful and I love it. It really means a lot to me."

And she meant it. Her own mother had never got something of this sort for her while Susan had just met her a few days back.

"You know, it took me quite some time to decide which charm to get for you. I decided to get you a bird yesterday morning."

"So that's where you went!" Exclaimed Emma.

"Yes. I went to get the bird charm. There's a simple reason behind it. A bird is the best way to remind yourself that sometimes freedom is necessary. Sometimes everyone needs to spread their wings and do what they want to do. What they feel like doing."

Emma knew why Susan was saying all this. She had been the only one who had noticed that Emma's behaviour changed around her parents.

"Should I put it on?" Susan said, breaking the silence which had followed her little speech.

Emma extended her hand so she could put it around her wrist.

The bracelet looked beautiful, slinking against her thin wrist.

"It looks really good." Emma said admiring the effect.

"I never thought my Alec would get married so soon. And I had thought that he would marry someone who was.... I don't know a little more like him...."

"Like Jade?" Emma interrupted the older lady.

Susan smiled, "Yes, I had always thought that they would end up together. But as long as he loves you and love him, how does it matter?"

Love?

The word had never been mentioned between Emma and Alec.

Emma cared about Alec and she knew that he cared about her too. But love...?

"And what if I say that we both are not in love with each other?"

If Susan was surprised by Emma's words she didn't let it show in her face. Her pretty face remained with a small smile on it, "Then I will say that it's better you both learn to love each other. Marriage is a big step and I atleast believe that love is necessary for it."

Emma thought about this. Maybe in a few years she would end up, not loving him, but atleast something which was pretty close to it.

But would Alec ever be able to fall in love with her?

"Life is very small Emma. And we're allowed to live it only once. It would be foolish of us to spend it without people who we really want to spend it with." Susan continued speaking, she held Emma's hand in hers. "In this life the best thing that you can do for yourself is spend it with the people who you love. I have spent my life. Alec, Julia, Amanda, Jade they have been there with me always. And of course Jackson. We had less time together. But it was good times."

Susan turned to look at the photo of her husband which was standing on her night table.

Emma wanted this.

She had never been a romantic person. Paula had never let her be one. But she wanted this in her life.

She wanted to spend her life with people who she loved and not regret a minute of it.

And Alec?

She wanted that for him too. And she knew marrying her would be the biggest mistake he could ever make.

She got up suddenly.

Surprised Susan also followed suit.

The first time when Emma had met Susan, she had been hugged. A very uncomfortable hug.

But this time when she initiated the hug she felt happy and relaxed.

"Thanks Susan. For everything." She said.

Susan placed a hand on Emma's cheek and smiled, "Don't thank me, honey! Just remember that you're a very sweet girl. You are!"

Emma smiled and ran out of her room she had to talk to Alec.

Before she could even take a step towards Alec's room her cell phone started ringing from it's place in her pocket.

She took it out and was surprised to see that the call was from her mother.

Instead of going in the direction of Alec's room she ducked into her room and answered the call.

"Hi mother." She said.

"Hello Emma. I just wanted to inform you that we are going to take the next flight back to London." Her mother's controlled voice came on.

"So fast?"

"Yes dear. Your father has some work pending. So we are leaving. How's everything over there?"

"Good.... Mother I wanted to ask you something."

Emma took a deep breathe. What she was going to say would take a lot of courage.

"Yes?"

"Mother.... Do you think it is necessary to be in love to get married and have a happy life?"

Emma anxiously waited for the outburst which was surely going to come and she was not disappointed.

"What is this about? Have you had a fight with Alexander? Give him the phone I will talk to him." Paula's voice sounded like she was speaking through gritted teeth.

"No mother. I didn't have a fight with Alec." Emma took another huge gulp of air, "It's just that... Just answer my question."

She heard her mother sigh into the speaker, "Well that is not what I believe. I didn't love your dad when we got married. And I had a happy life, didn't I?"

The life which her mother had lived was not the kind of life Emma wanted for herself.

Paula and Mark Burns were married only because the marriage certificate said so.

They slept in different bedrooms as soon as she was born. They never spent time together.

Her father was too busy with his work, whiskey and colleagues.

While her mom kept herself occupied with gossip, tea parties and shopping.

Neither disturbed or interfered in the other ones life.

"What is going on Emma?" Paula asked when her daughter didn't say anything.

"I think.... I think I'm going to break off this engagement."

"What?" Her mother almost screeched, "Have you gone mad?"

"No mother. Mother, I don't love him. And he.... He doesn't love me. What is the use of getting married?"

"Emmaline Maeve Burns, the use is that you can live a happy life. Imagine you can leave your job, you will be financially secure. You would do whatever you want to do."

"I love my job and about being financially secure, I don't need to married to be financially secure. I can take care of myself." Emma said, "And anyways I think Alec is in love with someone else."

Emma would not have believed what Paula next said if she as not heard it with her own ears.

"So?" Her mother asked.

"So? So I don't think we should get married. We both won't be happy. Why to trap him in a marriage he doesn't want to be in?" Emma sat on the bed.

Speaking to her mom was always infuriating. She just refused to understand.

"If he wants someone else, he can have a relationship with her. What is the need of breaking the engagement for that?"

Emma stood up. She couldn't believe her ears.

"Did you just say that? Really?" She asked in disbelief, "Is that the kind of life you want me to have mother?"

"Emma listen..."

But Emma didn't let her mother explain, "I don't want to listen. And I really don't care what you think. For the first time I'm going to take a decision for myself and not listen and agree to do every single thing you and father tell me to do. Bye."

She kept the phone before her mother could say anything more.

And in that moment she felt a sense of peace instead of the guilt she had expected.

Never had she ever done something like this before in her life.

Her conversations with her parents had been polite to the point of formal.

This was not the first time her mother had said something which had made her angry or hurt her. But this was the first time she had stood up to her.

The phone which she had dropped on the bed started ringing again. She looked at the screen and was not surprised to see that it was her mother calling.

She knew what the conversation would be like.

You're a disgrace on the Burns family.

Is this the way I taught you to speak to your parents?

We do so much for you and what do we get in exchange?

She didn't want to hear all these words which had been repeated over and over again every time she had done something wrong over the years.

She let the call go to voice mail and then switched off the mobile.

She needed time to talk to Alec and think.

She got out of the room looking for Alec.

But his room was empty. He was not there in the living room and not in the courtyard either.

She looked in the kitchen. Alec wasn't there but Steve stood with two cups of coffee in his hand.

"Good morning!" He said in his cheerful voice.

Emma smiled, "G'morning. Have you seen Alec anywhere?"

"No. Well not since he left." Steve replied.

"Left?"

"Yeah... He had some work at the construction site. He left about 20 minutes back."

When she had been talking to her mother.

"Is there a problem?" Steve asked noticing the frown on her face.

She shook her head, "No everything is fine. I just wanted to talk to him. I'll let you go. Julia must be waiting for her coffee."

Steve grinned and walked away with the coffee.

Maybe it was not such a bad thing that Alec was not at home. It would give her some time to think about what exactly did she want to do.

With this in her head, Emma made herself the cup of tea she had been dying for since morning and took it to her room.

Chapter 33

"Emma."

Emma was startled out of her thoughts by someone knocking on the door to her room.

"Yes?"

Julia poked her head into the room, "There's a call for you on the landline."

"Landline?" Emma asked surprised. Then she remembered that her mobile had been switched off for the last three hours. "I'll just come. Is it my mother?"

"No. It's some Marianne Jordan from Bridge and Co."

"Oh! I'm coming."

Emma got up and rushed down to where the phone was in the living room.

Marianne Jordan was Mr Bridge's personal assistant.

When Emma had gone to the Chicago office, they had asked for a alternative number they could contact on if she wasn't available.

Since she had already come to Millbrooke and she was staying at the Carter house she had called Alec and asked for the landline number.

She had give that number to them. So it didn't come as a surprise that they were calling her on this number.

She went to the living room and picked up the phone.

"Hello!" She said into the speaker.

""Hello. Am I talking to Miss Emmaline Burns?"

"Yes this is she. May I know who this is?"

"Hello, Miss Burns. I'm Marianne Jordan. We met recently at Bridge and Co. Chicago." The sweet woman replied.

"Oh yes. Hello, Miss Jordan. It's good to hear from you." Emma said. She propped her hip on the arm of the sofa.

"You too Ma'am. Mr Bridge wanted to talk to you about some important business. I couldn't reach you on your mobile."

"Yes my mobile is out of order at the minute. Do you know what Mr Bridge wants to talk about?"

"No Ma'am. But you can ask him yourself. If you wait a second I'll just transfer the call to his office."

Emma was surprised to hear from Mr Bridge. They had met just a few days back.

He was a fun man in his 50's with brown hair and a small bald patch.

"Hello!" Mr Bridge's jolly voice came on after Emma waited for a few seconds.

"Hello Mr Bridge." Emma said.

"Miss Burns, I was hoping to talk to you. I have a great opportunity for you. Great opportunity." He sounded really excited and happy, which was not very different for him, but it made Emma curious.

"Opportunity, Sir?"

"Yes. You remember you met Mrs Dimatto?" He asked.

Mrs Agnes Dimatto was an old lady who was at a very high rank in the company. The only person who worked over her was Mr

Bridge himself. She had around 30 people reporting to her directly, from Bridge and Co. from all around the world

"Ofcourse sir. I remember her." This was getting more and more interesting.

"Well she is planning to retire. We will soon be losing a very valued and hard working employee."

"That's unfortunate sir. Mrs Dimatto was the best in her job." Emma said.

"Yes she was. But her retirement means that we have a job opening here at the Chicago office and I want to offer it to you."

For a second Mr Bridge's words didn't register in Emma's head.

She replied after a few minutes, "What?"

"I know you're surprised, Miss Burns. But it's a golden opportunity for you and I don't think you should miss it."

"But sir it's a very high post. I'm... I'm not that..."

"Experienced? Good? Deserving? Which one take your pick. I think you are all those. You are the best at what you do and I think you will be he best for this job too."

"That's... That's... I'm...." She kept stuttering, she didn't know what to say.

It really was a great opportunity for her. It was a respected job and it meant a promotion for her, by a huge leap.

"I'm honoured that you thought I'm capable sir." She said atlast when her hysterics had subsided.

"Yes but Miss Burns, taking this job would mean that you have to move to Chicago from London. Will you be comfortable doing that?"

Emma had spent her whole life in London. She had never lived in any other city. Let alone country and continent.

But taking the job in Chicago would mean staying away from her parents for a few days. The Burns wouldn't definitely intimidate across the Atlantic.

"Yes sir. I'll take the job." She said immediately without any hesitation.

"Miss Burns, the job will be open for sometime. You can take some time to think over it before you come to a decision." Mr Bridge said, he sounded surprised at her haste to give him a reply.

Emma grinned, "I'm sure, sir. It's not a hard decision to make."

"That's great. That's really good. When is the soonest that you can come to the office? We have a lot to talk about and discuss."

"Tomorrow?"

"That's great. See you tomorrow then, Miss Burns. You're going to be a big shot pretty soon."

Emma kept the phone and couldn't help but grin like a psychotic person.

This was not only a very big leap for her career, it would help her settle her personal life, too.

She had to talk to Alec soon.

She was atlast going to do things she loved to do and wanted to do in her life. To occupy his mind and to keep himself from cursing at his life the whole day, Alec had worked his ass of at the construction site. Working along with all the workers.

After all the hard work he would feel his muscles cramping up as he sat on the front porch.

"Hi!"

Alec was snapped out of his thought by Emma who walked onto porch with two glasses of wine in her hand.

"Hello!" He said.

"Can I sit?"

"Sure." He moved a little so that Emma could sit next to him.

She handed him one of the glasses in her hand.

"Thanks."

They took sips of the wine in silence.

"I got a job offer." Emma said, breaking the silence.

Alec raised an eyebrow, "Job offer?"

"Mr Bridge called this afternoon." She explained about the promotion.

"That's great, Emma! It will be a great opportunity for you."

"I know. But I would have to live in Chicago...."

"Oh! Then what about the.... Uh.... Enga...."

"The engagement?" She smiled at the way he was stuttering, "That's what I actually wanted to talk to you about."

"Talk to me.... What do you mean?"

He was not looking at Emma.

"You love Jade. And for some unfathomable reasons she loves you too." Alec turned around to stare at her with shock written in block letters over his face. "And I've been the bitch who was coming in between both of you. Am I right?"

"Emma?"

"I know what you're going to say. There's nothing like that. I really care about you. You're not a bitch. But you don't love me Al!"

Alec didn't know what to say. He couldn't understand where Emma was going with this conversation.

He just kept looking at her face.

There was a smile on her face, which surprised him even more.

"One thing that I learned today is that if one wants to be without any regrets at the end of his or her life, it's necessary to spend it with the people who you really love."

"What are you saying Emma?" Alec asked.

"Al, this.... Relationship... Meeting your parents... The engagem ent... Till today it has been a game for me. An easy way to prove myself to my parents. To earn their love. That's the reason I turned a blind eye to what was happening between you and Jade. It was pretty clear. But do you think, telling Mark and Paula Burns that their daughter could not even keep a guy's attention till their wedding, would have proved anything to them?"

"It was not like that. Jade... Me.... I don't know... I'm sorry Emma."

"I should be the one saying sorry. It was a game for me. A quest. But today I realised something, children don't need to prove themselves to their parents. Parents love their kids anyways. And all the decisions I've been taking over the days, I have never made them as myself. I always thought, what would mother want me to do? What would father expect? And because of this stupid game I was going to spoil your life Alec. So I'm sorry."

"So you're saying that...."

"I'm saying that I'm taking the job. In Chicago. I'll live there, while you live here in Millbrooke with your family. Work on Wanderlust. And please go back to Jade."

Alec let his shoulders sag, dejectedly, "She doesn't love me anymore. It's not going to make any difference."

"That she does. She does love you. I don't know why... You're a fool. You jump to conclusions. You take stupid decisions. You never ever keep your stuff in the place where it belongs. You always throw the wet towel on the bed. You don't have a good fashion sense. But she loves you."

Alec smiled, "I do love you, you know?"

"I know. But you're not in love with me. I'm leaving tomorrow for Chicago. So before I leave, friends?" Emma held up her glass which was half filled with wine.

"Friends." Alec tapped his own glass to hers.

They sat together on the porch sipping from their glasses. They didn't talk.

Both of them had a lot to think about. "So bye Julia!" Emma said hugging her.

Julia hugged back, "We'll be living in the same city now. We'll meet up."

Emma smiled, "Sure. And all the best for the baby. I know he or she is going to be as beautiful as her dad and as clever as her mom."

Julia and Steve both laughed at that.

Next Emma hugged Steve, "All the best to you, because you're going to be living with a very hormonal woman soon. Please refrain from murdering each other."

"It will be difficult but we'll try." Grinned Steve.

Emma smiled and she walked to Susan.

"Bye sweetie." Susan said as they hugged.

Emma had once been uncomfortable with hugging these people, but in just a few days she had become like a small part of their family.

"Thank you Susan. For doing something even my mother didn't. And thank you for making me feel like a part of your family." She said.

"You are a part of our family. I got another daughter."

Emma smiled and held out her palm, the charm bracelet was lying in it. "I wanted to give this back to you."

"Keep it. It's yours now."

"But..."

Susan interrupted her, "It's yours now Emma. I got it for you. And it will always remind you of us."

Emma hugged Susan again and then let her put the bracelet around her wrist again.

"Bye stranger." She said when it was Alec's chance.

"Bye Emma." Alec replied, "I really am going to miss you."

"I'll miss you too. Here you go." She took of the ring from her finger and placed it in his palm, closing it over the ring. "You know what to do Alec. You have to talk to Jade. Apologise to her, tell her that we broke the engagement and please, please tell her you love her."

Alec grinned, "I will, I promise."

"If you don't I'm going to come back from Chicago and kick your ass."

"You can try to." Alec replied. "Emma you sure you're going to be fine alone in Chicago?" He asked in a more serious note.

"Yes Alec. I'm not 12. I'll survive. I need some time to stay away from my parents and figure out what I want to do."

"All the best with that."

They hugged each other for a little longer.

Their relationship had had it's ups and downs but overall it had been quite special.

They were coming out from it as friends, and that was what mattered.

Emma waved goodbye to everyone standing in the front yard for the last time and then got into the back seat of the cab.

She drove away with the whole Carter family waving at her till they couldn't see the car any longer.

She turned in her seat.

She was going to really miss Millbrooke and the quirky people that lived there.

She didn't really regret all that had happened in the last few days. Except for maybe the fact that she had made some horrible mistakes.

But she had met the Carter family and had come out from all the mess with new friends. And Susan.

They passed Jade's apartment building. She knew she should have taken some time to speak to Jade also herself. Apologise to her, too.

But she knew that she wouldn't be able to tell her everything face to face.

She took out the stuff she had out in her handbag and started writing a letter to Jade.

She started writing stuff, that till yesterday she herself had not known. Or believed.

Chapter 34

Alec could not wait to tell Jade.

He had been a jerk to her. Jumping to conclusions taking rash decisions, not talking to her about his feelings.

But he was going set all his mistakes right. He was going to tell her everything, even if she didn't love him. Or she didn't feel the same way about him.

He remembered the kiss from that day, he had a good feeling she had feelings for him.

The grin on Alec's face was stuck as he drove to Jade's apartment building.

The security guard of her apartment building said that she was not home and had left in the morning.

Alec sat back in the car and dialled Jason's number quickly.

"Hey Alec! What's up man?"Said Jason on picking up the phone.

"Hey man! Is Nicole with you right now?" Alec said without any preamble.

"Yeah she's here. Is something wrong?"Jason sounded confused.

"No. Nothing's wrong. I just need to talk to her."

"Just a sec. I'll give her the phone."Jason put his hand over the speaker and yelled, "Nicole! Alec needs to talk to you!"

"Alec? Why?"

Nicole sounded equally confused.

"Hey Alec!"

Alec sighed once her voice came on. There was only one person who was sure to know where Jade was.

"Hi Nicole! I called to ask if you know where Jade is. I mean I'm standing near her apartment building. But the security guard said she's not home."

"Jade? She's gone for a book reading at the new cafe across town. Alec don't go there. Just don't. She doesn't need that....." Nicole asked.

"I have to, Nicole. I'm sorry. Thanks!" Alec interrupted her.

Before listening to Nicole's reply Alec kept the phone and threw it in the passenger seat.

He started the car and drove to the cafe. Barely within the speed limit.

The new cafe was comfortable and smelt of coffee, as Alec entered the air conditioned room, he could see there was a huge crowd of people in there.

"Hello sir! Can I help you?" One of the employees came up to Alec and asked.

"Is this where Jade Tucker's book reading is happening?" He asked.

The brown haired girl looked confused. Most of the Jade Tucker fans were women.

"Yes sir. But the book reading is over. The question answer session is going on now."

That was a good thing. It meant he would be able to speak to her earlier.

"Thanks."

Alec flashed her a smile and hurried there.

The area was crowded with women all with signs of recent tears on their faces.

That's what Jade's novels did to women. One novel and they couldn't stop their tears.

And there in the middle sat Jade. She was wearing a plain white shirt and black trousers.

Her black hair was open and she was wearing her reading glasses.

Just as Alec was looking at her she laughed at something one of the girls sitting next to her said.

Alec couldn't believe he had not seen it before.

She was the one for him. And she was perfect in every way.

"Come on everyone we start the question answer session now ."Alec recognised Jade's editor, though he did not remember her name.

All the women gathered around Jade again and sat on the stools kept over there.

"Okay.... So... Go ahead ask me questions about anything... Go wild!" Jade smiled her usual goofy grin. Though the smile didn't reach her green eyes now.

All the women tittered. They started asking questions about all her different novels.

Alec tuned out the noise and just looked at Jade reply with smiles and nods of her head.

"We have been reading about love stories in all your novels. But no one knows if you have a love story yourself." A girl in a bright green sweater asked Jade.

The smile on Jade's face disappeared.

"You want to know about my love story?" She asked.

All the humour from her voice was gone. Alec started listening to what was going on from where he was standing.

He was standing behind one of the pillars, so though he could see Jade, he was not in Jade's vision line.

"Yeah... I mean your such a romantic person yourself. So I'm sure everyone over here wants to know." The same girl said.

"Being a romantic person does not mean I have a great love story." Jade said flatly, looking straight at the girl.

"So does that mean you're not in love with anyone?" Another girl asked.

"I didn't say that."

Alec's ears stood up at that.

"So who are you in love with?"

The first girl asked her again

"You'll really want to know?"

Jade eyes had become sad and downcast.

All the women and girls started nodding and saying yes.

"Okay. Here goes." Jade sighed. "I met him on the playground of my kindergarten school. Our first day. I was crying. He was grinning. We became best friends over a shared love for p b and j. We grew up. I fell in love. With him. He fell in love. With his dream. He went away and I didn't get a chance to tell him that I loved him."

Alec just gaped at her.

Did she really mean it? Had she really been in love with him?

Was she still in love with him?

"Now he's back." She continued, staring at her fingers, "And sensibly it means that this is my chance to tell him that I love him. Because the fool that I am I still love him. But guess what? He get this super hot, super glamorous girlfriend with a British accent with him. And me? I've had 15 boyfriends since he left. 15. And I'm still in love with him. He asked me to be friends with him again. Just friends. And me being the stupid person that I am I said yes. And then a few days later he comes and tells me that he is getting engaged to his girlfriend. And thought I want to hate her I can't. He is getting married. The guy who didn't believe in the institution of marriage or love is now looking at rings for his pretty blonde fiancé. And I just stand over there. Helplessly in love with him. I'm in love with my best friend who is getting married. And I'm the most hopeless stupid girl on this planet. So that's my story. Any questions?"

Tears had popped up in Jade's eyes while all the women just stared at her.

The green sweater lady looked like she was about to say something, but Alec beat her to it.

"Why didn't you tell him, before he left?" He asked coming out from behind the pillar.

Jade's eyes widened.

What was he doing here?

She had just spilt her sob story in front of a crowd of romantic women while he was standing right there with his hands shoved into his pockets and an expressionless face.

"Alec." Jade gasped.

"Jade, why didn't you tell me?"

All the women started gaping at him when they realised he was the one Jade had been talking about.

"I have to go..."

Jade got up and ran out of the cafe before Alec could say anything else. She didn't give one look to him.

She ran out of cafe blindly, while all hell broke loose inside. The women all turned to Alec, most of them yelling and the others glaring at him.

Alec turned to leave and follow Jade but someone caught his arm and stopped him.

He turned around to see Jade's editor standing with a firm grip on his elbow. Her face was hard and her eyes were throwing daggers at him.

The women behind her were being calmed down by the waiters.

"So you are the famous Alexander Carter? I'm sorry but I can't really say that it's nice to meet you, because it's not." She said.

"Look I need to go right now. Whatever problem you have with me we can sort it out later." Alec tried to free his hand.

But for a petite girl like her, Jade's editor, he still couldn't re-member her name, had an extremely firm hold on his hand.

"No. You're not going to follow." She snapped, "She needs to stay away from you. God knows you do more harm to her than good."

"Look Miss..."

"It's Blake. Blake Hastings."

Blake, quite a manly name for girl that petite and feminine, thought Alec.

"Okay... Miss Hastings. I don't know why you hate me so much, but I do know one thing. I need to talk to Jade."

Blake's expression hardened a little more, if that was even possible, "Isn't all the hurt you caused her enough? Why do you want to make it worse?"

"That's the thing... I want to talk to her so I can make it better. Apologise for what I've done..."

Blake's grip on his hand had loosened, Alec knew that if he wanted to he could remove his hand any minute. But somehow, he knew this was going to be his way of asking permission to make all his wrongs right.

"If you hurt her even a little bit more, I swear on God, I'll find and kick your ass so hard that you won't be able to walk, sit or lie down for the rest of your life."

With this vicious threat, Blake let his arm go.

Alec didn't know how he was supposed to react to the warning, so he turned around and started running, before she changed her mind................Jade sat in her car and drove home as fast as she could without being pulled over or killing anyone.

Her vision was blurred by the tears in her eyes and she could still feel the warmth on her cheeks from the blush.

After not seeing Alec ever since their confrontation at the engagement party, she had gotten used to the pain.

Alec was always there at the back of her mind, but she had adjusted and started doing her daily work around it.

When she had gone for the book reading, after a million requests from Blake, the last thing she had expected was to see Alec over there.

She reached her building parked the car and ran up to her apartment.

She closed the door and stood with her back pressed to it, breathing heavily.

Would he come?

She didn't know whether she wanted him to or no.

But right now, she sat down on the sofa and let the tears fall.

Chapter 35

Alec reached her apartment building and saw the car parked. He himself pulled over next to her Cadillac and got down.

He went up the stairs, his mind racing about what he was going to say.

He knocked on the door, "Jade it's me... Alec."

Jade who was inside still sitting on the sofa though her tears had stopped a few minutes back gasped.

"Go away! I don't want to talk to you." She yelled back.

She was not going to open the door. She was not going to talk to him.

"Please Jade. Just open the door once. Give me one chance. Listen to what I have to say. Please."

Alec was begging and he didn't care. He just wanted her to open the door and let him inside.

"Just go away!" Jade sobbed.

Alec pulled back his fist and let it bang on the door.

The loud noise made Jade jump.

"I'm not going anywhere till you don't open that door of yours. I don't care if it's today, tomorrow or the next month. I'm waiting here. Till you don't talk to me." Alec said.

Jade got up and walked into her room, closing the door behind her.

She needed to blank out.

She needed the comfort of dreamless sleep. She fell on the bed still fully clothed and fell asleep. When Jade opened her eyes there was an orangish light streaming in through the window in her room.

A glance at the digital clock in her night stand told her that it was 5:30 in the evening. She had slept for nearly 6 hours.

She got up groggily and walked into her kitchen.

Just as she filled a glass with water and took the first sip, her cell phone rang from inside her bag.

She pulled it out to see that it was a call from Blake.

She pressed the answer button, "Hello?"

"Jade! Where the hell have you been? I've been calling you non stop ever since you left. If you want to kill me just feed me some peanuts. Why worry me to death?" Blake yelled.

Had it been any other time, Jade would have smiled at that. Blake had a terrible allergy to peanuts and anything made from them.

"I'm sorry the phone was in my bag. And I fell asleep." She replied.

Her throat felt hoarse from all the crying and yelling.

"Why does you voice sound like...? Were you crying Jade? Is it because of Alec? Oh! He's going to get his ass kicked." Blake snarled.

The mention of Alec's name made Jade wonder if he was still outside her apartment.

She took another sip of water, "I'm fine Blake. Really."

"Okay. Though I don't believe you. But you won't let me help." Blake said, "Call Nicole once. She's been worried about you too."

"I will." Jade said, "Can I call you back later? I need to go now."

The urge to see if Alec was outside was unbearable.

She said a quick bye to Blake and went to her door.

She pulled it open and peered outside.

There was Alec sleeping on the floor outside her apartment.

His back was propped on the walk as he slept. His hair was ruffled and legs were sprawled so that it would be difficult for anyone to go past him.

Jade quickly closed the door before a sob left her mouth.

I'm not going to cry.

I'm not going to cry again.

She kept repeating the words to herself. She picked up her mobile to see that there were 15 missed calls from Blake, 12 from Nicole and 28 from Alec.

There were 12 voicemails from Alec. She clicked on the first one and let his warm voice flow over her, as she sat on the sofa.

Jade... Open the door once! Please. Let me explain. Let me talk to you. I'm not going anywhere till I don't talk to you.

The other voicemails were along the same lines. In some of them, he sounded angry and fed up, then the next one he apologised.

Jade listened to each one of them and curled up into the sofa.

The past few nights she had barely slept. Either she dreamt about Alec or she sat up writing till she was drop dead tired to stay away from the dreams.

With Alec's fading voice she let sleep catch up with her again. Alec woke up with a stiff back and a throbbing head.

Someone nearby was giggling for some reason.

He opened his eyes squinting because of the sunlight that was in his face.

There was two little girls standing in front of him. Both of them were dressed to go to school and were carrying bags.

Alec pushed himself up, "What time is it?" He asked the girls who were still giggling and were standing a few steps away from him.

They looked like sisters, with similar blonde ponytails and blue eyes.

"We're not allowed to talk to strangers. Especially homeless ones." Said the girl who seemed to be the elder one.

Alec smirked, "I'm not homeless."

"Only homeless people sleep in the floor outside." Said the younger one, "So you're lying. We're not allowed to talk to liars too."

Just as Alec was about to answer that, a woman came out from the apartment behind the girls.

She had to be their mother, because it was pretty evident that they had inherited they're looks from her.

"Melissa, Aubrey! You both forgot your water bottles." She said handing the bottles to the girls.

"Mom see!" The younger one said pouting a small chubby index finger at Alec.

The mother looked up to see what had gotten her daughter so excited and she was surprised to see a full grown man sitting on the floor.

It looked like he had spent the night there too.

"Hello ma'am!" Alec said pulling himself to his feet.

"What are you doing here?" The woman said before deliberately holding her daughters fingers and pushing her hand down. "Aubrey it is rude to point."

"He's homeless Mom." The elder one, Melissa, said gleefully.

"I assure you ma'am I'm no such thing. You're daughters seen to have misunderstood." Alec started to explain.

"I know. I heard you talk to Jade. Not that it was to hard to hear, what with both of you yelling." The woman shrugged.

Angela Webber had been living in the apartment opposite Jade for the past 3 years, and never had there ever been as much excitement as the last couple of weeks.

Alec's flushed a little, "I'm sorry about that."

"No problem. If you want something to eat, I could give it to you while you wait."

Alec looked up in surprise.

Why was this woman helping him?

"I know I know.... You're thinking why am I helping you. Well there's a simple reason." Angela said, "Only a guy who is in love would agree to spend almost 24 hours outside a girls door."

Alec didn't reply to that he nodded his head in the form of an answer.

"I'll just drop these little ones to the school and come back and give you something to eat."

Angela flashed a smile and walked away with the two girls bouncing along with her. An hour later, Alec sat down outside the door again and dialled Jade's number.

At least now his stomach was not growling from starvation.

While having ham sandwiches and cups of coffee, Alec had spilt the whole story to Angela.

He had learnt that she was a divorced mother, taking care of her two daughters alone and working at the same time, while their dad lived a happy life in New York.

Now he had to go back to trying to convince Jade to open the door and listen to him.

The cell rang.

But no one picked up. Instead he heard the door open and there stood Jade in a pair of shorts and a tank top.

Her eyes were blood shot and her face looked splotchy.

"Come in Alec." She said in a defeated tone.

Chapter 36

"Do you want coffee? Or something to eat? You must be hungry." Asked Jade as she walked into the kitchen.

His shirt was crumpled and his hair was standing. His eyes were red from lack of sleep. He looked like he had spent the night on someone's floor.

Which he actually had.

Alec followed her in, "No. Actually I just had breakfast. Your neighbour..."

"Angela has always been a kind soul. Have a cup of coffee to give me company?"

Jade had lived with Angela in the apartment next to hers for many years now and she had never seen her turn away someone who was in need.

"Okay."

They stood in silence in the kitchen while Jade made the coffee and poured it in two cups.

She handed one to Alec and took her own cup into the living room.

Once they were sitting on the sofas and sipping from their cups Alec started saying, "Jade I wanted to...."

"Wait Alec. Let me first say the things I wanted to say. Please!" Jade stopped him.

Alec nodded his head.

"Look I love you. And that became quite clear when you heard me say it in front of the whole cafe yesterday."

"You know that's what hurt the most. You could tell all those women in the cafe but you could not tell me?" Alec spoke up.

"But you... Alec... The reason I did not tell you anything is that, you were dating. Emma. You're engaged. To Emma. And you will eventually marry. Emma."

"And what about before I went to Thailand. 8 years back." He kept his cup down and looked at Jade.

Jade let her head fall into her palms, "You were so in love with your dream. Your dream of starting Wanderlust and making it big in the travel industry. I love you and your commitment to that dream was one of the main reasons I fell in love with you."

"And Matt?"

"Matt and I, Alec there's nothing between us!" Jade gave a small laugh, "He knows, he knows that I love you."

"He does?" Alec was surprised.

"Yes he does. Since the day we all met in the club." Jade said exasperated with his inability to understand anything, "I've been trying to tell you that there's nothing between us. Yes we were in a relationship. And yes he fell in love with me. And I'm not proud of that. I never wanted that to happen. Because I know that I won't be able to reciprocate those feelings. He wanted to move in with me... Eventually get married. But I... I couldn't cause I was in love with you. So we broke up. The day you saw us in Jo's was the first day after months that we had met. And he wanted... He wanted us to get back together."

"Then why didn't you?"

"Because Alec I knew you were coming back... And I hoped that maybe this time I would be able to tell you how I feel. If you wouldn't have come back, maybe I would have said yes to him."

"Oh!" Alec was speechless.

So there was really nothing between the two of them. Matt and Jade were not together.

"Now answer one of my questions. Why did you propose to Emma in such a hurry? Even though you told me that you were confused and that you didn't know what to do." Jade asked.

"I... After the two of you left from the club... I was worried about you. So I came here to see if you were okay. And Matt opened the door. He was not wearing a shirt... And..." Alec stuttered.

Jade interrupted him, "And you just assumed that we lied to you'll in the club and came home because we wanted to jump into bed?"

"Yes." Alec said ashamed of himself, "And it... I was... I didn't know how to cope with how I felt about that. So I ran. I went home and proposed to Emma."

"That was a very good reaction. Obviously asking me about the truth would have been too easy for Mr Alexander Carter." She said sarcastically. "You never could stop yourself from jumping to conclusions could you?"

Alec went to press the bridge of his nose, but as soon as his fingers touched it he winced and let his hand drop.

The soreness was still there, though the bruise had almost disappeared.

"Is it still sore?" Jade asked having noticed what happened.

Alec shook his head, "It's okay."

"I'm sorry... About the punch and the slap during the engagement party. You somehow always brought out the violent side of me." Jade said with a small smile, despite all that was happening.

Alec too smiled back, "We both have done something's which we regret haven't we?"

"Yes. You more than me." She replied.

"I want to be with you Jade."

"Alec... Please." Jade said. She felt a twinge in her heart when he said it.

She knew it wouldn't take much convincing on his part for her to give in.

But she couldn't. Because she had seen how happy Emma had looked during the party.

She had hated her the first time they had met, but somehow over the days Emma had made a small spot for herself in her heart.

She couldn't do that to her. She couldn't hurt her in that way.

"Look we both have made mistakes... Can't we just....?"

Jade shook her head, "No we can't."

Alec sighed, "Will you... Can you give me another chance Jade?"

"Alec, I'm tired. And I can't do all this anymore. Can we just agree to be friends again?" Jade asked, though it hurt her tremendously to say those words.

"What about the fact that we love each other?" Alec's voice was gruffer than normal as he spoke.

"I don't know."

Alec stood up and walked to the door of the apartment, "I don't know if you can... Be just friends. You know we can't be friends. I guess this is how it ends."

Jade saw a flash of hurt in his eyes, but before she could say anything he turned around.

He opened the door and walked out.

Before the door closed behind him he just called out one thing, "Emma broke off the engagement."

Before Jade could say anything else the door closed and she was left alone in the apartment.

Was it true? Was Alec really not engaged any longer?

Chapter 37

Jade had found out a way to stop thinking about Alec all the time.

She immersed herself in her work.

She had been writing feverishly. Going through the love story she was currently writing as fast as she could.

Thought she had to admit that the story had a little more depressing theme to it than her other novels.

She had been attending meetings with the representatives of the publishing house, spending time with her friends and the twins.

And completely avoiding any contact with Alec.

A recent conversation with her mom had surprised her when she had been told that Alec was still in town.

But she had immediately changed the topic. Alec's name always brought a pang to her heart.

She had a bad headache when she came back home from the meeting with the publishing house.

Jade seemed to be living on aspirin and coffee nowadays instead of food.

She went into the kitchen to make herself a cup of coffee, when she noticed that the post that she had got to her apartment the day before was lying on the table.

Jade went and picked up the letters going through them one at a time.

Bills.

A postcard from Cousin Maria.

A letter from Emma.

Wait... A letter from Emma.

Jade kept the other letters back on the table and tore open Emma's letter from the envelope.

There were two full pages filled with Emma's neat cursive hand-writing.

Why was she writing a letter to her?

Jade sat back and started reading the letter, her headache for-gotten.

Hi Jade,

I am sure you are extremely surprised to get a letter from me. But to be honest I do not know how to call you and tell all that I have to say to you. So a letter was my safest option. Anyways I am British, if we are taught anything, it is to write good letters. I am writing this letter in the car on the way to Chicago. I will drop it in the postbox as soon as I reach there. Well atleast I hope I end up with enough courage to do that. The main reason why I am writing this letter is that I want to apologise.

For everything that I have done since we met. The argument, the threatening. But more than that I want to apologise for closing my eyes and refusing to see what was happening in front of me. I knew from the first time I was introduced to you- maybe from before-that the thing between you and Alec was much more than just friendship.But I made a decision to close my eyes and ignore it. I was like the ostrich, who buries his head in the ground when enemies attack, thinking that if it can't see the problem the problem doesn't exist. I thought that if I couldn't see the connection between you both it was not really there. So I pretended.Pretended to think that you'll are friends. Pretended to be jealous when I saw you both together, when actually I just wanted a reason to tell Alec to propose to me.Now about that. I know putting blame on others is an easy way to get off.

I am not going to do that. But there is one thing I have realised, there were certain things that were put into my head from when I was young. Some very clear rules and expectations that were set for me. Expectations I wanted to live up to.My decisions were not really mine they were already made by my parents. You have met them. You know how they are.Susan did the thing what my mother should have done long back. She taught me what being in love was. She told me what caring for someone was.I broke the engagement. Not because of anything else but because I know I was not in love with Alec. And I also know that Alec was going ahead with the whole thing because he is too sweet to hurt me.I broke the engagement and that's the reason I am on my way to Chicago. I am taking up a job there. Not only because it's a promotion and a good opportunity for me. But because I want- I need- some time away from my parents.I have to decide what I really want from my life. And this time it has to be me who makes the decision.

I guess this is my second chance at the life I really want to live.And since we are on the topic of second chances... I know I'm not the best person to tell you this and I know there is absolutely no reason for you to listen to me.But Jade, listen to me and give Alec another chance. What you both have is hard to find and very easy to loose.I know he is stupid, reckless, and absolutely foolish sometimes- well most of the times- but he is caring and sweet too. And he really loves you.Susan told me one thing which will always stay with me.She said that the best thing we can do for ourselves in this life is spend it with the people we love.I don't know if I will find those people with whom I really want to spend my life, but for you... They are right in front of you. Alec is right in front of you.This is one long letter. And I don't even know what I have written. But please give what I have said- well written a thought.Give him another chance.I hope you have a great life ahead of you and I hope you forgive me for all that I have done.All the best! Emma.PS:- The green dress that I gave you the first night we met.... You remember? Well I hope it really reminds you of me.

Chapter 38

Jade let Emma's letter drop to the table.

She needed to talk to Alec.

Emma was right. What she and Alec had was beautiful and she was letting her stupid ego come in the way of her love.

This was her one chance to have the kind of love story she had always wanted.

And if she let it go.

If she let Alec go.

She was going to regret it.

She would have to stay like this, spending her whole life writing about perfect love stories when she let hers get away.

There was already a possibility that he had gone.

But she had to take a chance.

She didn't have the heart to call up Alec and hear from him that he had gone back. She didn't think she would be able to bear that. So she decided to call Julia.

As she picked up her cell phone and dialled Julia's number she remembered the way Alec had smiled the first day they met after he came back.

She remembered the whole day they had spent together.

The coffee he had left for her after that night in the pub.

The kiss on the playground.

The way he had slept outside her door waiting for her.

The look of hurt in his eyes before he left.

"Hello!" Julia's voice snapped Jade out of her thoughts.

"Hey Jules! It's me Jade."

"I know! Hi! You've been avoiding me haven't you? I'm going back to Chicago tomorrow Jade." Julia whined.

"I'm sorry about that." And Jade really was. "I promise I'll meet you today. But first tell me something. Is.... Is Alec still in town?"

She held her breathe waiting for Julia's reply.

"Yes he is.... Jade didn't you hear about...."

But Jade was not listening. A smile had come on her face as soon as she had heard that Alec was still in town.

He had not gone.

"Is he at home?" She interrupted Julia.

"No he's not... He's at the construction site."

"Construction site?"

"Jade let me finish my sentences!" Julia said on a laugh. She knew what was happening and she couldn't be more happy about it, "Alec is opening an office of Wanderlust here. In Millbrooke. That's where he is."

"Really?" Jade asked in disbelief.

"Yes."

"Where is it?"

Jade was already up and on her way out of the door with the car keys in her hand.

"Near the kindergarten playground. Can you please tell me what is happening?" Asked Julia though she knew everything.

"I'll explain everything to you later. Now I got to go. Bye, Julia! I love you!"

"Bye!" Julia said.

She kept the phone chuckling to herself, before going to the living room to give the good news to her mother and Steve.

Alec stood on the playground and looked at the deserted swings. He felt desolate and exhausted. The last couple of weeks had completely drained him out.

Suddenly he heard the crack of a twig breaking into half. He turned around to see the person he was thinking about standing at the gate of the playground. Jade.

She was wearing a grey tank top and blue jeans. Her clothes were crumpled and her hair was all ruffled, as if she got dressed in a hurry.

"What are you doing here?" He had to yell in order to be heard as they stood on almost opposite ends of the playground.

"I went to the construction site. The guys told me that you're here." She yelled back.

She had made record time to the construction site after keeping Julia's call. But she couldn't find him anywhere over there.

At last she had gone up to one of the men working over there and she was told that he was in the playground.And there he was standing under the same tree under which they had met a few days back. Wearing a black t-shirt and dark wash jeans and with his brown hair fluttering in the air.

"And why were you at the construction site?" Alec yelled.

Neither of the took a step towards the other. They just continued standing where they were.

"I wanted to talk to you."

"About?"

Jade looked at her feet nervously, then looked up at the sky, "Nice weather isn't it?" She stammered.

"Seriously Jade. You came all the way to speak about the weather?"

"Yes." She said before thinking again and shaking her head, "No. Actually... Alec I'm sorry."

She said in a hurry. Without stopping even to take a breath.

"For what?" Alec replied simply.

He dragged his fingers through his hair and looked at her expectantly.

"I was a fool. Not as big as you but still a fool. I let my anger, my ego come in between us. And right now when I thought that maybe you had gone back to London.... I was so scared. Scared that maybe I had lost you for real this time."

"I'm not going back Jade." He said softly.

"I realise that...." Dragged Jade. "Why didn't you tell me?"

"You didn't give me a chance to." He replied simply.

"I'm sorry." Jade turned red again.

"Do you still love me?"

"Yes." Jade looked down at her feet.

"Why didn't you tell me before?" He asked.

"I would have told you if you wouldn't have got Emma with you in the first place." Jade replied with a huff.

"Seriously?" Alec asked, "Emma was not there before. You didn't tell me back then."

"Ummmm.... That's there." Jade looked up at last, right at him. And she said the first thing that came to her mind, "Can we start again?"

Alec didn't reply. Instead he smiled and walked towards Jade.

Jade just stood where she was, stuck to the ground.

Finally when he reached her, he stood and stuck his hand out, "Hi! I'm Alec. And I love Mickey Mouse too."

The same words he had said to her on the first day of kindergarten after seeing her Mickey Mouse lunch box.

They were standing on the very same playground. And the smile on his face was also the same mischievous one.Jade put her hand in his shyly and said, "Hi! I'm Jade and I have p b and j sandwiches."

Jade repeated her answer.Back then Alec had jumped up and said, "Will you spend the rest of the break with me? We can even become best friends!"

Now Alec smiled before hooking a finger under Jade's chin and pulling up her face till she looked into his eyes."Will you spend the rest of our lives with me? We can even get married!"

The tone was the same but the sentence was so different.

Jade didn't know whether to laugh or cry. She just opted for her original line, "Okay!"

Alec slowly bent his head and touched his lips to hers in a hesitant kiss.It was a sweet kiss and when they came up for breath, Jade asked, "Do you really mean it?"

"I wouldn't say it if I didn't." Replied Alec, "I love you Jade. I really really do! And I was a fool to not realise it. I was stupid to do all that I did. I jumped to conclusions. I took rash decisions. And you were a bigger fool to not tell me when you realised it. Since we spent almost half our lives being fools let's do one clever thing. Let's be fool's in love. Together."

Jade just looked at his handsome face. Her eyes were burning with unshed tears.

"Well it's okay if you don't love me!" Alec replied.

Since Jade was not replying he suddenly got nervous.

"I love you idiot!" Jade yelled, crying and laughing at the same time. She threw herself at him.

They kissed once again and this time it was a deeper, knee weakening, chocolate- melting hot kiss.

"Hey! What are you doing here?"

The yell of the caretaker brought them out of their embrace.

The caretaker was standing at the entrance of the kindergarten and looked angry.

"Trespassers are not allowed!" He yelled before he started running behind them.

Jade turned to Alec, "Want to do another clever thing?"

"What?" Alec asked with a smile.

"Run!"

The two of them ran, their fingers entwined till they reached the construction site. The caretaker having given up long back.

The stood in the middle of the half built office, panting with stupid grins on their faces.

Suddenly Alec hit his forehead with his hand.

"What?" Asked Jade.

"I asked you to get married to me, and I don't even have a ring for you."

Jade laughed. She was still wearing the fake ring on a chain around her neck.

"Don't worry. See what I have here." She pulled out the the chain out from inside her top opened the clasp and let the ring fall into her hand.

Alec gingerly picked it out from her hand and grinned, "This ring? Where did you get it?"

"A little boy and a little girl were saving it for us!" She replied.

Alec took her hand in his and put it on her ring finger.

"It fits!" He smiled.

"I love you!" Jade said looking into the eyes of the only guy she had loved in her whole life.

"I love you, more."

Chapter 39

The day was finally here and unlike what she had thought, Jade was uncharacteristically calm.

Her heart wasn't pounding in her chest. She didn't have a mild panic attack and she was definitely not getting cold feet.

Instead she had this heady, floaty feeling that made her feel like she was the luckiest and possibly happiest person alive at that moment.

She was going to get married today. To her best friend. To the man she loved with all her heart and then some more. To Alec.

And she felt wonderful as she stood in front of the mirror as Nicole and Blake helped her into the dress.

How many times before had she written a very similar scene in her books? The heroine getting ready, surrounded by her loved ones and the lovely radiance on her face.

Blake buttoned the last pearl along her back and stood up straight to look at her best friend.

Jade was glowing. She had been smiling ever since she woke up that morning. Her eyes twinkling, dimples winking on her cheek and a radiance that only love could bring.

"Time to look at yourself, Jady."

Jade smiled nervously and tugged on the neck line once before turning around to face the mirror. Her bridesmaids, Nicole and Blake had forbidden her to look at herself till then.

"Oh!" Jade gasped when she turned around and for a second was stunned. Was that really her reflection in the mirror?

The white dress had belonged to her mother and it had needed only a few alterations. It was the colour of snow, bright and sparkling.

The dress was off the shoulder which left Jade's creamy shoulders on display. The bodice was form- fitting and had a long row of pearl buttons at the back.

From the waist the dress opened up into miles and miles of flounces, glittering with small pearls on it too.

Nicole had forced her to leave her hair open instead of the chignon, she had thought would suit the dress more and Jade had to agree that she had been right.

Her black hair, curled just at the end lay messily on her shoulder and the only head adornment she wore was a small tiara made up of peach carnations.

"You look beautiful." Nicole said with a smile that was almost as big as Jade's.

Blake gave an enthusiastic nod, "I'll have to agree with Nicky. You look like a princess."

Jade placed a hand over her heart which for the first time since morning was pounding, "Thank you. Thank you so much." She had tears in her eyes as she turned around to face the two best friends a girl could ever ask for.

"There's no need to thank us." Nicole waved a hand under her own eyes, trying to stop the wave of tears that were threatening to come out.

"No no... We can't have tears now." Blake stopped the two of them before they could start on a sentimental crying fest. She never did well with crying women, "We don't want to spoil the make up. And Anyways we don't have the time."

Jade gave a small laugh and dabbed her eyes with the tissue Blake handed her in a mild panic, "Yes, we shouldn't be crying. Oh! I look so lovely."

She turned back to the mirror and admired the handy work of her friends with a smile.

"Alec's going to fall to his knees when he sees you." Nicole wiped her own eyes and poured three flutes with sparkling champagne, "A toast before the ceremony?"

"I don't think I want to be drunk before going out." Jade hesitated.

Blake who had happily taken her glass from Nicole nudged Jade's toward her, "One drink won't make a difference, Jady."

How was Jade to explain to them that she already felt dizzy with the wonder of actually getting married?

But still she took the champagne flute. Nicole grinned, "To Jade and Alec. The fools who took so many years to realise that they were in love with each other." She held up the flute and the two others laughed as they clinked the glasses.

"To Alec and Jade, because true love knows how to get through all the troubles. Even if it means waiting outside her apartment for almost 24 hours." Blake said with a mischievous look at Jade, making the bride blush and giggle.

"To Nicole and Blake, the two prettiest bridesmaids ever." Jade said, lastly and all three of them took deep gulps of the bubbly liquid.

Jade had chosen pretty knee length dresses in a peach colour for her bridesmaids and they both really looked wonderful in it.

Just then there was a knock on the door and Amanda pushed it open holding the flower bouquets in her hand.

"Your flowers are here, girls." She said, trying to hold the three bouquets at the same time, "Just five more...."

But words stopped when her eyes fell on her daughter.

"We'll need more tissues." Blake announced as she saw the emotional look come on Amanda's face.

"Oh! Jade, baby you look so pretty." Amanda sniffled, handing all the flowers to a surprised Blake and hugged Jade tightly, "You look better in the dress than I did."

"Thanks mom, but you look so good too." Jade took a long look at Amanda in her peach morning suit, with the cluster of carnations in her front pocket.

There was no more crying and heart break in Amanda's life. She had found her Stuart back and In the process Jade had got her father back.

"Come on Amanda! We don't need tears." Blake almost shoved the tissue into Amanda's hands, "You don't want runny mascara even before the ceremony starts."

Amanda nodded and gave a short laugh, "Yes... Of course. And you two look lovely as well." She informed Nicole and Blake.

"Thank you." Nicole said and then as an after thought added, "Have you seen Noah and Nadia anywhere?"

Amanda nodded, "Noah is with Jason and Alec. They seem to be having an all boys meeting. Nadia is being dressed by your mother. They should be done by now. The little girl looks like a doll."

"Yeah yeah... Till she dumps the basket of petals on someone's head." Jade had chosen Nadia as her flower girl and Noah as the ring bearer and Nicole's only worry was that they were going to end up doing something to embarrass their mother completely.

"I'm sure she'll be an angel. And if Noah drops the rings, well at least my old ruby ring won't break." Jade said, making everyone in the room laugh. But while her back was to them Blake exchanged a knowing look with Nicole and Amanda.

"I had to give you something." Amanda told Jade before turning to smile at Nicole.

Nicole got the hint and immediately said, "Blake here are your flowers and we should leave Amanda and Jade alone for a few moments." Nicole said, carefully placing Jade's bouquet on the table and pulling Blake along with her.

"But if we leave them alone I'm sure there's going to be crying. We'll have to do Jade's make up all over again." Blake protested as she was dragged outside the room and the door was closed behind her.

Amanda and Jade laughed.

"Blake never did well with tears." Jade said still giggling as she turned to the mirror one last time and looked at the beautiful dress.

While Amanda fidgeted with the pocket of her pant, "Wait I got something for you."

She took out a box from her pocket and opened it. Sitting on the blue velvet of the box was the prettiest earrings. They were little studs with tiny, dangling pearl drops.

"Mom, those are beautiful." Jade gasped, as the small diamond on the stud glittered.

Amanda took out one earring and placed the box on the table, "They are mine. They were my moms until you were born and she gave it to me. One day they will be yours, but till then I thought you could borrow it from me." She clipped on the earring on Jade's ear lobe and then did the same to the other one.

"Thanks mom, it looks just right with the dress." Jade looked at herself in the mirror and then looked at her mother's reflection.

"So you have something old, my dress. Something borrowed, the earrings. You just need something new and something blue."

"And that's what I'm here for." Said Susan coming into the room with an equally big grin on her face and holding a jewellers box in her hand, "Jade you look lovely. My poor boys going to be speechless."

"Mrs Carter, everyone's eyes are going to be on you and mom. No ones going to even look at me."Jade said indicating Susan's off white dress which she herself had picked out for her.

"Oh not at all. You look like a princess." She walked into the room and held out the box to Jade, "My gift."

Jade smiled and took the box she offered. Opening the lid she saw the prettiest little bracelet inside. There was a tiny charm dangling on it, a blue book with the pages open.Jade already knew about the tradition of giving the charm bracelets that had always been in Susan's family.

"This is so cute." Jade lightly touched the delicate bracelet worried that it was too fragile.

"Come here, I'll put it on for you." Amanda took out the bracelet and put it around Jade's wrist while Susan placed a hand on Jade's cheek.

"The charm that I gave you is a book, because you of all people need to remember that if the end is not happy, it's not the really end as yet." Susan said and placed a soft kiss on her cheek.

"Thank you."

Just then they were interrupted again, by a loud knock on the door.

Stuart poked his head in, "Everyone ready? It's time for the ceremony."

"Yes yes! Here take your flowers!"

Amanda exclaimed handing the flowers to Jade.

Jade had chosen a simple arrangement of peach carnations for her wedding bouquet.

She went out of the room and stood next to her dad while her mother and Susan headed out to take their seats.

"You look like the most beautiful bride ever, Blade."

He said, his voice was gruff and he had a huge grin on his face.

"Thanks dad."

Jade smiled back and placed her hand in his.

She was really glad that she had managed to make her relationship with her dad better. And that he could be there to walk down the aisle with her on her wedding day.

It was not that she had completely forgiven her dad, it was not easy to forget the hurt from so many years. But they were working towards it.

And someday soon, Jade knew, she would have a good relationship with her dad.

Nadia walked down the aisle first sprinkling petals a little too enthusiastically but without any mistake.

Nicole gave one last thumbs up and started walking down the aisle in front of them to take the place of the bridesmaid.

"See you on the other side, Jady." Grinned Blake as she followed Nicole next.

Soon it was their cue to start walking. Jade's heart was thudding so loudly that she almost feared that everyone in the church would hear it as they started walking.

She looked up and there at the end of the aisle was Alec. He was looking at her as if she was the only girl on the planet. With a huge smile and twinkling eyes.

And Jade forgot all her nervousness. She was going to spend her whole life with the person who she loved. Her best friend. Alec and she didn't have any fears. The ceremony was going perfectly. And now it was time for the little proud ring bearer to bring the rings.

As Noah walked down the aisle, with his tongue out in concentration, Jade was surprised to see Alec grin.

Suddenly something happened and Noah dropped the rings he was carrying.

"Oh!" Everyone in the church gasped.

"It's okay sweetie! We'll get it!" Jade said, worried that Noah might start crying. But instead Noah had a huge proud smile on his face as he stood over there.

Everyone started looking around, except for Alec who was just standing and grinning while Jason, who was the best man gave a short laugh and picked up Noah like a proud papa.

When finally everyone was going to give up, Jade exclaimed as she saw the ring at the edge of the stool on which Father was standing.

She bent and picked it up, "I got it!"As she stood back up she looked at the ring, instead of the fake ruby ring.

There was a ring which looked exactly like but it had one little change, it was real.

"Alec?" She looked at him, whose grin had become even bigger.

"Let two little best friends have their one dollar ring." He said taking out the old ring from his pocket, "I couldn't possibly give my wife such an old ring. What would my mother- in- law say!"

Everyone in the church laughed while Jade started crying and smiling.

The ceremony continued.

Jade had two identical rings one real and one fake, and a very happy besotted husband by the end of the ceremony.

She felt like the luckiest girl in the world.

"I love you, bestie."

Alec said once he kissed his bride.

"I love you, more!"

Epilogue

J ade looked at herself in the mirror as she put on her earrings.

The tan from the honeymoon in Bali was still visible and the white colour of her sundress brought out the brown colour even more.

She had brushed her hair back in a loose braid.

"Hi beautiful!" Alec said coming into the room.

He was dressed in jeans and plain black shirt. But he managed to make the simple clothes look fabulous.

They were living in Jade's apartment in a few days till the construction of the new house was completed.

The new house that was at the moment being made at one of Jade's favourite places.

Near the lake.

Even now whenever Jade thought of the prospect of living in the beautiful house with the stunning view of the lake and the silence and peace she felt an army of butterflies fluttering in her stomach.

"Hello." She said turning to her husband.

Her husband. She had still not gotten tired of saying or thinking those words everytime she looked at Alec.

"I love the dress." Alec said as he walked up and placed a soft kiss on her back which was left bare by the dress.

She turned around to face him, "Now do you, really?"

"Yes Mrs Carter." Alec laughed and touched his lips to hers.

Just as the kiss was getting a little heated the door bell rang.

Alec groaned while Jade laughed moving away, "Can't we be late for dinner."

"Yes we can. But since it is being held at our own house...." She laughed and started going out of the room.

"But the kiss was just getting heated up." He whined following her out.

Jade chuckled again at his tone, "Didn't you have enough heat in Bali?"

"I can never have enough heat Mrs Carter... Never."

Jade smiled as her heart filled with love for her stupid, stubborn handsome husband.

They had invited their friends for dinner, to celebrate their homecoming.

She pulled open the door but not before Alec could sneak in another kiss.

Matt nervously stood out side the door to Jade's apartment.

This was the first time he was going to meet Jade ever since the wedding.

And to say that it was going to be difficult would be an understatement.

Suck it up, Matt!

He rang the bell and waited for someone to open it.

The door was pulled open and there stood Jade. Looking beautiful and tanned in a white summer dress.

"Hi Matt!" She exclaimed and hugged him.

Her scent enveloped him as he hugged her back.

It was difficult to see her, but the happiness that could be clearly seen on her face somehow made it better.

"You look lovely, Jade." He said once they moved away.

Jade took his hand and pulled him into the apartment, "Thanks! Now come in! You're the last one to arrive. Everyone is already here."

The living room was already filled with people with glasses in their hands.

Nicole was sitting Julia on the sofa as they talked. Julia had a glass of water in her hand while Nicole sipped her wine.

On the other side of the room Steve and Jason stood near the window chatting excitedly about something.

"Guys Matt is here!" Jade said.

A chorus of hi's and hello's rang out while Steve and Jason came to give him half hugs and pat him on his back.

"Matt you know everyone over here. Except.... Wait where is she?"

Just as Jade looked around for someone, a petite girl came out of the kitchen followed by Alec.

Alec grinned at Matt as soon as he saw him. After the wedding things had somehow become a little less awkward between them.

They carried a bottle of champagne and champagne flutes with them.

The girl who Matt didn't know was short, just till his shoulders, with chin length black hair and dark brown eyes.

She was dressed in a short electric blue dress and high sky scraping heels in the same colour.

There was something in the way she walked that reminded Matt of the pixies that they showed in movies.

"There she is. Come here." She pulled the girl by her hand and made her stand next to them. "Blake this is Matt. Matthew Damon. I told you about him."

"Of course. Nice to meet you." The girl gave a smile that was a little too big for her face, it brought out the dimples in her cheeks.

"And Matt this is Blake Hastings. My editor." Jade said.

"You're Blake Hastings?" Matt asked.

"The last time I checked." There was an amused look on Blake's face.

"It's just that I though you were a guy."

"Do I look like a guy?"

"Well no…. But you're name…." Matt stuttered.

"It's Blake. Is that a problem?" She raised an eyebrow.

"No…. I mean ofcourse not." He shook his head, "Why would it be?"

The girl might be short but she was as intimidating as a giant.

"That's good."

Jade clapped her hands once gleefully, "Well then why don't you'll get to know each other while I get you a drink, Matt."

Jade walked away to the kitchen to make a drink for Matt.

Alec followed her in, "I see what you're trying to do."

"What?" Jade tried to be nonchalant.

He laughed, "I know you very well Mrs Jade Carter. You're trying to patch them up."

"Was I too obvious?"

"No…. Very subtly done." Alec said sarcastically.

She laughed, "Well you see I think that they're perfect for each other so I'm just giving them a push in the right direction."

"Why do you think they're perfect for each other? They're completely different."

Jade walked up to him and placed a hand on his cheek, "I know. They're poles apart. That's why they're perfect."

www.ingramcontent.com/pod-product-compliance
Lightning Source LLC
Chambersburg PA
CBHW070752190726
48292CB00002B/515